IMMORTAL

BOOKS BY JACK DANN

IMMORTAL

Short Novels of the Transhuman Future

EDITED BY

JACK DANN

HARPER & ROW, PUBLISHERS

New York, Hagerstown, San Francisco, London

For the Doctors:

Ed Rem
John Harding
Leonard Barron
Leon Payes
Robert Brooks
Michael Ashman

Library of Congress Cataloging in Publication Data

Main entry under title:
  Immortal.
  1. Science fiction, American. 2. Immortality—Fiction. I. Dann, Jack.
PZ1.I44 [PS648.S3]   813'.0876   76-26264
ISBN 0-06-010962-9

78 79 80 81 82 10 9 8 7 6 5 4 3 2 1

CONTENTS

Introduction:
The Transhuman Condition

What manner of writer attempts serious fiction about immortal supermen? First off, he must have a giant ego, to deem it within his powers; this rules out nobody. Second, he must make a nearly superhuman effort, and this rules out almost everybody. So it goes: Many are culled, and few self-chosen.

And what do we owe these men of La Mancha? To begin with, a little appreciation of the sheer audacity of their ambition.

H. G. Wells, for one, remarked on the near-paradox of man trying to foresee superman. A character in *The Star Begotten* says:

> ... these coming supermen are ... altogether wiser than we are. How can we begin to put our imaginations into their minds and figure out what they will think or do? If our intelligences were as tall as theirs, we should be making their world now. ... You make me feel like the sculptor's dog trying to explain his master's life to the musician's cat.

But for all that, Wells barked, and some of us cats listened, and felt we learned a little.

Yet hints no longer suffice, nor isolated tingles of excitement. Consider this passage from Robert Heinlein's *By His Bootstraps:*

> It had not been fear of physical menace that had shaken his reason, nor the appearance of the creature—he could recall nothing of *how* it

looked. It had been a feeling of sadness infinitely compounded . . . a sense of tragedy, of grief insupportable and inescapable, of infinite weariness. He had been flicked with emotions many times too strong for his spiritual fiber and which he was no more fitted to experience than an oyster is to play the violin.

Magnificent! This is classic science fiction, the "sense of wonder" *par excellence.* And yet, with no disrespect to the master, it isn't enough—not in these days of our lives. Now that some of us are beginning to take seriously and *personally* the prospect of life extension and radical improvement of people, we need more. If we are to become practicing immortals and nascent transhumans, we need at least rough outlines and a few details.

These are almighty hard to come by. Even Heinlein has made only a few contributions, and—like everyone else—many bloopers. In one of his more recent novels, *Time Enough for Love,* the protagonist has lived one thousand years, give or take, and the most interesting project he can think of is to start a new restaurant! Another time, he starts a new farm. When really inspired, he fornicates with his mother and clone-daughters.

Well, I don't mean to knock new varieties of fornication; I've even invented a few myself. But *restaurants*? And *farms*? In the *far future*? This, from the man who gave us *Beyond This Horizon*? It's enough to drive a poor human to think.

Let's think first about the easiest (?) type of immortality story. Posit greatly extended life *before* important improvement of people's minds. It's still just you and I, but now we don't have to die. How will our interactions and feelings change, and how will our clumsy institutions evolve? What if aging can only be halted and not reversed; will those already beyond the prime of physical life find it worthwhile to hang around? This scenario lends itself to pessimism, to *Weltschmerz* and sing-the-blues, so I don't like it—but the world doesn't always accommodate itself to my preferences. It could be this way—for a while—and forewarned may be forearmed.

(Personally, I will be delighted to stick around, if necessary, with my present cheap, broken-down body and feeble mind, for as long as it takes. A man should live forever, or die trying.)

Another easy (?) type of near-future story postulates that some people are coming out of cryonic suspension before humanity and society have changed much. Remember the atrocious TV series about the thawed man who was younger than his son? This theme is not very ambitious, but minor art can also be useful and enjoyable. It can even be important in the political and life-saving sense, if it helps build active interest in the freezer program.

A variant of the foregoing types sets the near future in the far future—that is, the author assumes the immortals will remain more or less human indefinitely. Alan Harrington *(The Immortalist)* explicitly predicts a game-playing or dreaming future, individuals choosing roles or sequences or rebirths at whim, with no purpose beyond amusement. Harrington seems to imply that the games will be played in real space and time with real matter, but others have noted that, if you want only to play, it may be easier and safer to simulate everything in your own skull.

It has not escaped notice that game-playing can be hazardous to your health, mental and physical. An immortal opium-smoker—or the electronic equivalent—might feel pretty good for a while, but what will he do when the rent comes due? When the aliens land, or the sun goes nova, or a neighbor goes berserk? Possibly his robots would protect him for a while, but robots that capable are apt to have their own fish to fry. At the first crisis, our opium-smoker is likely to deanimate. Still, mere humans being what they are, some will certainly choose this route, if the rest of us permit them to. With *laissez-faire* and I-don't-care a good bet, it's very possible there will be some game-players.

Moving right along, let's add transhumanity to immortality; now we are in the big time. But it will tax any writer's skill just to convince a human that the way from here is up.

Remember Joshua Lederberg's definition of disease? It is "any deficit relative to a desired norm." *Desired* norm. This means that any difference between yourself and your own ideal represents disease, although Lederberg himself may not have been quite so explicit. How marvelous! How right! Not only is cancer a disease, but the susceptibility to it. Nervousness is a disease, of which we must soon proceed to cure ourselves.

To be born human is an affliction; it shouldn't happen to a hog. Of course the disease is enjoyable, and everyone still has it; that's what makes it so confusing, and why the writer needs all of his cunning. He must show that *Homo sapiens*, like every other species, is a botched effort, a partial and temporary success, barely adapted to conditions that are rapidly changing.

In particular, man's psyche is a patchwork of makeshift adaptive compromises. We have no true natures, but rather a mixed bag of instincts, tendencies, and drives, some of which are mutually inconsistent. The left and right hemispheres of our brains and the various layers of the brain are scarcely on speaking terms with each other.

This is the source of the highest art concerning the "human condition": Our various parts and aspects are not reconciled with each other. For example, both domination and submission have their occasions, their satisfactions, and their prices. Alertness and serenity are at best uneasy bedfellows. There are endogenous drives both for self-preservation and for self-sacrifice. Man *cannot* be true to himself because he has no single, unified self; hence he must always compromise and frequently fail.

Now we know where to look for a very rich lode of literature on the transhuman condition. That is in stories of *becoming* more than human, stories of the sculptor sculpted, of the wild and wonderful transition period between man and the first complete superman.

But there is also another aspect of the "human condition" which is quite as poignant, and much easier to capture in art. In fact, there are countless songs and ditties, a bit banal, maybe, but true and touching all the same. Remember, from *Fiddler on the Roof?*

> Sunrise, sunset, sunrise, sunset,
> Quickly fly the years,
> One season following another,
> Laden with happiness and tears.

Or, from *Happiest Girl in the World:*

> Here we are, adrift on a star,
> And what is the journey for?
> ....
> Why the rain, and why the rose,
> And why the trembling heart?
> ....
> Music of the spheres,
> Are there words to your song?

All such songs, and the reactions they celebrate, constitute the "wha' hoppen" syndrome. We scurry around, and every now and then we pause, look up and around in stunned amazement, and wonder, "Wha' hoppen?"

True enough, the "wha' hoppen" syndrome has two parts to it, and one of them is mortality, which we are about to leave behind. But that still leaves the other part: "What's it all about, Alfie?"

In my personal view, we are almost ready—in one sense— —to deal with this second part also. The purpose of life is to discover the purpose of life. That is, we adopt the following point of view. First, we admit to ourselves that, in all likelihood, the "secret of the universe," if any, is much too complex or subtle for such paltry creatures as ourselves. The Celestial City, if it exists, lies in all probability at the end of a very long and winding road atop a mountain not yet even visible. Hence our strategy, for the foreseeable future, should simply be to explore and study and build and improve ourselves without limit, uncovering and attaining as long a succession of intermediate goals as necessary, until at last, if we and the cosmos both survive, we will either attain everything or prove it is unattainable.

But we must remind ourselves how this challenges the writer. The storyteller must interpret the transhuman condition to *humans*. He must convince the tired wage earner, relaxing with a beer and baseball, or watching Mary Hartman's friend drown in a bowl of chicken soup, that superhumans are interesting and simpatico.

If the writer is political—that is, if he takes immortality seriously and personally—he must try to convince the beer-bibber that the struggle is worth it, and that transhumanity can be fun. Or contrariwise—if that is his opinion—he can try to show that more is less and different is probably worse. The density of nightmares in the future, I think, will be far lower than in the past—but they could make up for it, I suppose, in quality. The future-as-nightmare certainly makes legitimate speculation, and it tends to please many readers, who can feel snug and comfy in the now and patronizing toward those supermen who turn out not so smart after all and get their comeuppances.

Is it even possible to make many readers sympathize with a full transhuman? How many will wax enthusiastic about learning and growth as the mainsprings of motivation? Who will really like a being that fully controls his emotions? Most people like children and puppies, and at best are very uneasy with their superiors. So what is the answer?

The answer, I suppose, is that the writers must lie a little, as they all do anyway. They must be a little inconsistent, as they all are anyway. They must pretend—just a trifle less than the hack writer—that the far future is merely the present with a little more chrome and a few novelties. They must imply that transhumans are almost the same as you and I. By focusing on only a very few significant changes, they can keep within bounds both the task of designing a future and the strong aversion of most humans toward anything really different and superior.

This point is worth belaboring a bit—the extreme difficulty of selling transhumanity to humans, or even making it emotionally understandable. I recall a letter to Ann Landers (or perhaps it was Dear Abby) from some poor woman who detested sex. Her problem—as she saw it—was *not* how to learn to enjoy sex normally, but just how to persuade her husband not to bother her!

Now consider today's humanity, raised to admire warmth, generosity, and impulsive friendliness. I am not saying that tomorrow's transhumans will be altogether cold or selfish or inward; but they will *certainly* have better control of their impulses and more ability to make calculated decisions. We love vulnerable protagonists, for there go we. H. G. Wells's Martians were "intellects vast, cool, and unsympathetic," and they were cordially detested by their readers. Even with the "unsympathetic" toned down, would his skill have sufficed to make us identify with such creatures?

Our writers' task is not quite so hard, though, as trying to convince an oyster that he should learn to play the violin. Humans are closer to any conceivable transhumans, or even inconceivable ones, than oysters are to humans. The reason, of course, is that we have reached the critical stage of self-awareness. Some of us are beginning to grasp the notion of progress, and a few even have a personal appreciation of the possiblities in biological and mechanical improvement, not only for the race but for individuals.

Yet the political writer—as opposed to the pure entertainer— must do more than make transhumanity somewhat plausible and mildly appealing. He must ram his pen, if not his head, through the brick wall of human inertia and dread of responsiblility. Remember Dostoevsky? "Men prefer peace, even death, to freedom of choice in the knowledge of good and evil." So it goes: Many are cold, but few are frozen.

Most people fear struggle and hazard more than defeat and death, except in the very short term. They will dodge tigers and taxis, but will not quit smoking or help raise funds for gerontological research. Somehow, the writer must persuade them to get their butts in gear, set aside funds for a cryonics trust or whatever. And he must do it without explicit polemics, through his art; he must depict the joy of open-ended life and the glory of transcending humanity. In short, he must reach the emotions.

As for the apolitical writers, we have set a neat trap for them, or they for themselves. Most writers will claim they have no axe to grind, and indeed very few are immortalists. Nevertheless, we activists have them by the short hairs, and they can't get away. After all, literature of quality usually includes complex villains who gain considerable reader sympathy. Likewise, even the dreariest dystopia, if honestly and imaginatively constructed, must necessarily include some notes of cheer and glimmers of hope, for realism and contrast. Good writers do not set up straw men, but must reveal genuine opportunities even if in the end they close them out. Some readers, then, will focus on the opportunities and reject the author's conclusions. Q.E.D.

And there we have it. At one end of the spectrum—trying to interpret the fullness of transhumanity to humans—our writers' problem is unsolvable. (Not "insoluble"; that is chemistry.) But the other end of the spectrum is within view, and there are some strange and splendid colors in it, even if some of them are the colors of darkness. (Someone said that, but I can't remember who.)

Let there be light.

Chanson Pérpetuelle

THOMAS M. DISCH

Author's Note:

"Chanson Perpétuelle," which is excerpted from a work-
in-progress, is set in the year 2098. The human race has
become immortal as a result of genetic alterations
caused by a plague that swept the earth in the twentieth
century. However, a small but genetically dominant
minority of mortals has survived and perpetuates itself in
this world, among them the heroine of this story, Emma
Rosetti.

The title is the same as that of a poem by Charles
Cros, which was set to music by Ernest Chausson.

One summer, gods, is all I ask:
  One summer—and one fall to give
    To song. Once my heart is sated with
      Singing, I will die willingly.

How, if I have not here received
  My due, shall I cease to long for it
    In hell? Yet let me once achieve
      My uttermost of song—and then

Welcome, you Silences! Welcome, Night!
  I will be happy. Even if no music
    Follows me down, still, once I lived
      Among the gods. Once—I need no more.

—FRIEDRICH HOLDERLIN,
To the Fates

Clouds roofed the landscape like layers of sheet metal—below the mid-gray of steel, above the glowing half-white of aluminum. Around her, rust-red crumbling stone, brown ferns, withered but not yet beaten down, and mosses intenser now than in the helter-skelter of summer. Across these certainties the wind dragged a ragged mist. In the shifting light the surface of the tarn behind her flashed unread, unreadable semaphores; ahead the rockface of Lingmell loomed, a thicker, steadier gray amid the vapors rolling up from Wasdale. Now for a while the path rose, and now it fell. The newly nailed boots scrunched comfortably against the rocks. She walked through a sequence of privacies, rooms and tunnels cut through the mist, filling them with the calm rhythm of her walking. At the cairn that marked the start of the traverse she stopped, removed the topmost rock from the loose heap, and heaved it outward into the gray. She was walking again before it hit the slope below with a dull-edged *click*. As though, during a phone call, one were to hear the shutting of a door half a world away.

Here ferns and grasses had left off: only the moist and mossy rock that rose on her right in ever steeper and more massive formations. She paused at the base of a single perpendicular block of schist so awesome that it had a name all to itself, she'd forgotten what. Even the two cracks up the length of it had proper names, and though just a year ago she'd clawed her way up the more indomitable of these, their names too were lost to her. Here it was again, the same; herself the same. Really, did one *want* them to have names? With a smile of regret she touched the first handhold. But her plan did not admit any delays or detours from what was plotted on her map: up Great Gable and along the highest ridges till the plunge past the old quarries into Honister Pass, then a final hike down the highway into Buttermere: eight hours from the village where the bus had let her out.

One last brief descent through a maze of slippery boulders, and then the traverse mounted upward into the mindlessness of mild exertion. More often now the patches of dampness had glazed to frost. The first tentative icicles were forming on the crags, though only inches away water still trickled freely down the face of the rock.

At each cairn, as at the first, she would remove the topmost stone and throw it with the full strength of arm and back out into the sheer space left of her. She had to put on mittens, but for a while yet she let the cold nip at her ears.

The cold, the mist, the height invisible but felt, the planetary presence of the stone: the day was beginning to assume a certain shape, when from somewhere near, a voice hailed her:

"Hello? Down there—hello!"

No.

"Hello!" More desperately.

She kept straight on.

"Please, I need a bit of help. I'm up here on the Needle, and I can't seem to . . . get down."

Nape's Needle? This soon? Above her the mist had thinned sufficiently to allow her to see, if only intermittently, the top of the rough cone of rock. On it, like a mouse on a milestone, a figure signaled to her with comical, conscious pathos.

"Are you stuck?"

"No. Well, yes, in a way. I can't find the toehold."

"It's over to the right of where you're sitting. You'll have to hang down by your hands and feel for it. I can direct you from down here if you like. As soon as"—he had disappeared—"the mist clears off again."

"Really? I mean, *you've* done it?"

"It would seem that you have too. At least the way up."

He acknowledged this with a weak laugh. "Actually. What I thought. . . . There are some pitons in my bag. If you could toss up one or two . . .?"

"Pitons? Don't be ridiculous. Now, while it's clear."

Shamed, he lowered himself til he was hanging flat against the rock and she directed his feet to holds. Once in motion his form was good, the smoothness of the descent inflected with small, telling cautions. At the shoulder he paused. "I did it!"

"You did it." She set off on the path, but before she'd gone three yards he was calling after her:

"Hey! Hey, I'm not safe yet. You know?"

Though the better part of the lower stage was on the far side of the Needle where her eyes could be no help to him, she consented to wait till he'd got down to the path.

The nearer he came, the younger he seemed. Fifteen, and that was being generous. He was dressed cap-a-pie for his climb in a blue Davis jacket jittery with badges, plus fours, and red socks, a bobcap, and, incredibly, goggles. His rucksack, propped against a nearby boulder, was no less complete: ice axe, rope, nailed boots, and (when he was round the other side she hefted it) a good twenty pounds of ironmongery. Enough to take you up the Matterhorn.

He jumped the last eight feet. "Thanks. I mean it." He pushed up his goggles, held out his raw hand. He'd scraped some skin from the knuckles, but it was not a climber's hand. She found herself liking him.

She bit off her mitten, shook his hand.

"My name is Clive. Clive Crespin?"

She wondered if she ought to have assured him that his name *was* Clive Whatever-He'd-Said. She smiled, not unfriendly.

"A second more, okay?" He tore at the laces of his vibrams with stiff fingers. "Where you going? Up to the top? I'll go with you, okay? With this ice, you know, it's a better idea. For a while up on the Needle there, I was really . . . I guess I owe you. . . ."

"Oh, if I hadn't come along, you'd have had to make it on your own."

"Do you think so?" He grinned drunkenly.

Despite herself she had to grin too. Of all ages the least possible is fifteen. Or so, at twenty, it seemed to Emma. For arrogance, for ignorance, for sheer vaulting silliness, no one can match a fifteen-year-old, and yet it is also the time when, if ever, one begins to be human.

Clive got his boots on and they set off. As he took the lead, Emma had occasion to study the little autobiography sewn to his jacket: Helvellyn, Scafell, Harrison Stickle—even a few lakes and valleys thrown in to fill out the meager story. And then to brag about it!

While he had breath he talked. She didn't resent it as much as she might have, remembering how she'd rattled on after her first real scare. Soon enough the work of climbing steadied him and he quieted down, though he would always, as they approached any distinct landmark, feel obliged to announce it. "Ah, that's Eagle Nest Ridge up there. You can't see all of it now, but it's really way up there." And a moment later: "This is Eagle's Nest Gully coming up." And then, "This is Eagle's Nest Gully now that we're in."

At Sphinx Rock he suggested a break. "I don't know about you, but *I* am beat."

"You won't feel any better for stopping."

"Just a second. Till I get my breath. Hey, where are you staying? If you don't mind my asking. I'm at the Brackenclose." He gestured at the gray void stretching out below them.

"Is it nice?" she asked.

"Yeah. But right now it's sort of . . . I mean, I'm the only person there except for the caretaker. You can only stay there, you know, if you're a member of the Fell and Rock."

"You're a member, are you?"

"The youngest." Then, less brightly: "But I guess if they'd seen me today . . . " He shook his head, and a lock of black hair fell down becomingly across his acned forehead.

"It happens to everyone, Clive. The whole trick is not thinking about it too long. Now *we'd* better get a move on, right?"

"Right!" He would have agreed to anything. As he followed her, he thought how already, without even knowing her name, he'd fallen in love! The way she moved. Her eyes. Her voice. Everything! And not an inch taller than he was either.

Each time he came to a cairn he would stop, find a rock the right size, and place it on top. He realized, as the gap between them widened, that she strode on right past the cairns. So, calling another halt (he was short of breath anyway), he explained how it was a custom always to add one stone to a cairn when you passed it.

"Why is that?" she asked.

"On days like this they help you keep to the path. I'm surprised you didn't know that."

"I always come here by myself."

"Yeah, I do too. The feeling of solitude is incredible sometimes, isn't it? But you know, it isn't a good idea to do any of the really difficult ascents on your own. Even two people can be dangerous. By the way, I don't think you mentioned your name."

"Emma."

"Emma, I'm really glad to meet you." He frowned prettily. "You know, the people you meet here, they're not like other people."

"Oh? I never meet people here."

"Yeah, that's a difficulty. In the old days they had whole *cities* of tents in every damned valley. But what I mean is, when you do meet someone, a climber, they're always a special kind of person. Different. Why is that, do you think?"

"I wouldn't know."

"My mother says I'm crazy to keep coming back here. Maybe she's right, I don't know. You can't deny there's a risk involved. But maybe short people, like you and me, maybe we have more of a need to prove ourselves. But even so, there has to be some kind of limit, right? I mean, nobody's going to go up fucking Everest again." He glanced sideways to see if she objected to his obscenity.

True enough, she thought.

"On the other hand, the way I explained it to my mother, if a person doesn't do something that involves *some* risk, he could just spend his whole damn *life* with a feeling of . . . a feeling that—"

She stopped listening. All her misgivings had come to focus in the peculiar emphasis of that one word, *life*. She'd been misled by his youth, by his presence on the Needle—or, indeed on the mountain. But he was not, for all that, a mortal.

He'd come at the same moment to a complementary realization. "Oh, I thought—"

"Good-bye."

"No. Hey, Emma, I didn't mean—Wait!"

She took a direct route up the side of the crag. The ice made it a bit treacherous, but that was something to think about.

Clive followed as far as the first awkward ledge, where he slipped. Then he went back down to the track.

She moved well, but without feeling her muscles connect to the rock. The momentum of the morning was lost. The rock and the light that moved across the rock were just something to look at. Even at the summit, with Scafell Pike ideally present across a plane of mist, her mind was a clutter of words, of mere wistful longings that time would stop and her soul become one with the stillness of the stone. Instead, this triviality of beauty and, from below, the boy shouting her name. She hurried down the northern path into the gap.

✳

She had thought to wait for the next car, but once the doors opened, the mass of people behind her swept her in with them. The train lurched, oozed a few feet forward, and stopped. There was a communal groan. Wriggling round so as not to be quite groin-to-belly with an overwhelmingly lemon-scented executive in a gray surtout, Emma got a grip far down on the pole just as the train began to move again. One of the few advantages of being so short was that down here one didn't compete for the same few inches of elbow room with the whole mob of the middle-sized.

At Tottenham Court Road more people bulled in to make an even greater crush. She kept her place on the pole, but all the hands above hers changed.

A dark green stone stared at her from a setting of dull gold, a red vein slanting across the green. The train braked and the compacted bodies swayed with a single massive motion that pressed Emma's cheek against his hand. She jerked back.

His hand flexed: a vein flickered beneath the bright skin, the chilly stone glinted. Both the hand above his on the pole and that beneath were gloved, so that his seemed peculiarly physical. Naked.

Usually, in a crush like this one was spared those discomforts of curiosity, one's own and other people's, so inescapable at other, roomier times of the day.

Mornington Crescent. The man in the surtout said, "Excuse," and his briefcase caught Emma in the ribs. As she opened her mouth to protest, his shoulder—"Getting out!"— smashed against the back of her head. Her teeth scraped the ringed hand.

"Oh! I'm *sorry*." She looked up to see if he was as angry as she felt he ought to be.

His eyes flicked away.

"I really didn't mean to . . . The man behind me—"

"That's quite all right." Smiling. His eyes pretending only now to meet hers. "No harm done."

But he had (she *knew*) been watching her since that first inadvertent touch. At least since then.

She looked dead ahead into the calm green eye of the ring. The very smallest droplet of blood formed on his knuckle next to the ring. She watched it swell and slowly swoon down the curve of bone, into the dark crevice at the finger's base.

The most embarrassing . . .

And yet: Wasn't she just the least bit pleased she had bitten him? Albeit accidentally. They all thought *they* could stare at *you* and think whatever they pleased and that you were never supposed to mind or even notice. Some of them even seemed to expect you to be flattered, as though their attention were a kind of benediction.

Her stop. She fought her way out. As the doors were closing she looked back. His eyes were waiting. The train just stood there with the doors closed and she stood there too, rooted in a sudden and absolutely powerless rage.

It was gone as quickly as it had come. By the time she was on the escalator, laved by the long cool wind that lived there always, it was almost as though it hadn't happened. On the High Street it was still snowing as it had been fifteen minutes ago when she'd gone down into the Underground.

"You're late," August said before she was quite inside the room. But she wasn't. It was his way of saying hello.

He returned to the Twelfth Programme and Emma concentrated on supper. With the telly going and both heaters churning out calories it would have to be cold: cold Plumrose from Sunday, four nice little potatoes, and a plate of mixed pickle, which, when they sat down, was the only thing August touched. Undoubtedly he'd been to his pudding club.

"Nice day?" he asked.

The day had vanished behind her in a haze of small motions. What could be nicer? "Quite. And you?"

"Oh, nothing. I walked over to Talat's, wasn't a soul there, the weather, I suppose. So then I thought I'd come right back but you know how cold it was. I went upstairs and . . . " He lifted a gherkin up into the ever-diminishing cone of visibility. His pause swelled to a silence.

Emma quartered a potato neatly, waiting for him to resume. Whatever thoughts might occupy him in these intervals, August was always consecutive. So much so that at times his speech seemed printed on a tape: he could choose between On or Off, but beyond that the message was mechanical and inevitable.

" . . . played a game right hand against left hand. Left hand won. The high point of my day. Then I came home and listened to the bats."

This was a signal that he wanted to argue. August claimed he could hear the bats. Emma insisted that the noise they made was inaudible to human ears (it certainly was to hers) and that what he probably heard was the whistle of the heater in the other room, since August never heard bats except on the coldest days of winter. His theory was that the bats were especially sensitive (as he was) to the cold.

Emma refused to argue. With resolute cheerfulness she reconstructed, more from probabilities than any distinct memory, her own day at the shop. Ruthven had been off during most of the afternoon making deliveries, and he'd let her finish the work on a badly pitted muffineer by herself. Ms. Bateman had come upstairs once with a set of flatware. She described Ms. Bateman's new frock, and August, always eager for a bit of bon ton, forgot to be petulant. Though Emma was sometimes disloyal enough to complain to Ruthven about the old man's bad weathers, secretly she cherished them. They were her day-to-day equivalent of a scramble across some scree: an obstacle of known and manageable difficulty. Emma thrived on difficulties.

"I don't suppose you remembered to stop in at Foyle's? They're still holding that book."

"I'm sorry, I forgot. It was so cold I just went straight into the tube." (In fact, as August ought to have known, she wouldn't have the price of his book till Friday. Half her salary ended up on his bookshelves: an investment, such was his rationale.)

"There's no hurry. I'm an old customer."

"The tubes were beastly tonight. Just beastly. I've never seen them so—" Almost as vividly as if she were still there, she could remember the green ring staring at her.

"There!" August said, pushing back his chair. "I told you! Can't you hear them?"

"The bats?"

"Don't you hear *anything*?"

Obligingly she strained to hear anything. Her ears popped, and she could hear more distinctly the ordinary household hummings and creaks but nothing like what she supposed bats must sound like. She smiled in deprecation of her deafness, but August, too near-sighted to read such nuances, left the table in an ill humor, thinking she was once again denying the evidences of his senses.

"Bats" was the code word for all their discontents. After Ms. Harness, cured of teaching, had set off for Oregon and a new life, a pharmaceutical concern had moved into the Inverness School's empty shell. Now instead of flowers the smell of bats pervaded the building. Great crates of flittering pipistrelles were regularly delivered to the mobile sheds parked all about the former playing field; smaller crates of vaccine issued from a side-door sporadically. It all had to do with some dread disease that people could still get in Africa, and Emma was certain that one day all the bats would escape from the sheds and wire cages in what had been the greenhouse and that she and August would come down with whatever gruesome symptoms and die in fits. Meanwhile you couldn't breathe.

After the dishes, a rosary. The Glorious Mysteries. August, meanwhile, would probably be doing his exercises, scrunching his face up evilly, then loosening the muscles to slack idiocy. He claimed that it accomplished the same thing as her prayers.

He called her when the news came on. There is nothing like following the crises of fifty years ago to give you a healthy indifference to the crises of today. For all the shortages and revolutions and terrors of the past, the world had gone on, and it went on still. This, at least, was the lesson Emma drew from BBC-12. People who'd lived through those times (August had been her own age then) must have entirely different reasons for following the Twelfth Programme. Nostalgia? Ms. Harness had once said it was more in the nature of an exorcism, the pine branch that a hunter drags behind him to destroy his tracks.

August fell into a doze.

At nine, a comedy called "Deedle." Emma turned off the dubbing and listened for a while to the restful senselessness of the original Japanese. Then the squeaky voices woke up August, who switched back to English, and the lilting frog-croaks became sexual innuendoes. Emma went into the other room.

August was more present here amid the silt and debris of his seventy-three years than when she'd been sitting next to him. The heater wheezed and coughed, the windows rattled, a clock ticked. Yards of memoirs and biographies darkened the walls and ballasted a makeshift desk. He'd read them all, underscoring the choicer passages, inveighing in the margins, and very occasionally awarding one paragraph the encomium of a five-pointed star. A lifetime: an allegory: and, since he didn't let Emma tidy up in here, an awful mess.

When they had set up housekeeping together, August and Emma had drawn up a model constitution that defined most explicitly their individual rights, duties, and spheres of influence. For two years they'd lived by these laws, but when Joanna Harness had closed the school and flown away, their little commonwealth fell apart. Gradually August let Emma assume all the chores they'd so rationally apportioned, retaining only the direction of the budget. In fact, this more feudal relationship suited both of them better than their first formal utopianism. Emma kept busier and that suited her. August could collapse, and he asked no more.

Emma, though she thought Ms. Harness guilty of the blackest

treason, never said so to August. He protested, nobly if too often, that he didn't blame his aunt. Joanna had her own life to live (and Emma must never forget that *she* did too), the chimera of her own happiness to pursue. August fully intended to enjoy his new independence. He had his pension, which was modest but sufficient, and thanks to a clause his aunt had written into the sublease with Cowper Biochemicals, he would retain the same cozy flat he'd lived in most of his life, and for quite a nominal rent. Furthermore, and crucially, he had Emma. No doubt Ms. Harness had oiled her conscience with the same arguments.

For her part Emma swore she would never abandon August. She loved him dearly and deeply. In a way she considered herself married to him. In the way a nun is said to be a bride of Christ.

At ten o'clock, "Deedle" having given way to the Cup Finals of 2048, August peeked into his bedroom. "Emma?"

"Yes."

"I thought you were asleep. Why are you sitting in the dark?"

"Oh. So I am."

"I wondered if you wanted to go on with our book."

Since August's eyes had begun to fail, Emma would read every night twenty or so pages aloud to him. Presently they were halfway through Southey's *Life of Nelson*.

"Really, August, not tonight. I have an absolutely splitting headache."

"Can I get you something? An aspirin? Some tea?"

"I think I'd just like to go to bed. If you don't mind."

"What's wrong, Emma? Ever since you came home tonight . . ."

"It's nothing."

He stood in the doorway, squinting into the dark.

She touched her cheeks to be certain they were quite dry. "Actually"—she stood up—"I think I *would* like to read for a bit."

"Oh, not if—"

"I'd feel better. I would. And we can't just leave him there, can we, in the middle of the Battle of the Nile? He'll win, won't he? You must promise me that."

"Nelson? He never did anything else."

"There, you see! My headache's gone already."

He handed her the book.

✳

Emma worked at Bateman's Antique Silver ("In Kensington Since 1952"). Ann Bateman, the granddaughter of the shop's founder, was an alumna of the Inverness School. Without that and Ms. Harness's aggressive sponsorship, Emma would never have found such a plum of a job.

Following the discovery of the Ragnhild Lode, the art of silversmithing had enjoyed a renascence unequaled since the time of De Lamerie. Now, as then, the monuments of the past fell victim to a living art. Despite the influx of Antarctic silver, the demand for workable metal soon outstripped supply, and most old plate was melted down and refashioned a la mode. The last two centuries had been annihilated, the nineteenth was heavily eroded, and even earlier periods could fall victim to the passion for novelty. Against this tendency Ann Bateman fought a resolute and losing battle. She would buy up whole collections to save them from the rolling mill only to find herself obliged to dispose of them as ruthlessly. From the vast river that flowed through Bateman's she was able to skim off only the finest or most idiocratic pieces, for which there was still a market among the conservative, unhappy few; but the multitude— of flatware and cruets, of salts and chafing dishes, of sauceboats and loving cups—these, after a brief stay of execution, were consigned to oblivion and the vat.

Ms. Bateman and her husband tended the shop. Emma worked upstairs with Ruthven Melzer. Officially she was apprenticed to him, which meant that she did the polishing while Ruthven was responsible for all but the most routine repairs. Occasionally, at the request of a regular client, Ruthven undertook work of a more creative nature, as when he had transformed a Dublin sugar basin into a very feasible teapot, but Ms. Bateman was too much the purist to tolerate such carnival goings-on very often.

The fifth member of the staff was an affectionate, attack-trained Alsatian named Elizabeth, who looked after the shop at night and spent her days dozing in the repair room with Ruthven and Emma.

Emma enjoyed the work, which required the utmost attention and very little thought. Few tasks are so innately satisfying as the transformation of uneven or mottled surfaces into smoothness and regularity. Painting a wall is, *a priori*, a good experience. Refinishing woodwork is rather better. Polishing silver is best. The rhythms of the hands' caresses are modulated and varied by a system of concavities and convexities that become, as one's attention is engrossed by the work, not so much gigantic as absolute. The object, whether a bowl or a knife or a chocolate pot, enters into a new relationship with the light, becomes noumenal. Just as only the interpreters of Bach truly understand his music, so only one whose fingers have followed, hours long, the cartouche of an Abercrombie tray can know its value, its intelligence, its wit. The fact that most of Emma's work was in vain, that all but a few of the pieces she polished went to the making of more ingots, did not distress her in the least. The notion pleased her, for it was a proof that the pleasure she took in her work was selfless. After loyalty, selflessness was the virtue she prized most.

Socially as well, the job was agreeable. Aside from a few deliveries she didn't have to deal with the customers, a mercy for which, when she'd first begun looking for work, she hadn't dared to hope. Ruthven was an exacting master, but once she'd learned not only to do the work but to believe in it, his initial hostility thawed to an indifference out of which Emma was eventually able to force, as from the rockiest soil, actual friendship. It was Ruthven who'd first taken her to Snowdon and the Lakes; who, with the same calm and care with which he'd shown her the use of a polishing wheel, had taught her the use of rope, pitons, and her body's strength; who, on the occasion of her first Very Severe, certainly had saved her life. Everything she valued most seemed to be a gift from Ruthven.

As for the Batemans, they could be ignored, and this was a considerable virtue. They'd hired Ruthven and Emma not because they were mortals but because they were willing to accept low wages. It was a conscious arrangement on both sides, and not a little cold. But, as Ruthven always said, the cold is good for you.

A Tuesday late in February. Business had been slack. All morning Ruthven and Emma were as idle as Elizabeth, who lay sleeping in front of the red coils of the heater. Sometimes her ears would twitch, her tail would thwack the herringbone floor: a dream. At noon Ms. Bateman made their *de facto* holiday official so that she could close the shop and take her husband to an auction. Elizabeth was roused and brought downstairs.

"Going right home?" Ruthven asked, slipping into a vaguely military twill jacket. All winter long he wore nothing else, on principle.

"I don't think so. August doesn't care for departures from the norm."

"Good. Let me take you to lunch."

"Oh no. I thought I'd just walk about."

When he asked again, she agreed. She liked to walk, but not through midday crowds, in Kensington, on the dismalest day of the year.

The bell tinged as they left the shop. Drizzle—the fifth *day* of drizzle. At the curb, polly shovel and pail in hand, Ms. Bateman's husband waited patiently for Elizabeth to shit.

"Derry and Tom's?"

"That would be nice."

But on their way there Ruthven dodged into the High Street arcade to keep out of the wet, and in front of its garish windows he asked Emma if she wouldn't like to try Wimpy's for a change. She was sufficiently in command of herself to be able to stop, to look inside, to seem to consider the suggestion.

Any city where one has lived for long will have these trapdoors through which one can tumble into the oubliette of the past. The soundest policy, perhaps, is to brazen out such confrontations. An assumed indifference will harden to sincerity. Emma, unwisely, had tried to cordon off the past, and so it still had power over her. London had become a mosaic of taboos—shops she wouldn't look at, doorways she couldn't pass, streets to be avoided, whole boroughs she refused to enter.

Ruthven looked at her queerly. "What do you say?"

"I don't know. It doesn't look very nice."

"It's so-so. A more personal sort of place than Derry and Tom's. I've been here once or twice with Beau and Conrad. They do good curries, as I recall."

As he stepped up to the menu blazoned on the door, her distress edged toward panic.

"Can you read French?" he asked. "Half this damned thing's in French."

She pretended to study the menu. "Oh, for goodness' sake, look!" She pointed to a word in the "Legumes" column. "Four bob for mushrooms."

"That is rather dear, isn't it?"

"It's all frightfully dear, Ruthven. Really, we ought to go to Derry and Tom's. As we set out to."

He was persuaded. They went down the High Street to Derry and Tom's Rooftop Garden. It was there that Emma encountered Joseph Regan the second time.

Emma liked the Rooftop Garden because she felt safe amid the tiers of potted coleus and spider ferns, the clumps of never-flowering rhododendrons, the book jackets and authors' photographs. You couldn't imagine anything very interesting or unpleasant happening here. Ruthven liked it because it was cheap. Up till six o'clock you could have high tea for four shillings, and for five shillings thereafter.

After only twenty minutes in the queue they were led to a small table in the Tudor Court. With agile good manners Emma took the inside seat so that Ruthven had the holly to look at. It showed the great vine at Hampton Court. Instead of acoustical partitioning, the din and crash of the place was smoothed over by the plaint of a krummhorn, the scrape of rebecks. It was all very period. Ruthven punched in their orders, and then they both sagged with relief into the shaped and slightly yielding polly, she with a smile, he with a sigh. His eyelids drooped shut: The first prefiguring of those abrupt dozes that overtook August nowadays during dull programs and soured conversations. Then he squared his shoulders and they were, effectively, the same age once again. In fact, Ruthven was forty.

They talked about their next climb, somewhere in Scotland. It was another of Ruthven's mighty principles not to discuss anything but silver when they were on Bateman's premises, so that days like this when they could lay their plans and be lyrical were all the more precious for being rare. Where? That was the first thing to consider. They were wavering between the Cuillin of Skye and Ben MacDhui.

The former promised a more classic magnificence, the latter, a ghost—Ferlas Mor, the Great Grey Man.

"I don't believe in ghosts," Emma declared, eager for rebuttal.

"You can say that now, in London, with this mob around you. Wait till you're up there in the snow and you hear him."

"Hear him! Is that all?"

"Oh, he's been seen too, a kind of shadow. Anywhere from ten to forty feet high."

"Really, Ruthven."

"But it's the sound of him that people fear."

A waitress in sleek mourning and a starched cap came with a tray and began laying tea. Ruthven stared at the holly, Emma at the crowd. It was then, her gaze drifting across the faces, she became aware of Joseph Regan's presence. Too late she looked away—at the waitress, at Ruthven, at the steam curling from the hot water jug.

Once, on the Waterloo Road, she'd stepped off the curb without looking and almost been struck by a bus. Then as now, the whole useless armory of terror had taken hold of her. Messengers ran screaming the news from nerve to gland, gland to muscle. By the time the bus was out of sight, her body was totally mobilized for danger.

The waitress went away.

Ruthven reached for the teapot. "Shall I be mother?"

"What are you thinking of! Leave be, I'll pour." She busied herself with the tea things, astonished at her own ostensible control, while her heart, like some poor, flightless bird fallen into a trap, plunged and clawed in unwitnessed despair. "You take two lumps, don't you?" Tongs poised above the bowl.

Ruthven nodded.

She handed him his cup of tea.

"You were saying, about that ghost."

"Ferlas Mor. It's a Gaelic name."

"Yes. That's so interesting. I don't suppose"—she scalded her lips—"that you've talked with anyone who's actually seen him? Or heard, if all he does is squeal and gibber."

She risked another look, over Ruthven's shoulder. Not to be certain, for it was just the completeness of her certainty that was so awful, that from two brief glimpses in the Underground she should have retained an image of him so indelible that memory could filter that one face out from all these others. Not to be more certain, but because she had to know if he'd seen her.

Joseph caught her glance and smiled.

" . . . a matter of fact, not once but twice. And I can vouch for both of them being sober, levelheaded boys, not the kind to be making up tales."

"Oh, I'm sure." A polite, half-teasing smile accommodated the curve of the cup.

Mashing up the half-dissolved lumps with his spoon, Ruthven went on in his solemnest fireside manner to tell how the first of these two witnesses, coming down from the summit of MacDhui late of a winter's night, had heard the crunch of footsteps following him down the snowy slope. The peculiarity of these footsteps was that, without ever falling behind, they matched his own in a ratio of one to three.

"An echo?" Emma suggested.

"So I thought, at first. But think of it. One in three is an odd sort of echo."

"And the next person who heard these footsteps heard the same one in three?"

"He did not—and that's the strange thing. What *he* heard was more like one footstep for every two and a half of his own."

"Well?"

Ruthven placed his cup back in the saucer for the denouement. "You see, the second fellow was long-legged, almost six feet tall. But the first chap, he wasn't any taller than you."

"It makes you think."

"It does, doesn't it?"

"And of course there's no question now but that *we* must go to Ben MacDhui. I wouldn't miss the chance of having the Fearless Morgue stalk *me*, not for the world!"

From the way he twinkled as he agreed to this, she knew it was the choice he'd wanted her to make. From sheer gratitude, Ruthven even tried to top off the previous wonderments with some inventions of his own, but they were rather pale. Fancy was not an important component of his character.

Emma had never felt so grateful for another physical presence as now for Ruthven's. His stolid, beaten-up and utterly invulnerable face; the scarred hands piebald, like her own, from the polishing compound; the grubby grey jacket—he was like some great pile of a Norman wall, a barbican from whose safety she could survey, unscathed, unworried, the tents and fluttering pennons on the plain below.

Loud laughter cut across a jittery courante. Both of them— himself and the busty woman with him—were howling and carrying on. She was sure he'd just told her of their first meeting, of the bite she'd taken out of him. She was about to excuse herself to the loo when Ruthven stood up to announce the same intention.

A moment later he came over to her table. "Hello again."

She nodded stiffly.

His hand was extended toward her: the same hand, the same ring.

"My name is Joseph Regan." There was nothing gloating in his voice, nothing bullying in his insistence that she take his hand. She did and it was as though instead of being run over, the bus had stopped for her and she'd gotten on. "I was sure I'd meet you again. Every night on the tube I expect to look up and see you."

As he made no threat against Ruthven's seat, Emma, to see any more of him at all than the helicine embroideries on his codpiece, was obliged to tilt her head back the way one does to see the top of a tall building. A hectic complexion; a smile at once extravagant and overdelicate; lank, light blond, unpowdered hair tied back in a stiff Hessian tail. His clothes were, in the very simplest way, all wrong. By no means was he so heroically handsome as she'd remembered him, nor were his eyes so annihilating. They didn't simply bear down on her as if she were not more than the target of some unswervable, impersonal awareness. In fact, he seemed quite human, and much less dangerous.

"Is that your usual train then?" she asked.

"Yes. Isn't it yours?"

"No. I take the Bakerloo Line usually." Which in a way was true. For the past two weeks she'd gone home each day by this longer route just to guard agiainst the likelihood of meeting him again. "I like to walk across the park." Need she have said that?

For the longest time he just stood there. The pressure of his silent attention made her avert her gaze again, down to the garish helices, orange paired to sky blue, crimson to lime: In the same way, in a light rain or when the sun is too intense, one walks along without looking up from the pavement. It was not an unkind attention, but it was, in the same natural-seeming way as rain or too bright light, uncomfortable. She told him her name.

By the time Ruthven had returned from the loo, their acquaintance had progressed no further. Joseph returned to his companion, and Emma was obliged to tell the story of that first encounter.

Ruthven thought it a damned funny thing. Like all very tactful people, Ruthven often chose to be regarded as a simpleton.

They returned to their plans for Ben MacDhui over the second infusion of the tea. Five minutes later Joseph left with his blowzy ladyfriend. He didn't embarrass Emma by more than a nod.

They'd barely left when Ruthven said, "I'm going to say something I probably have no right to say."

"Ruthven. Not now, please."

"It isn't what you think."

"It isn't what *you* think either. It was a completely utterly ridiculous *accident!*"

He looked at Emma in a baffled way. She let her own face go all stony with resentment.

"What the hell, Emma. I didn't mean . . . "

"Ruthven, I have no more interest in him, or he in me, than . . . than *you* do, if that's what you're hinting at. And I don't want to hear one of your disgusting, silly sermons about the Greeks or whatever."

"All I meant to say, Emma, is that the whole business . . . well, it isn't that awful. Or important. It comes and it goes, like a bit of rough weather, and the thing to remember is stay planted on a good ledge and keep your grip."

"Is that all?"

"That's all. Sorry."

"Then if you don't mind I'd like to leave. No—by myself."

Ruthven stood to help her on with her coat. In another corner of the Tudor Court two couples rose at the same moment and began to perform a cramped saraband. Emma had to duck under the bridge of their arms to get out.

Almost the moment she was on the High Street, regrets sliced at her like so much crushed green glass underfoot—not for what she'd said to Ruthven or even what she'd let him guess, but for having let him see her lose control. She flinched from the thought of going back to the shop tomorrow—the necessity of apologizing and being apologized to, and then of matching Ruthven silence for silence the rest of the day. Easier just to call in sick! Or disappear!

But this was such an abject and explicit weakness that it served, like a whiff of ammonia, to clear her head. By the time she'd reached the gate to Kensington Gardens, her good intentions for the future had elevated her to a mood of grim, do-or-die buoyancy. Indeed, her spirits were on such a rapid boil that even if she hadn't gone through her ordeal at Derry and Tom's, just the shifts and changes of the weather (a fine gusty wind blew out of the west and the sun burst out fitfully through rifts in the clouds) would have sufficed to plunge her to the depths or lift her up rejoicing. It was the first hour of the spring.

Pale purple crocuses starred the margins of the Flower Walk. It was too soon for anything else. Twenty yards on from the gate Joseph Regan was sitting on a bench set back from the walk, arms draped on the orange slats, head tilted back to take in the coursing clouds. Either he was genuinely unaware of her approach or he was a good actor. In either case she felt secure enough, that instant, of her own strength to walk right up to the edge and say hello.

"Hello, Joseph Regan."

"Why hello!" He had a scattered look. Was he trying to remember her name? "Rose!" A smile spread gradually across his whole face. The clouds had smoothed everything overcomplicated from his features to make of him now a thing as simple and gorgeous as sunlight on summer grass.

"Better not sit down," he said, rising. "The bench is wet, and cold as . . . " He seemed to have to reach for the comparison. " . . . ice."

Where he'd been the rain was wiped off the slats; the bench, thus acted on, became a work of art.

"Or better yet, here—sit where I've dried it off. And I'll"—he sat again, a polite interval from the dry spot—"sit here."

"Thank you."

Like a perfume, the ghost of his warmth still clung to the orange polly.

"I was surprised to see that you're by yourself," she said. "Though I suppose you could say the same."

"What, surprised? No. I mean, of course I'm happy to see you, Rose. Whenever I do."

"You weren't waiting here?"

"Ah, you know, perhaps I was! Did you think I would be?"

"I don't know. Perhaps I did." Her smile tipped delicately sideways from sincerity. Now who was being Byzantine? But wasn't it a grand feeling, after all this time, *not* to be serious? Like being barefoot after a day laced into heavy boots, like getting on a bicycle when you haven't ridden one for years.

"Actually," he said, "I did ask Veronica if she wanted to stroll about the park, but she had some shopping to attend to. She's only just come to town."

"Were you telling her about my biting you in the Underground? Is that what set you off like that?"

"When?"

"At Derry and Tom's just now. When else?"

"No, that was something malicious she said about Daryl. My second wife's older brother. Veronica resents him for being so rich. But it was a very complicated joke, and if you don't already know the guy and hate his guts it's not very funny."

For a long time he just watched her knees, which she crossed left over right and then reversed, not nervously but by way of keeping up her end of the dialogue and keeping warm. Seated here, the west wind seemed less certain a presage of spring.

"This is incredible weather today," he said. "You can forget, looking about you, that it's still February."

"It's deceptive that way," she agreed.

Could he actually be as slow, as stupid, as stumbling as he seemed right now? She hoped so. Whole realms of hearsay widened into reality from this new vantage point. She could imagine herself a femme fatale, a Circe enchanting herds of lovers, ringing their noses, driving them to their sties with a wand. Not that she ever would, but she could now imagine it.

"In fact," she said, as though he had suggested it, "a walk *would* be a good idea."

She set a brisk pace past the newly turned plots of mud. It

occurred to her, as they approached the Albert Memorial, that Ruthven would almost certainly be taking the same route to his dorm in the Knightsbridge Barracks. She veered north, and Joseph followed tamely, always lagging a step or two behind, always looking at her.

She kept walking faster and only the conviction that he would be able to catch her and that he would probably try kept her from breaking into a run.

They were standing on the wooden bridge that spanned the narrowest part of the Serpentine. One swan and then another sloped out from the bridge's shadow, crackling the silvered surface into coins of light. Joseph reached into the pouch slung from the straps of his codpiece and removed a hard roll. He gave half of it to Emma. They fed the swans.

"What's that?" he asked, "at the end of the pond?" They were still on the bridge.

"Some kind of pine? I don't know trees at all."

"No, that."

"Nelson's column, you mean?"

"What I mean is, what's it doing here?"

"Oh, they had to move it when they put up the big development in Trafalgar Square. Haven't you been to see that? It's quite grand."

"It looks incongruous, I must say."

"You get used to it. I have anyhow. The way it reflects in the water is very nice. Rather like that obelisk in Washington."

"It wasn't put here recently then?"

She saw belatedly what he was driving at, but not so late as to lose the advantage. "Not very. 'Eighty-three perhaps?"

"No, it would have to have been after that. It was still in Trafalgar Square the last time I was there. And that was in 'eighty-four for the *Extrovert*'s send-off."

"Oh yes, you're right. I remember: they'd strung up Union Jacks and all different countries' flags from every part of the column. Well, they must have moved it here immediately after that, because it has been here forever and ever."

"You were at the launching?"

"Just the parade. I loved that. One of the astronauts gave me *such* a look. I've never forgotten. I wanted to fly away with them."

Joseph gave her a look nearly as memorable. "How old *are* you?"

He might, she thought, have fallen into her ambush more gracefully, but never mind.

"Why," with feigned surprise, "how old do you think?"

For answer his eyes attempted once again to enter her, to wrest an admission by main force, but today she was prepared for him. She turned him away as dexterously as any maid answering the door with a message that her mistress is not at home.

"Not a day over twenty, I'd have said," he answered at last.

For all its staginess her laugh carried conviction. "Then you've been supposing that I—oh, my Lord. Because of Ruthven, is that why? The fellow I was lunching with?"

"I hadn't sorted out the reason, but I did assume that—"

"Well, I'm not. I hate to disappoint you, Joseph."

He insisted it was not a disappointment. "But you still haven't answered my question, Rose."

"If it *must* be answered, then I'm sixty-four."

"Oh."

She patted his hand in mock condolence. "No, no apology is necessary. I do understand. I used to feel the same way about Ruthven when he wasn't looking *quite* so worn out. They're not like us, are they? And I regard your mistake as the sweetest of compliments. I really do."

As they walked on to Marble Arch his every glance would seek to verify what he suspected still, that she had lied to him, that she *was* mortal. But the mask of her irony was not to be dislodged.

At the gate he said, "I must leave you here. I've an engagement at four o'clock to see the gentleman Veronica and I were making fun of. And it's almost that."

"We're bound to meet again, Joseph. These things happen in threes."

"I hope so." But the kiss he gave her this time suggested that it was no very fervent hope.

The pleasure of her victory was slowly but wholly attrited by the stream of faces moving eastward along Oxford Street. Whom had she been taunting, whom deceived but herself? For all the cleverness

of her retreat, the single moment that remained alive to memory
was that on the bridge across the Serpentine: the minute bread-
crumbs still clinging to his fingertips, the softness of his hands, her
terror that in kissing her he would force himself into her mouth and
then, instead, his lips had touched her neck, not even touched: a
breath. Ah, if this were a victory, she would have preferred death.

✳

Once across Waterloo Bridge she found that even the most
hallowed sights of childhood had no power over her—Festival St.
John's, say, or the Tesco Monument that she'd spun round almost
every day on her way home from school. The touch of memory was
neither brutal nor caressing now, but neutral, like a nurse's or a
dishwasher's.

Ninety-eight, where the taxi let her out, was the only recent
addition to the street, a brand-new high-rise with long hollies and
files of windows striping its sides. The hollies were aerial views of
warm ripe fields of wheat; the windows reflected the pale February
afternoon. Huge in the foreground, crows hovered above the wheat
fields, as gulls swooped through the intermittent winter sky. Emma
could not decide if it was worth such a lot of trouble.

She identified herself to the buzzer and was let in through the
gate. Flat D was in the second sub-basement and so immediately
magnificent that Emma almost ignored the woman who opened the
door to her, though she was, surely, no less magnificent. The woman
smiled and gold dazzled from deep, dark Madagascan flesh that
seemed, so grainy it was and wrinkled, to crumble away even as you
smiled back, like some long lost sandstone bust fished up from the
ruins of Ca d'Oro. A wrap of cobalt crepe de chine streamed down
from a collar of pearls to a froth of simulated down. Receiving the
vase from Emma with a rather legato grace, she carried it toward,
and placed it on, a tall guéridon table.

She slipped off the flannel bag, boosted the lights, and beamed at
her treasure. "Oh yes. It is ravishing."

It was a fluttery, top-lofty piece by Paul Storr, overwrought with
anthemions and masks and animal legs. Atop the whole soaring
mythological heap a water nymph reclined, invulnerable and nude.
Emma agreed that it was very nice, and quite sincerely.

Ms. Adoko (this was the name on the invoice) pointed Emma to a couch. She circled her acquisition hungrily, running a silvered fingernail along the beading, quite as if it were the frosting on her wedding cake. She touched the breast of a supporting sphinx, breathed on the water nymph, desired it.

"You don't think it's too busy?"

"Not any more than it tries to be," Emma assured her, with a fine sense of her own diplomacy.

A fat cream-colored tom wrapped himself round Emma's ankle. She flinched. The cat was in her lap in one bound.

"Godwin," Ms. Adoko scolded, "you know better than that!"

"Oh, but I love cats."

"As a rule, perhaps, but Godwin may prove the exception. For one thing he isn't a cat. Are you Godwin? He's an author. Look at the way he's studying your face. Taking notes already. He can be quite ruthless, but he can also be a dreadful sycophant. You're Irish, aren't you?"

"Well, I was *born* in Ireland," Emma said, as though she might, by another criterion, not be Irish at all.

"I can always tell. As for me, it must be obvious that I'm Madagascan."

"And Godwin?" Emma asked, steering back to shallow water. "What nationality is he?"

"Very *echt* English. But a fair novelist for all that. Have you ever read *Caleb Williams?*"

"No." With an uncertain smile, for she was beginning to fear that Ms. Adoko might intend these whimsies in earnest.

"Neither have I, actually. I often wish I did have time for books and such, but ah, my mind's a butterfly." She stooped to ruffle the cat's throat with butterfly fingers. Godwin purred and squirmed in Emma's lap. "Flower to flower, the story of my life."

"It's a real book?"

"Indeed: *Caleb Williams, or Things as They Are.* Metempsychosis, you see. Centuries ago there was this novelist, William Godwin, who must have lived a very unregenerate life, because coming back as a cat, even a Persian, even *my* Persian, can't be too fulfilling. He still wants to write, poor darling, but he can't of course, not physically. So he has to do all his work mentally and project it to me, telepathically. Usually, though, I can't be bothered and so none of it gets written down, which must be very frustrating to him, but after all I have my own life to live. Don't I?" Silver nails tweaked Godwin's nose. Godwin snarled. His claws tensed, pricking Emma's thigh.

Ms. Adoko pushed herself to her feet. "But to get back to the vase, you may tell Ms. Bateman that her taste is preternaturally right."

"You want it?"

"Passionately! But—" Waving aside the invoice that Emma began to unfold. "Do give me half a moment, my dear, before I sign my life away. I've asked Gerald to make us some tea, to which you unconditionally must submit. Besides, there's everything you still haven't seen, my famous silver turtle and a *glorious* tureen from the Deccan service. Oh, there are rooms and rooms. You must, if you're human, be a little curious. In any case, I am." She winked, and wrinkled.

A bell tinkled.

"That will be our tea. No doubt Ruthven has told you about Gerald?"

"No. He makes it a rule never to gossip."

"Not even about me! How cold-blooded."

A tall, lanky, pink and black teddy bear entered the room and laid tea on the low table beside the couch. Ms. Adoko sat down beside Emma, with a gesture to her butler that he should pour. As he stooped over the tray, a massive pectoral cross swung out from his pink plush chest. Synthetic fur had been implanted everywhere except around his eyes, mouth, and genitals. By these evidences he too was Madagascan.

"Milk, my dear, or lemon?" Ms. Adoko asked.

Emma just stared.

Gerald tipped milk into both cups. Ms. Adoko reached across the couch and scooped Godwin from Emma's lap to the floor.

"Sugar?"

"One, please."

Taking the cup and saucer, Emma's hand brushed against the furred fingers.

Gerald placed a plate of petits fours between the two women, made a little bow in proper teddy-bear style, and sashayed from the room.

"Now, you see, if Ruthven had gossiped just a little, he wouldn't have left you quite so unprepared."

"Oh, but I wasn't . . . I mean, you see them on the street like that. Sometimes."

"Do you? I don't get out as much as I used to."

"Well, not exactly the same." Emma took a sip of tea and, thinking about the giant teddy bear, gave a muffled snort. Her nose filled with tea. She began to choke.

When she'd recovered, Ms. Adoko explained that Gerald was studying to become a priest. He had been studying some twenty years already (he was an American Negro, *not* Madagascan), and it would probably be another twenty before he became a professed member of his order, the Society of Jesus.

"Are you in the same church?" Emma asked in a tone of the grayest politeness.

"Goodness, no! Me? I'm still *years* from needing religion. Fifty-four, the prime of life. No, having Gerald is a testimony rather to my wickedness than to my piety. They have to take vows, you know. Poverty, chastity, and obedience. I'm obedience. Thank heaven." She nibbled a crumb from the edge of a petit four. "In any case, you know, it's not the sort of church for the likes of us. From the strictly *Catholic* point of view they're all heretics, and yet they're so orthodox in their own peculiar way that they *agree* that they're heretics."

"It does seem a strange sort of religion," Emma ventured.

"Isn't it? Though I'd never say so to Gerald. He's mine for two years yet so long as I don't tamper with his inner life. In any case, I'm not inclined to, provided that he keeps it out of sight. God bless Ignatius Loyola, say I, and God bless my teddy bear. Did you notice his pectoral?"

"The cross?"

"It's fourteenth century. When the Ashmolean was closed, I picked up several very pretty things. It has the soundest possible pedigree. Various people who get mentioned in footnotes in history books owned it at one time or another. Dr. Fox, the Bishop of Winchester. Mrs. Oliphant. But you still haven't seen any of my treasures. Come!" Ms. Adoko rose in billows of cloud-colored crepe.

As she conducted Emma through the flat, her patter was nonchalant as any tour guide's, and almost as inflexible. She was shown the famous silver turtle, the tureen from the Deccan service, and a cabinet of chalices and mustard pots.

Why is she doing this? Emma wondered. Was it sex?

They returned to the vase on the guéridon table.

"Well?" Ms. Adoko asked.

"It's all quite magnificent."

"But not, any of it, quite so magnificent as this, eh?"

"I couldn't say."

"Oh, you could, you could. Should I plunge? Would I like it for my very own? Tell me."

"Well then—yes. Buy it."

"Good." Then, turning her head but not raising her voice, "Gerald, bring me the money."

Godwin appeared in the doorway, and a moment later the teddy bear, holding a blue envelope. He handed it to Ms. Adoko. Ms. Adoko handed it to Emma. "A thousand pounds for now. Tell Ms. Bateman I'll bring by the rest when I'm next in her neighborhood. Or perhaps you'd like to phone her?"

"No."

"You should at least count the money."

It was already in her pocket. "Don't be silly."

"It may not be the right amount."

"I'll trust that it is."

Ms. Adoko smiled, stroking her pearl collar. "Shall I make a little prophecy, Emma?"

Emma glanced down from the too-intent, too-friendly brown eyes. Godwin, beside the feathery hem, gazed up at her. She glanced from the cat to observe that the butler had a hard-on.

"Someday, if you should ever think it worth your while, you will have so much money, my dear, such an incalculable amount of it, that all this, and there's quite a lot more than I could show you, all this would be invisible beside it."

Emma looked up with some relief. "Thank you. It's a lovely prophecy."

"I'm quite serious. You're beautiful, you're mortal, and you're bright. That, plus a certain respect for money, is what it takes."

"Thank you again." She glanced back at Gerald, who seemed as oblivious of his own erection as any piece of furniture.

"You *don't* take care of your hands, but I suppose it wouldn't be possible, working every day with the silver. Maude Gonne had poor hands too. What are the lines?

> You are more beautiful than any one,
> And yet your body had a flaw:
> Your small hands were not beautiful . . . .

Still, there's never any excuse for torn cuticles."

Emma nodded.

"I shan't bore you now with any more good advice. You'll have to fall in love, fall out, and generally lead your own original life. Another person's experience is never of any use. But would you, when the time comes that you're *interested* in money and manicurists and such, remember me—and try to get in touch?"

"If that time should come, of course."

"That's very generous of you, my dear. Gerald, take off your cross and put it on Emma."

"Oh. No, I—" Fuzzy fingers brushed her cheeks. A cold line cut the nape of her neck, as though an executioner were lightly to position his axe before the stroke.

"Remember, Gerald, to send Emma the documentation."

"Really, Ms. Adoko, I can't possibly accept this, not possibly."

"Baiba—please." She planted a businesslike kiss on Emma's right cheek, steering her meanwhile to the door. Only now did she notice the deadfall over the lintel.

"Pardon?"

"Now that we're friends you must call me by my first name, which is Baiba." She got the other cheek, held open the door.

"But I cannot—" She reached back to remove the cross. Links of chain snagged in her hair.

"My dear." Ms. Adoko laid her hands across Emma's, preventing her. "First, you ought never to refuse *any* gift. People will suppose you have nothing with which to retaliate. Secondly, this is not a gift at all, so far as I'm concerned. An investment, rather. I may not see you again for some time." The door began to close. "I want you to remember me. This way perhaps you will."

✳

Beautiful?

But what, in a way, isn't? The pavement was beautiful, with all its lumps and cracks; the stars on a manhole cover worn smooth as an old ten-penny bit; brick walls, windows, an old sign flaking away almost to silence:

BUY YOUR
WET FISH
HERE;

another, perpetually orange, the polly bonded to brick:

ALL SPECIALTIES;

and people, of course: the way, when they stepped off the ped belt and entered the arcade, they seemed to awaken, eyes and mouth narrowing to attention; the way, getting on, they seemed to enter a dream common to them all, like so many shallow skiffs swept off on the current of some mild, sluggish river.

Yet Emma doubted that Ms. Adoko had used the word in this all-inclusive sense when she'd said *she* was beautiful. An hour later the remark still lingered, irritated, itched. Beautiful? No, even discounting all her diffidence could contrive by way of mute clothes and careless haircuts, she didn't think so. Not "beautiful." Of any of *them* you could tell at a glance whether the word applied, and more often than not it did. Mortals seldom realized their potential in quite so final a way, though her mother had been "beautiful" off and on. And Ms. Adoko, at one time, must have been . . . . ravishing.

She stopped before the windows of THE BRIDE STRIPPED BARE, where half-size blank-faced mannequins marched back and forth and sat and stooped and embraced each other in miniature copies of this season's offerings. She remembered once wanting something that had been in this window, wanting it just desperately, but for the life of her she couldn't remember what, or why, or exactly when. There seemed to be no connection between who she'd been then and who she was now.

Now, if she had wanted to, she could have gone inside and outfitted herself head to toe. What wouldn't a thousand pounds buy? Her imagination balked before such an expanse of possibilities, but, just as once, roped to Ruthven on the side of Pavey Ark, she had made herself look down into the dull-gleaming mirror of the tarn until she'd balanced her fear against a countervailing strength, so now she forced herself to consider how, if it were hers, she might spend a thousand pounds. Not, she knew at once, here. THE BRIDE STRIPPED BARE was not that acme of deluxe she'd thought it at age thirteen. Nor anywhere in dreary old London.

Travel, that would be the way. One should be able to get to a good many of the world's wonders on a thousand pounds. If nothing else, she would have liked to trace de Saussure's footsteps up to the summit of Mont Blanc, or follow the path that Leslie Steven had taken up the Matterhorn. What with train fare, hotels, equipment, and (why not? it was only a dream) a guide, she could imagine devouring the whole thousand pounds before she was arrested. Oh, easily.

Having imagined as much, she was free to continue on her way. Up from the arcade and down along the High Street, past flower stalls and junk shops and all the other relics of her childhood spread out like a box of broken toys on a bedspread, and all of them, wonderfully, powerless to hurt. The freedom of it! The strength!

On the Borough Road she went into Maggy's. She took a stool at a counter with forty tulip glasses, each a different color, representing the forty flavors of Campbell's Fortified Puddings. The counterman asked her what she wanted.

"Eels." Anything seemed possible today.

"Small bag?"

"Please."

She spun her stool a quarter-revolution to the left. Four stools off the man who had been watching her turned back to his companion.

The counterman brought the bag of jellied eel. Emma reached into her pocket past the envelope and fished out two half-crowns. She waited till he'd gone to the register before she peeked into the bag.

They looked more loathsome than she'd remembered. Maybe if she bit off just a teensy bite from one end? She lifted one of the droopy cylinders from the bag. It slithered like a bar of waterlogged soap. She feared that within its gelatinous coating it would be too rubbery to bite through. So, closing her eyes, she took in the whole length of it at once.

Pressed between her tongue and the roof of her mouth, the eel dissolved slowly into a slime of salt and smoke that her throat refused to swallow. It remained in her mouth, a motionless mulch, and its inassimilable flavor laved her body with tides of nausea. It was easier, finally, to force it down.

The man who'd been looking at her was now only two stools away. He nodded to her, smiling. His eyes moved in an ironic arc from her face to the bag that still contained three more lengths of eel.

She couldn't.

She would throw the rest away when she want back to the tube. She'd take the ramp across St. George's Circus and drop the bag down into the Vacancy.

Just as he was about to say something, Emma grabbed up the bag and spun her stool round in the opposite direction. Halfway to the door she threw up. She stared at the vomitus for a moment (bits of orange icing from the petits fours dotted the undigested scraps of eel), then returned to streets that seemed, once more, altogether as terrible as she remembered them.

*

The third was rainy, and then the tenth and seventeenth. Emma would have prayed for the twenty-fourth to be rainy too, but it seemed a kind of impiety, like praying for the sermon on Palm Sunday to be shorter. No, if it were sunny, she would go along to the zoo. And cheerfully, she told herself, cheerfully.

Actually once you were there it could be amusing if you forgot the injustice of the animals being caged. Some of them, anyhow, were still half alive. The jerboa, for instance, spanning its vivarium in a single sudden ping, like a quantum jump. The gibbons swooping. Her special favorites were the wild goats on the Mappin Terraces. She could watch them for hours, bounding about on their artificial rocks.

August, however, preferred larger animals of a less anthropomorphic stamp, who mostly just lounged in their cages with an air of crazed indolence—lions and tapirs and slow-motion stacks of giant tortoises. Since it was for his sake that she came to the zoo at all, Emma felt obliged to sacrifice her preferences to his.

It hadn't rained and they were there, on a bench in front of the lion house. One of the lions had come out, if not exactly to bask, as a sign of encouragement to the sun. August unwrapped a toffee and sucked it audibly. The lion stared.

Some haze slipped from its face and the sun fractionally upped its wattage. People seemed to move a bit faster, and the lion's tail flicked once against the bars. Emma thought that in another hour she could fairly suggest that they leave.

The tradition of a visit to the zoo on the first non-rainy Sunday in March dated back to August's own childhood, when each year had witnessed the miracle of another and another extincted species resurrected from its frozen chromosomes. It must have seemed a veritable golden age after the harsh decades of the Second Famine, a time of prodigies and phoenixes. Perhaps for August these visits still were celebrations of the world's perpetual renewal, a kind of atheist's Easter. But for Emma, this time, the zoo served only to memorialize all those creatures who had not found sanctuary in the freezers' ark: the yak, the panda, and the ocelot; the egret and the flightless cormorant; the otter, the coypu, and both the white and black rhinoceros. Cage after cage in all the houses, whole paddocks and compounds remained untenanted; just the animal's name on a marker and the dagger   that symbolized its extinction.

"You know." August cleared his throat. "One never is aware of them as individuals. This one, for instance—he might be the same lion I saw when Joanna brought me here in 'thirty-six."

She had decided that August had indeed come to the end of his thought and was about to remark that the attendants, working with them every day, probably did have a clear sense of each animal's unique character, when he resumed. "Of course, one doesn't see most individuals as individuals."

The lion shifted his massive head on his paws. Where had she read that they could kill an ox twice their own weight with just a single motion of their claws and jaw? She tried to imagine the motion.

"Perhaps," she said (August had coughed for her attention), "if we could see them in the wild, when they're living the sort of lives they were meant to. . . ." If you thought about that (she hadn't while she'd said the words), it actually made sense. The idea had just spilled out of her, like tea from a pot. "Perhaps then."

"Perhaps," August agreed.

The lion was looking at her. He was. People would cross back and forth between them, but the focus of his eyes didn't shift. Emma pretended to pay attention to August, who, having attained to his midday spate, needed only phatic encouragement. In fact, she was teasing the lion. The lion remained implacably interested. She winked at him, wriggled her fingers, smiled. August noticed none of this. The lion glared at her, unteasable, melancholy, mad.

August was discussing the advantages of being omnivorous.

"August," she said.

He didn't hear. She stood up. The lion fractionally raised his head, setting his great mane to swaying.

"Excuse me, August. I must get to a lav. Really."

At the end of the row of benches she glanced back. The lion had stopped noticing her. She felt disappointed and a little contemptuous. The lion faded from her imagination like a song before the commercial comes on.

She couldn't remember where the toilets were and anyhow she didn't need one, so she walked inside the first building she came to, which was the Elephant and Rhinoceros Pavilion. She would wait five minutes and return to the bench. Time to breathe.

Both the elephant and the rhinoceros were extinct, and their pavilion did not attract many spectators. It was like going to church in the middle of the afternoon, a resemblance heightened by the peculiar architecture of the place. Facets of ceilings joined at unlikely angles high overhead. The cages, raised and set back like a series of side chapels, were separated from the central space by the merest of iron railings. You could imagine going up to them and taking communion. With a few candles and a bit of incense. . . .

"Why, hello!"

Who in the world?

But she smiled at her provisionally, hoping the woman would say something to spare her the embarrassment of having to ask outright. The likeliest theory was that she was a customer of Ms. Bateman's, but her clothes were a mite too unconsidered, not to say shabby.

"You're Emma, aren't you? What a lovely coincidence!" She extended her hand. "I'm Veronica. You probably don't remember me. I was an element of the background."

"Oh?" Warily Emma accepted her hand.

"At Derry and Tom's."

"Oh!" And in fact it was the same frowzy dress she'd seen her in then.

"I've an unfair advantage, I know. Joseph was so taken with you he talked of nothing else for days. One dance at the Capulets and *wham,* you were *imprinted* on his libido."

"Less than one," Emma said. Though she couldn't remember who the Capulets were (some kings of France?) she was certain she wanted to get away from *wham.*

"Joseph is incorrigible."

Emma allowed that he was very nice. Then she asked, "Do you come here often?"

"This is my longest vacation in years. Usually I find myself in Tübingen. Or did you mean come to the zoo?"

"I meant to this pavilion, actually. You see, I practically *live* here."

"Really?"

"Really. I have a passion for architecture"—that much, at least, was true—"and this is one of the ideal forms of architecture. Like one of those big abbey churches: a vast complicated empty space that serves absolutely no purpose. It's pure." The conceit had sprung from her unpremeditated and whole, like the page that appears on the screen when you slip a library book into a viewer.

"Well, it *did* have a purpose," Veronica said, with a glance toward the commemorative bale of never-to-be-eaten hay at the back of the white rhinoceros's cage.

"So did churches," Emma countered, "though they continue now and then to be built. If I should ever take up architecture seriously, this is what I'd like to do—rhinoceros pavilions."

Veronica conceded her a small unamused laugh. "You do know the story, don't you, of how this actually came to be built? No? It's a lovely story, and quite hilarious."

Emma could not fathom the woman's hostility. Why? Because of Joseph Regan? But she had gone out of her way not to *mention* him. What more did she want from her? A vow of chastity?

"Shall I tell you?"

"Please."

"Rhinoceroses used never to breed in captivity. Whether from shyness or a general zooish sense of alienation, no one ever knew exactly. All kinds of creatures do lose heart when they're put in cages. Then some bright research assistant found that all it was was that they'd always been put in buildings with relatively low ceilings. When the rhinoceros was just browsing around and mooning, this didn't matter, but sometimes a new rhinoceros, when he thought himself to be alone with another rhinoceros . . . . Have you ever seen one, by the way?"

"Stuffed."

"Oh, that's right. You're only sixty, a stripling."

Emma smiled.

"Well, the bull rhinoceros *would* try to mount the lady rhinoceros with the best intentions. But when he did—*Whump!*—he'd hit his horn against the ceiling. And the next time—*Whump!* After a few tries, any rhinoceros simply deconditioned himself from ever *thinking* about sex. When they designed this building, they raised the ceiling ten feet, and the rhinoceroses began to breed like crazy."

"It *is* hilarious," Emma said levelly.

"Yes, I thought so. *Whump!*" Veronica pantomimed a male rhinoceros.

"I must be getting on. I have a friend waiting by the lions."

"I'll go with you. I only ventured in here to look for my cat."

Outside the sun had cut through the haze to lay crisp shadows across the pavement.

"Niobe!" Veronica called loudly.

Emma felt she was being led into a trap. She thought of excusing herself to the lav again, but Veronica seemed capable of following her right into the stall.

"Niobe!"

"Niobe is your cat?"

"Yes. I thought a visit to the zoo would expand her horizons, but then she slipped away from me, and I've been terrified that she'll find her way into some predator's den, or attack a penguin. So we both—Oh! There she is."

(She had said: "Both.")

Niobe looked up coldly from her nest in August's lap. Seeing Emma, August left off petting the cat to wave. "Emma, come here! There's someone I'd like you to meet."

Joseph Regan rose to his feet. As Niobe's leash was twined round his right hand, the cat was obliged to jump down from August's lap.

"This is my very old friend, Joseph Regan. Joseph—my niece, Emma Rosetti." For years August and Emma had employed the simplifying fiction of their being uncle and niece.

Reluctantly Emma offered her hand. Because of the leash, Joseph accepted it in his left hand. The sun shone through the thin Indian cotton of his tunic like an X ray. Goosebumps constellated his bare legs. He wouldn't let go of her hand. Finally she thought to say, "How do you do?"

Joseph inclined his head. The sun aureoled his blondness.

"What an extraordinary coincidence," Veronica said.

"Oh, excuse me. August, this is Veronica Quin."

Only now, so that August could take Veronica's hand, did he let loose his grip. Emma stared at him across the barrier of their clasped hands. A strand of coral circled his neck like a tiny kabob of glistening beef.

"It was August," Joseph said, without ever shifting his eyes from Emma, "who stopped Niobe, and with only moments to spare. She was about to feed herself to the lion. Apparently she did not regard him as being essentially different from herself. It was an altogether heroic action. August's, that is—not Niobe's."

Veronica bent down and scooped up the cat. "*Du Schreckliche! Undankbar* kittycat!" As she rose, Niobe struggled to get out of her arms. "Naughty . . . foolish . . . and too curious!" With each adjective she rapped the cat's forehead with her knuckles. "I don't know how to thank you, Mr. . . .? I'm afraid I didn't catch your name."

Joseph's eyes flicked to Veronica. The shift of his attention was so entire, so fierce, that he seemed to vanish. "Where are our manners?" he said, in a quietly threatening way. "Veronica, this is August Harness. August's mother taught my son Oliver in the third grade. Almost a century ago that must have been."

"My aunt, in fact," August interposed dryly.

Vortices opened before her. Emma found herself standing on the brink of an abyss of time. August and herself stood on the hither, desolated side and far away, mere specks of light on the canyon's other rim, were Joseph and Veronica, as opulent as gods, and as uncaring.

She wanted him to look at her. She wanted to wear his blood agate eyes on a string around her neck. She wanted to die.

He looked at her.

"Later, many years later, my son came to work at this zoo, helping to resurrect the rodents. But it's a very long story, the moral of which is that old friends seem to be fated to go on running into each other. Are you still living at the Inverness School?"

"Yes," August said, "though it isn't the Inverness School any longer. Joanna finally liberated herself."

"Ah, yes, I remember her threatening to."

Veronica shrieked at the cat.

Once again, in the same words, Joseph told the story of Niobe's rescue, and once again, but more amply, Veronica thanked August.

"You had already met my niece?" August asked her.

"Yes, in the rhinoceros house, where she'd come to study architecture. I recruited her to help me find Niobe." She glanced sideways at Emma. "So you can imagine *our* surprise coming out here and finding the two of you having a *reunion,* for heaven's sake."

August frowned. "I didn't know you were a student of architecture, Emma."

Emma could think of nothing to say. In the sunlight Joseph's face possessed a hundred tincts and intensities she'd never seen by the Serpentine, never imagined. All kinds of paintings suddenly made sense.

"Actually," Veronica said, "I forgot all about Niobe, and began lecturing your poor niece—"

"Veronica is a vicious lecturer," Joseph said.

Undaunted, she finished her sentence. "—about the sex life of the rhinoceros." Once again she pantomimed, in an abridged form intelligible only to Emma, the crash of the rhinoceros's horn against the ceiling.

The humor of it shattered inside of Emma, pierced her with shards of crystalline hilarity. Though at the first telling she'd felt no more impulse to laughter than if she'd been listening to a table of random numbers, now it seemed devastatingly funny. She could see the poor darling rhinoceros rear up—and then, *Whump!* She began to laugh. She couldn't stop laughing.

Veronica laughed along with her, but more mildly. "I told you! Didn't I tell you?"

Tears came to her eyes.

"Emma," August urged nervously. The people on the benches were beginning to notice her, and he dreaded scenes.

But whenever she tried to stop, the thought of it would come back to her, the desperate rhinoceros and the look on Veronica's face as she went *Whump!* and the hilarity of the whole wide incredible and agonizing world.

Finally Joseph had to help her to the bench.

Talat's on Camden Road was one of the oldest pudding clubs in London. Emma had walked by its scruffy bush many times, had wondered what it would be like inside (the club rooms were tucked away in back of and above a betting shop), had even gone so far as to express her curiosity to August, who never had more to say about it than, "Talat's? Oh, it isn't much." Or, in a mellower mood, "It's a friendly place, Talat's." Then, the evening of their Sunday at the zoo, August asked her if she'd like to go there with him.

The nature of the crisis Emma was undergoing was as indistinct to August as the hands and figures on their one functioning clock, and though he'd become quite shameless about asking, every quarter hour, what time it was, he couldn't bring himself to ask Emma, outright, what was upsetting her. Not so much for fear of finding out (she would have said she wasn't upset) as because he sensed a tactical advantage in remaining, at least ostensibly, unaware. Even so, the question nagged at him, and as soon as they'd taken their bowls of blancmange to a table in the little downstairs cafeteria, he began to probe and poke at the likeliest areas.

"You've heard the news, I suppose?"

Her mouth full of the sweet synthesized froth, she tilted her head to the side, crinkled her forehead: What news?

"About Ireland?"

"Mm. M-no. You know I never listen to the news. Who's always telling me there *isn't* any news anymore? 'S just delicious."

"There was this week. I'd have thought that Ruthven..."

"Ruthven doesn't fuss about"—Emma waved her spoon in contented indifference to the world beyond her pudding—"the news."

Because August came to the club almost every day, they never had desserts at home. You could almost feel each little molecule of the blancmange dispersing inside of you and zooming around to find the right kind of other molecule to hook onto. Or was this a form of regression? Was she reliving all those heavenly and forever insufficient Public Health puddings she'd tasted at the Anckers'? Whatever the reason, she did love a good pudding.

August wasn't eating his at all.

"What *was* the news?" she asked, trying to sound interested. The tone she achieved was nearer condescension.

"The Vatican has sealed the borders."

"Again?"

"This time they seem to mean it. Cardinal Marchesini, the new Secretary of State, has thrown out the whole UNESCO contingent, half the members of—"

"Marchesini? For heaven's sake, I think I've *met* him! He preached my great-grandfather's funeral sermon. The Right Reverend C. S. Marchesini, S.J. He knew my name, which somehow seemed very mysterious and grand, so I've always remembered him."

"Maybe they'll make some special dispensation for *you* then," August said sarcastically. She was spoiling his story.

Emma laid her spoon down and leaned forward to show that she was concerned. "It probably isn't the same person. Ireland must be full of Marchesinis. Anyhow, what did this cardinal *do?*"

"He ordered all the non-Catholics not attached to an embassy in Dublin to leave the country. Even mortals who've been living there less than a certain length of time, converts, as you might say, will have to go, unless the Rota gives them a special visa. That's just a way to thin down the ranks of the Liberal party, of course. But the part that I thought might have upset you . . ." He squinted to catch her reaction. "They won't allow native-born Catholics who've been away from Ireland more than two years to reenter. There's already been a test case."

"Really. It does seem unfair. I suppose there'll be a protest and all that."

"There have been two already."

"But I can't see that it affects me. I've never planned to go back there. Why, there aren't even any *hills* to speak of."

"And your cousins?"

"My cousins! What a bizarre idea, August! *You* haven't been thinking of going there—have you? I mean, because it *is* all Catholic or something like that."

"No, of course not."

"Because it wouldn't suit you. Not at all."

Emma returned to her pudding. The news seemed to have left no impression. Reluctantly August dismissed his first theory. He could think of no tactful way to approach other, less pleasant possibilities.

"This is our library," August said.

"It's very nice."

She tried not to show her disappointment. Except for a much denser population of chairs and couches, most of them unoccupied, the upstairs club room looked like nothing so much as enlarged versions of August's own room at home. The space was fractured into fifteen or so acoustical compartments. People talked and tellies flickered in a silence of white noise.

"And in here—"

She followed him through the door.

"—we have our game room."

Tables and chairs, chairs and tables, and the same unnerving hum. The sole occupant of the game room looked up from her jigsaw puzzle and waved. August smiled to her.

He always referred to the other members of Talat's as his "cronies," which had suggested to Emma that they were his own age and, by and large, mortals. They weren't. With a mounting intensity of awareness, Emma was being forced to bear witness to the whole awful continuum of August's life: the years, the loneliness, the sealing silences, the horrid waste.

"Let's sit here," he said.

Between them mismatched chessmen confronted each other across a polly board.

"Is this where you usually . . . ?"

"Yes. If I'm just playing left hand against right. The light is better in this corner of the room. Would you like a game?"

"Please, not tonight, August."

"Actually, I'm feeling a bit done in myself. The zoo."

"But you enjoyed it?"

"Oh yes, it was a proper holiday. And meeting Joseph too, after all this time, that was nice."

She stared down at the chessmen, not daring to ask, certain August must already know, and giddy with the syllables of his name.

"A little distressing as well, perhaps," August went on. "That he should look so entirely unchanged after such a stretch of time. You think that you'd get used to it, but you don't."

"When, exactly . . . ?"

"I must have been no more than twelve the last time I saw him. They had an affair, you know."

"Joanna and . . . ?"

"I find it just as hard to believe. He isn't much to look at, but then neither was she. First, you see, she had had an affair with his son. That, as I gathered many years later, was something of a disaster. Then with this Joseph, who proved a happier choice. At one point she was about to chuck up the school, everything, and go off with him to some cottage in Surrey."

"Why didn't she?"

"Lost her nerve, I expect. Understandably she didn't care to discuss that part of it with me, since I must have been one of her reasons. I don't think she bore Joseph any hard feelings, but the son, Oliver, dear me! She would *revile* him!"

"It sounds incestuous."

"Rather. The son, by the way, went on to join the *Extrovert* expedition. At one time or another I've met three of those astronauts, as well as one other who'd been to Mars. He used to be a regular at Talat's, sat right over there where Ann is. Larry . . . oh, I can never remember. He said it was very dull. Would never go back there. But would he have gone on the *Extrovert* if he had the chance, I asked him. Lieberman, that was his name! Lawrence Lieberman. And he would never play anything but draughts or gin rummy, children's games, said he only thought beyond a certain intensity of thinking if he was paid cash for it."

August, reminiscing in his maundering, post-meridian way, did not return to the subject of Regan *père* and *fils*. The pauses between each monad of memory and its sequel became longer and longer till at length he'd fallen into a doze.

Emma walked across the room to observe the progress of the jigsaw. It was holographic: every piece represented, ever so dimly, the whole picture; as they were united each to each, the distinct elements of the picture emerged, as from a mist. Already one could make out a large speckled fish that seemed to be floating above the surface of the table. Behind the fish blurry seahorses swarmed round a branch of coral. The woman working the puzzle remained either oblivious of, or indifferent to, Emma's presence two feet behind her chair.

Four people came in the room and began playing bridge. Emma watched the first rubber. They took no notice whatever of her.

Emma had always liked the idea of the pudding clubs. They were the one place you could go in London where sex just didn't exist. Even at church people would proposition you, which was the main reason Emma had stopped going to church. The pudding clubs, however, because they functioned as an elective form of an exogamic clan, were as safe as the combined forces of taboo and good manners could contrive. She still liked the idea. But Talat's?

Not at all.

✳

April 18, a Wednesday, and when she came in the room there were August and Ruthven and two of Ruthven's friends from the Knightsbridge Barracks, Beau and Conrad, in the full-dress uniform of the Royal Horse Guards. Before she could think why they were there, Beau lifted his arms and conducted them in a rousing chorus of "Happy Birthday." Then, twenty-one times, they hip-hip-hurrahed. When it was over, Emma was too limp from embarrassment to be capable of any kind of protest.

Conrad opened a bottle of Moët-Almaden and poured it, frothing, into five proper champagne glasses.

August raised his glass, slopping foam on his liver spots. "To Emma!"

"To Emma," the others concurred.

Conrad demanded she make a speech.

"The only speech I've ever given in my whole life was one of Pitt's that I memorized in the fifth form. All I can remember of it now is: 'I rejoice that America has resisted." Will that do?"

"Rejoicing is the general effect we're after," Beau said, "though as to the particular cause, I can only say that in my own experience America has *never* resisted."

August frowned. "One's twenty-first birthday is a solemn occasion, Emma. We couldn't let it go by without . . ." He paused to deliberate a mot juste.

Conrad filled in the blank (and filled, as well, his own and August's glasses back to brimming): "Without some solemnities. Cheers!"

"The Batemans said they'd drop by in a little while, too," Ruthven announced.

"And *all* the dear fairies, each with a different gift," Beau said. "Except for Calaboose, whom we decided not to invite." Seeing that he'd drawn a general blank, he added a footnote. "That's act one of *The Sleeping Beauty*."

It was as much as she could do to smile at their banter, nor did August play any very extravagant part in all this, except to match the Horse Guards glass for glass. By common agreement she and August did not celebrate each other's birthdays, and so their ambush had come as a genuine and by no means welcome surprise.

At the uncorking of the second bottle Emma was obliged to open her presents. From Conrad she received a rainsuit of gossamer-light polly, from Beau a pair of Bass hiking boots.

"Note," said Beau, "the laces."

The laces were tipped with gold. Beau's own personal touch.

A year ago the two Horse Guards had gone with her and Ruthven to the top of Sca Fell, no more than a day's stroll in the Lakes. That was the extent of their acquaintance with Emma. How was she to account for their largesse? Even Ruthven seemed nonplussed by his friends' prodigious gifts. His own, a forty-yard hank of nylon rope, seemed trifling by comparison.

"And this is from me." August handed her an envelope. "Can you guess what it is?"

She held it up to the light. Money? A lottery ticket? Or could it be (no, not possibly) a life insurance policy. That, according to one of her mother's favorite anecdotes, had been what she'd got from

Granny for *her* twenty-first birthday.

"I can't imagine."

It was a one-year membership to Talat's.

"Oh, August! August, you shouldn't—"

August interpreted her tears as the overflow of too thorough a happiness. He glowed with self-conscious generosity. And indeed, the membership had cost more than all the other presents combined.

"Hey, Emma," Beau prompted, as Conrad tipped more champagne into her glass. "I rejoice, remember? How does the rest go? I rejoice that America . . ."

"I rejoice"—quaveringly—"that America has resisted. Three millions of people, so dead to"—she snuffled back tears—"to all the feelings of liberty, as voluntarily to submit—"

The phone rang.

"I'll bet I know who it is," August said. His hand hovered above the receiver.

Whelmed by panic, every false feeling she'd been indulging fell away from her—the silly self-pity, the luxurious frustration, the patronizing compassion.

When August answered it was a moment before she could order the dots on the screen into the face of Ms. Harness's husband, so certain had she been that it would be Joseph calling. The Harnesses had lost the directions Ruthven had written out for them and wanted to know how to find Inverness Street.

It was only eight-fifteen. In an hour she would remind her guests, if there were any still about, that she and Ruthven had to be up early to catch the train. She could have August tucked away by nine forty-five. It might be a tight squeeze, but she could make it.

August hung up. "So, where were we?"

"As voluntarily to submit—" Ruthven prompted.

"I forget the rest."

Her eyes refused to meet Ruthven's. How could she accept the familiar assurance of his wry smile, its promise that they two were allies against a world of fools and madmen, on the evening she meant to join the other side?

Conrad popped another cork, and Beau, in the same spirit of stoic good fun, stood on the settee and belted out two stanzas of "*Le veau d'or.*" The plumes of his helmet brushed the ceiling, the lion's head embossed on his cuirass gleamed, but Beau himself, within the impermeable, glistering screen of his motiveless energy, seemed not to exist at all. Emma simply fell in love with him, the way, when long ago her mother had taken her to see *Cinderella* at the old Haymarket Theatre, she had fallen in love with its lobby.

"Bravo!" she called out when Beau finished his song.

"Bravissimo." August patted his hands as though he were brushing off crumbs.

"Encore," she insisted.

As he took his bow, Beau's spur snagged in Joanna's needlepoint. He wavered—and crashed, gutting the upholstery and spilling the ice bucket in a single stupendous *jeté*.

The disaster allowed August to regain control of the party. He played a tape of Pol Plançon for Beau's especial edification, and afterwards, assuring Ruthven that the Batemans were bound to arrive at any moment, he took it on himself to open the last bottle of Moët-Almaden. He gushed unremittingly over Southey's *Life of Nelson*. He made Emma unpack the Ordinance Survey maps and show them all the route by which she and Ruthven planned to conquer Ben MacDhui. Then, though they'd all heard it at least once, he made Ruthven tell the story of Ferlas Mor.

By the time the Batemans arrived with Elizabeth, Beau and Conrad had drunk themselves into the carpet, from which Beau raised himself just long enough to bellow: "Calaboose!"

Elizabeth snarled, ears pricked, tensed to spring.

"Aus!" Ms. Bateman shouted, as her husband hauled back on the leash.

Ruthven apologized for there being no more champagne. Ms. Bateman said she understood and it was perfectly all right since champagne had always been her undoing.

On the tag nestling in the bow of their present, Ms. Bateman's husband had written: *Wednesday's child is fair of face.*

August, who would have known better had he been sober, disagreed. "Isn't it Monday's child who's fair of face? Wednesday's child is something else. Can't remember what though."

"You see!" Ms. Bateman said vindictively. "Monday's child—didn't I tell you Monday's child?"

"Then, full of grace. That's even nicer."

"I expect that would be Tuesday's child," August said. "Fair of face, full of grace—they rhyme. But I can look up Wednesday's child if—"

"Oh, August, don't *bother*," Emma protested. "The sentiment is all that matters."

"Stuff the sentiment," Conrad advised, "and open the fucking present."

"Exactly," said Ms. Bateman.

It was the candlestick Emma had polished that afternoon and, at Ms. Bateman's insistence, polished twice again, even though, being only a Tiffany copy of de Lamerie, it had seemed a certain candidate for the vat. Emma had never been so furious with her employer as when, having brought it downstairs for the third time, Ms. Bateman had grudgingly allowed that it would have to do.

"I don't know how to thank you," Emma said. "It's *so* nice."

Ms. Bateman offered her cheek, and in fealty Emma kissed it.

"I've found it," August announced, returning from his room with a large green book. "On page 368, the index says, though with this damned small print . . ."

"Let me." Ms. Bateman's husband took the book from August.

Beau rolled over onto his back. "Time, everyone. Drink up, it's time."

Elizabeth growled.

"Monday's child *is* fair of face."

"You see!"

"Tuesday's child is full of grace. Oh dear."

"Well?" Emma said. "You can't stop there."

"Wednesday's child is full of woe."

Emma, who'd known as much for years, enjoyed the look on their faces.

The phone rang.

This time, she was certain, it would be Joseph, but no, it was Joanna, calling all the way from Vancouver to wish Emma a happy birthday.

Then there was the cake, which Ruthven had baked himself in the kitchen of the Knightsbridge Barracks. Surreptitiously Emma fed most of her icing to Elizabeth. When, too late, the party was over and Emma had conducted the guests to the foot of the stairs, Beau hugged her tightly against his embossings and nuzzled her neck with his moustache. She thanked him again for the boots and wished him good night.

She closed the street door, locked it, leaned against it. Half an hour ago, as she had forced down the birthday cake, forkful by sodden forkful, the Brighton Belle had left from Waterloo Station. Already it would have reached its destination. The last passengers would be going through the gate, and she not among them.

And if there had been no birthday party? If her past had not mustered its scanty army to defend her? Would it have made any difference?

Upstairs she could hear, ever so faintly, odd screaks and squitterings. The bats? she wondered. It seemed fitting that they should have manifested themselves to her at exactly this moment.

It wasn't, after all, the bats, but August, who, sprawled sidelong on the ripped settee, could neither cry nor keep from crying. His head rocked back and forth on the frayed arm. His fingers would clench the torn fabric, then relax to trembling. Yet for all this effort, for all his groans and keenings, he could not find his way to the release of tears.

She sat at the end of the settee and made him lay his head in her lap. He let himself be calmed, but with a decorous appearance of reluctance, lest the whole apparatus of his grief be called into question.

"Emma?"

"Yes, August."

"Emma, don't leave me."

"Why? . . . Why did you think I would?"

"Don't leave me, Emma. I don't have that much longer. I'm seventy-three."

"I won't leave you, August."

"Promise me."

"I promise."

"Oh, God, I'm sorry. I have no right to—It's not dying, I don't mind that. It's what's happening to me now. I don't *want* to be senile. Sometimes, when I see myself—" He began to rock his head again and whimper.

I should touch him, Emma thought. But she couldn't. Her hand refused to stroke the knotted forehead or smooth the ruffled sparseness of his hair.

"The ugliness!" he cried. "The awful ugliness. That's why Joanna had to leave, you know. She couldn't stand to see it anymore. And myself, I can't stand to see it. Old people, when I see them, they disgust me. They always have."

"August, please."

"But what can I do?"

"What anyone does, August. Get by from day to day."

"Yes. Yes, I try to. I'm sorry, it's the champagne. I'm just not used to—Help me sit up, and I'll be better."

Tipped upright, August's eyes opened as though by an arrangement of counterweights inside his skull. He exercised his smile. "There you see. It was only being horizontal. But dear me, will you look at the two of us! We're covered with stuffing."

"August, *please.*"

"I'm all right now. Really I am." He began to pick spongy wads of batting off his cardigan. "It's like flakes of giant dandruff, isn't it?"

"It's not enough just to say you're feeling better. You owe me some kind of explanation, August. Not now, if you don't feel equal to it, but—"

"Yes, I suppose I do." He sighed. "There was a phone call."

"Oh."

"Earlier today. It was that woman you met at the zoo. She left no message, except that she wanted to talk to you. I believe I wrote down her number on the pad."

"What did she want?"

"You, I expect, my dear."

"But that's ridiculous. Why ever would you suppose—"

August's entire attention was focused on removing the last specks of batting from his trousers.

"Because of *Charmian*?"

"Emma, I never accused you. And I would never even have mentioned it if . . . but I can't keep from *thinking.* I'd rather not discuss anymore about it tonight. I feel more than ordinarily a foolish old man. Couldn't we just go to bed now? I *am* very tired, and you have to be up bright and early to meet Ruthven."

"I hope you don't think I intend to go off to Scotland now?"

"Of course you shall. Heavens, it isn't my intention to become your jailer. In fact, I realize that I've been taking up your time much too selfishly and I do mean to try and reform. Your birthday present was a step in that direction."

"It was a lovely birthday present, August, and a lovely birthday."

He snickered.

August was asleep by the time Joseph called. Emma explained what had happened.

"I thought you'd decided not to come."

"I thought so too." Then, blithely but seriously too, she asked, "Do you love me?"

Joseph said, "Tilt."

"I *know* I'm not supposed to ask."

"The last train's at twelve."

"I know that too."

"I'll be at the platform." He smiled and vanished. She touched the glassy greyness where his lips had been. As if the Sacrament, by being doubted, were to become, again, mere bread and wine.

It was the softness of his skin that so astonished. With each touch, touching the cushion of flesh above his hip, touching his shoulder, this awareness would be the distant echo of each caress. It was disconcerting. She had expected to be lost to such itemizings once she'd surrendered herself to him, had thought that thoughts of every kind would be demolished, swept away and drowned in some vast flood of love. The songs of St. Theresa, which were by all accounts authoritative, promised exactly such annihilations, a bliss beyond all reckoning. Perhaps, then, she had yet to cross the threshold to that region of absolute, transcending joy. It was wonderful, of course— there was no denying that—but she did wonder whether it would become still more wonderful. She didn't really see how it could.

The waves shimmered in the endlessly shifting radiance of the six orbital mirrors. Faculae of darkness, acres large, flitted across the surface of the sea, like fragments of the authentic night, obliterating sails, pitting the silver water with fields of ebony, as, thousands of miles above Brighton's beach, the mirrors, themselves pitted by the dust of space, performed their endless gyrations.

They walked at the very edge. The water would come frothing over their bare feet to vanish into the rough and shifting shingle. Regularly at each third step, a new roaring would commence, as the undertow churned tons of flint, sand-stone, quartzite, shale and chert.

"Now?" he asked, as they drew near the pier.

"Yes, let's." It was an unconditional assent, for she had no idea what he wanted.

"What are you hungry for, then?"

His words seemed immense with meaning, as if they had been plucked, ripe and round, from the pleasantest tree in the garden of philosophy.

"Anything. Everything. You."

At the restaurant on the pier they were lucky enough to find a table by the railing. Joseph had cockles that he ate with a pin. Emma had eels, which were not more problematical now than pork sausages or mange-touts. Below them, visible through the polly floor, the ocean heaved, alive with scavengers. Their appetites, illumined by her own, seemed not to contradict the general blessedness of all things everywhere. Endlessly, epicycle within epicycle, the world involved.

Joseph rose, discovering his torso to her. As often as she'd seen men naked on London streets, or even in museums, transformed to stone or bronze, she'd never been able to regard their sexual organs as other than unseemly excrescences—as though some vagrant tube or vesicle had been extruded from its proper station in the dark labyrinths of the nether gut to dangle down between the legs, a mere impediment to motion. Now how necessary, how irrefutable that same form seemed, not only in the single case where love could exert its special influence, but everywhere that it appeared, throughout that restaurant and in the pavilion that adjoined and where, without a word of protest that she'd never learned the simple figures of the contre-dance, she danced with him. She knew the song from years before: Mies van der Rohe's "Shepherdess."

"One," the singer whispered perpetually over the serene sine curves of a figured bass. "Two. Three. Four."

They were on a ledge thirty floors above the beach, one cell in the great cormorant-nest of the Brighton Wall. The orbital mirrors had turned their faces from the imminent sun, to disclose, within the archway looking out on sky and sea, an hour of the monumental night.

She was silver beneath the rippling of his hand, stone in which he discovered, meter by meter, his careful purchase. When, too soon, too consciously, she sought to exert a reciprocal influence, he caught hold her wrists and pinioned them; it was as if he'd pitted his strength not against hers but Time's, and she thought she could begin to feel those great machineries shudder and slowly, slowly yield to his superior force. His face was all that she could see, and then his talons tore into her side and she was borne up aloft into the brightness of his purpose. What does she see now, as Ganymede, as Semele? When the clouds roll back, what is there? A beautiful absence, a blue sky, a burning sun. A creature that lives without illusion, without plans, without longings, driven by the clarities of habit, of wishes immediately and forever fulfilled—or driven not at all except, as clouds are, by the wind. A wind: his flesh became an endless prairie which she passed above, a wind, unconscious of the bounties it bore: the seeds and spores, the chill spring rains, the mists of summer mornings, the high, bright, tangled webs of cirro-stratus cloud, the exfoliations of the cumulus, their slow shadows staining the golds and olives of the plain to deeper tones and bringing a silence and a coolness to the creatures of the grass. She did not think what meaning her limbs might have for his, her weight and warmth, pauses and relinquishings, the abrupt ascensions and dizzying declines. She did not think. The morning sun was framed within the open archway of the balcony. Supported in his hands, her back drew taut, a bow: but neither away from him nor towards. As though the sun, as it rose, were to become unplaneted. As though she herself were now no more than an immaterial radiance, the glory streaming from his face.

*

His head was pillowed in the tumble of their clothes, and the salt breeze played with his hair. The sea permeated the morning with its vapors and immemorial roar. Emma looked down on the white dissolvings of the waves. In her mouth lingered the conjoint savors of Joseph and of the eel, and in her heart, persistent as the sea, she felt the old resolve, the foolish, inescapable pledge.

Foolish, but now, for reasons she could not have suspected when the purpose first had shaped itself, so right, so necessary. Already the sea seemed to be spreading its calm influence within her. To surrender to it now would be no more difficult, no less delightful, perhaps, than the surrender already achieved.

Yet she did not want him to suppose she acted from remorse. Neither reason nor feeling compelled her suicide. All that was cleansed away, and her mind was scoured to the whiteness of bone, of cloud, of godliness. What was left was a kind of hilarity, a laughter in which kindness and cruelty were reduced to the faintest blue-green smudges on the horizon of her soul.

She found a pencil in her pack and wrote to him on a scrap of the dress she'd worn last night:

"Dearest,

How can you sleep? In so lovely a world as this! I'm going swimming. I love you.

Emma."

Then, as a footnote: a poem! For poems, in contrast to the raw declarations of letters, must be believed.

Jellied Eel

Having breakfasted on it,
One wonders what there was
To be so frightened of,
All this time. So now I've filled
My icebox
With jars and jars
Of this delicious and popular
Cockney snack.
And I hope you'll come and visit me again
Real soon.

She went down to the lobby and out onto the beach without clothes. The sun had not yet burned off the haze. There were few bathers on the beach and only three in the water.

She looked back at the Wall. How easy it would have been, how nearly riskless, to have returned to him up the facade of the building, climbing from balcony to balcony. In effect, wasn't that just what she'd done? Mounting higher with each new accession of strength until at last she'd reached this summit, the highest and most final.

She stepped onto the darker shingle at the water's edge and waited for the first wave to claim her for its own. How cold! Colder than the cold of glaciers. Yet it caressed, offering its all-sufficing answer like a cup that could never be emptied: Yield! Only yield!

She began swimming southward toward a horizon that was never more than a few yards away. At first she feared the animal pleasure of motion would waken too soon the responses by which she knew she must eventually betray her purpose. She would, no doubt, turn back to the shore, but by then her best strength would have been exhausted.

It proved a needless fear. Her purpose outlasted arms and lungs, and she hung at last, feeble, gasping, triumphant, in the dazzling ocean of her death. It lifted her to view the white unbearable expanse of the Brighton Wall, and let her sink and lifted her once more.

She took a breath and dove. Though her eyes smarted from the salt water, she forced herself to peer into the featureless depths, as if, with constancy, she might pry from death some intimation of its true form. And, as she opened her mouth to accept the world's last sacrament, it appeared—it approached her—a black tube some eight feet in length with a red cross blazoned on a circle of white.

Useless to strain against the web of arms that grappled her into the humming hull, as useless to resist the reflexive spasm of stomach and throat as the water was pumped out. The lifeguard mechanism bore her living body up to where the molten sun was spread in vortices upon the surface of the waves, and then, puttering cheerily, to the shore where Joseph, still asleep, awaited her return.

The Doctor of Death Island

GENE WOLFE

"You shall read them, if you behave well," said the old gentleman kindly; "and you will like that, better than looking at the outsides,—that is, in some cases; because there *are* books of which the backs and covers are by far the best parts."

—CHARLES DICKENS,
Oliver Twist

Night, and prisoner orderlies halt in the bright hospital corridor to talk.

"Did you know Alvard?" the older man asked, pulling at his chin. He contrived to lean on the push-bar of his cart in such a way that it did not roll. "No, I guess you didn't. He'd pushed his partner out the window. Used to be a big blond guy—face like a big kid."

"What were they doing, Stan?"

"I never had an idea. He was on days when I got here. Hell, I didn't know where it was at. He got it—the long string—and he rode it all the way. Clear out the gate. Only a couple years ago, I think it was."

"Is he out now?" the other man inquired.

The beginning-end of the string, when it comes, is not readily recognizable. It is cancer of the stomach; and it begins as a long bellyache that hurts even when he and dark Jessica, no longer jealous, tumble over one another on the big bed in Visitor's Cottage #3.

"In the evening," (Alvard wrote) "the shadows come into the yard like furlough men: not talking, dragging their feet. They are as gray as we. It's getting colder now, and the days are shorter. The shadows lapped all around my ankles when I crossed the yard tonight coming back from the hospital. I'd like to read *A Christmas Carol* again in December—if I can get Jessie to find a copy for me—and renew acquaintance with old Scrooge."

He had been going to write something beautiful about the shadows; but he had forgotten now what it was. Instead he wrote: "It will be two weeks now until Jessie can return. My stomach still hurts. She rubbed it while we were together, and it felt better then. I think I'm getting an ulcer. I never did when Barry and I were starting up the Genre Jinn.

"Glazer is coming tomorrow. I'm going to make it plain to him—either he does something for me—gets the case reviewed, or at least gets me on the furlough list—or he loses me as a client.

"There's a new man in the ward, emptying bedpans. His name is Stanley (Stanley Johnson or something like that) but he wants to be called *Snake*. Seems like a nice enough kid, but he says he killed—he says *cooled*—a little girl in the course of a holdup. He asked me what I did. How can you explain to a boy of nineteen?"

He remembered then, and wrote: "The shadows are like tall and beautiful women, drawing an old gray blanket over the dead."

The people over whose faces the shadows drag their gray blanket are not dead; many are not even sleeping. They lie in their beds, some of them, and think. Others pace their cells—four steps long. Still others do their duty in the various departments of the prison—tending the boilers in the powerhouse, telling the warden's children it is time to turn off the light. In the hospital, where Alan Alvard worked by day, others tend and wheel and feed by night, and tell their prisoner-patients that the doctor will be there in the morning, and that they can tell him then.

Dr. Baldwin, who was on duty to deal with emergencies, saw Dr. Margotte, who was not supposed to be on duty at all by night, come in; he asked him if he wanted some coffee.

"Thanks," Margotte said, and reached for the plastic hotcup with his ruined hand. His white hair glimmered beneath the fluorescent lights.

"Don't you ever sleep?" Baldwin said.

"All the time. I nap. This is my excuse." Margotte blinked bulging, hyperthyroid eyes. "When Devereaux knows I was in during the night, he doesn't mind if I snooze." Devereaux was the administrator and that was the way Devereaux was; but Margotte did not snooze.

One of the prisoner-orderlies approached Baldwin when Margotte was gone. "Somebody's passing over tonight."

"You mean *dying,*" Baldwin said.

"That's what I said—passing over. We always called it that—my mother did, I mean. It still doesn't sound right to me to say right out that a person's dying. It isn't decent; it is what dogs do."

"How do you know someone's dying?"

"Doc Margotte knows. He comes in to see them go—or maybe they go when he comes in. They'll take somebody off the top floor with a sheet on his face tonight. You watch and see if I'm not right."

Alan Alvard lies sweating in his bed. The sheet has gotten over his face somehow, and perhaps it has lent his dream a character of suffocation. A black box with plug jacks over all the surfaces like the scars of smallpox is on his bench. He knows that he has designed its circuits, though he has no idea now what it may be. And he knows he must repair it, though he has no notion of how it is intended to function when working correctly. He takes up a screwdriver, which slips and chatters along the black surface. At once there is a slipping and clattering thunder across the ceiling of the room. He cannot breathe, and understands that he is dead, and inside the box. His stomach hurts.

For a moment he could not remember where he was. Then he heard Riemer snoring in the upper bunk. "Barry was coming," Alvard said. He whispered so that he would not wake Riemer. "He was coming to see if I had fixed it."

Riemer asked, "What'd you say?"

"I was talking to myself. I'm sorry."

"It's all right."

"I had a dream. I was working, and Margotte was the boss."

"That's not much of a dream." Riemer worked in the hospital too.

"It was eight or ten years ago. I'd never heard of Margotte then. But in my dream, he was coming to see if I had done what I was supposed to. I was holding something—I forget what it was—and something was scratching across the top of the room. I couldn't breathe—it was as if there was no air. And Margotte was coming to see if I was finished. I wasn't facing that way, but I could see his hand on the knob; it was Margotte's, with the two fingers gone."

A new voice that was neither Alvard's nor Riemer's, a thin, sibilant voice, said: "You are quite correct. It was Karajan. I trust you know how it was done?"

Riemer laughed. "I thought that would shake you up."

ALBANY, New York (AP) The State Board of Correction disclosed today that Alan Alvard had become the first prisoner in U.S. penal history to undergo cryogenic freezing. Alvard's attorneys successfully contended that since he could afford the process and was suffering a terminal illness, to deny it would constitute a *de facto* sentence of execution, contrary to the intent of the court. Alvard, an inventor and publisher, was given a life sentence two years ago.

His waking, which he had thought would be agony, is not. He is conscious of his body only as a presence, as he might be conscious of the scent from an open spicebox in a cluttered, hole-in-corner shop, or of lying between blankets instead of sheets. But he is awake. Awake.

That thought circled in his mind for a long time. He could not be sure whether his eyes were open or closed; but he believed them closed. If so, he could not open them—not because they were gummed shut, but because the muscles would not respond. Similarly, he could not be certain of where he lay. He could not move his body, but he could feel his body move, against something . . . something.

"You're going on a journey," his counselor says. She is a clean, starched, stiff young woman, and a prisoner; she speaks with what sounds like a down-east twang. Everyone does. "A long, long

journey; and you can't come back."

Alvard said, "That's what they used to tell people who were dying."

"How interesting. Look at it this way. All your life has been spent in a remote country—the past. Now you have to live here. The world has changed from what you were used to; but it's where you have to live from now on."

"And how long will that be? Can you cure the cancer? You wouldn't have waked—"

"Revivified," the young woman said. "I've told you all this, but you've forgotten. That's normal."

"You wouldn't have revivified me if you couldn't cure me, would you?"

"That was done before you were conscious." She paused. "Do you remember what I told you about life expectancy, Alan? The doctors used a technique we call cell therapy. They could give you the details better than I can, but it means that certain substances were introduced into your system that have altered your DNA. The result will be to hasten the death of old body cells, while stimulating the growth of new ones. It's a process that eliminates cancer—more or less as a side effect—while circumventing aging."

"And I've already had this treatment?"

"Everyone has. When it was discovered, the government tried to keep it from the people. That was the government you knew about. There was a revolution, of course, and now we're even using the technique to produce parthenogenetic children—clones."

"You mean I'll live forever?" The thought was almost too great for him to grasp. Words in his mind became fleeting pictures of a hillside covered with long, sweet grass. A hillside smiling in the sun. Day always. No night ever.

"Think of yourself as a porcelain vase. The vase can be broken at any time; but if it is not, it may last a thousand years, or ten thousand. If someone blows you apart, or a building falls on you—perhaps in an earthquake—or you drown or burn, you'll be every bit as dead as if you had died back in your own time. Eventually something like that will happen to you by sheer chance, as it will to all of us." He said nothing, and she added, "Is there anything else I can tell you?"

"I want to think about it."

"I can't go—I'm supposed to spend a certain amount of time with each patient on my list—but we don't have to talk if you don't want to."

"Ten thousand years."

"Perhaps."

It was longer than all recorded history. He said, "How long have I been gone?"

"Forty years."

"Is that all?"

"That's all. Many of the people you knew must be still alive."

"I see." He wanted to ask how much things had changed, but he was aware of the fatuity of the question. For a time he lay back, resting on his pillow, breathing and staring at the ceiling. "This building . . ."

"Possibly you remember it. It must have been here before you were frozen. I believe they say it's sixty or seventy years old."

"The hospital."

"Yes."

"I worked here. My job inside." Alvard was exhausted. It seemed only a few days ago—yet immensely remote. He had had the same reaction when he had begun to serve his sentence; when his trial was over it had seemed, in less than a week, to have receded far into the past. This time it was real.

An orderly began to perform some operation on the floor, using an implement that was not a broom or a vacuum cleaner or anything else Alvard was familiar with. For a time his eyes followed it; then he noticed the man's clothes, and looked back to his counselor. She wore the same stiff, wide-legged trousers and slightly Russian-looking tunic.

"Yes, I'm an inmate too. I work here in the hospital, just as you did."

He stared at her—soft blond hair, rounded chin, wide blue eyes.

"I've been in prison for eighteen years, Alan. Some of us were lucky enough to be young still when C. T. was released; I'm forty-four." She stood up. "It's nearly time for your lunch now, and it's not good—yet—for you to talk too much. I'll be back tomorrow."

"Can I eat solid food?"

"You already have. Several times."

"I don't remember."

"Don't worry about it." Accidentally, the orderly cleaning the floor bumped against her. She pushed him away violently, making Alvard think, for a moment, of children on a playground. As she went out the door, the orderly glanced at her. There was resentment in his look, but no surprise. Alvard wondered how old he was. He was of medium height or a little less, and had paintbrush-stiff black hair, like Hans in the old comic strip. After a moment, Alvard asked, "How's it going?"

"Slow."

Some things, at least, had not changed. "In the old days," Alvard said, choosing his words, "we didn't have women in here."

The orderly grinned. "Pretty soft. Say, you want your chow now? I'll get it for you."

Lunch came on a tray of some green material that was not plastic (at least, as Alvard had known it) or wood or metal or any other identifiable material. The covered dish and the cup there, however, would have been commonplace in his own time—china, thick and cheap. A metal pot held a hot drink that was neither coffee nor tea.

"I got to go now," the orderly said. "There's a buzzer on your right. Push it and the nurse'll ask what you want."

Alvard lifted the cover: a meat patty, an unidentifiable reddish orange vegetable, and something that might almost have been an artichoke. With a red fork of the same smooth, temperatureless stuff as the tray, he cut off a bit of the patty and put it in his mouth. It was unlike anything he ever remembered eating—bland as shortening on his tongue, spiced in the back of his throat. The orange vegetable tasted like spoiled straw soaked in milk; but the artichokelike one was delicious, crisp yet meaty, and delicately flavored. He smiled to think of himself propped up in bed like Miss Havisham in the novel, eating from a tray; and after a time he slept.

✳

It is dim in the room, but not dark. Alvard sits up, feeling stronger than before, and listening.

He could hear nothing. It was as though the entire world outside his room had ceased to exist. He tried to recall the hospital by night, as it had been when he worked there; there had been night-sounds, he felt certain: the soft trundling of carts in the halls; someone snoring; the noises, mostly faint but sometimes very horrible, of pain. Now there was—or seemed to be—nothing.

Greatly daring, he threw the blankets back and looked at his legs. They were covered with bruises, and as thin as stilts. He gripped the mattress and tried to swing them over the side of the bed; without warning he found himself plunged in a waking dream of his own childhood, of sliding from the straw stack. For a moment the sun shone again in his face and the air was full of dust, and a rich, dry odor.

His feet touched the floor, pain flashed through them, and the straw stack was gone. He felt that he had groaned or screamed. If so, there was no response; the hospital was as silent as before.

Half an hour later he was able to stand. For a time he held on to the headboard of his bed. When he could make his way over to the window, he found it closed by double panes of glass. The catch was of a design new to him, but not difficult; he loosed it and swung the halves back. In his own time, he was sure, such a window would have been covered with a grille of steel wire. Now there was nothing between his face and the night. It was dark, cool but not cold, and a gusty wind blew. Outside he could see nothing. There was no sound but the wind's sighing—nothing at all. No far-off jets; no trucks on distant highways.

What floor was he on? He tried to remember the layout of the hospital. Somewhere near the top, it seemed. Near the incurable ward, then.

There had been a goldfish bowl in the cottage, on the bureau in the bedroom, with a little cardboard box of fish food from Woolworth's; once or twice Jessie had mentioned it when they lay panting in the much-used bed. He had pretended each time that he had never noticed it; yet the truth was that that insignificant thing had become one of the central images of his thought. So that now, when it had surely been broken and forgotten for two generations, it reappeared as he stared out into the windy night—presenting itself so vividly to his imagination that he felt he could smell its dank marshiness and see each bit of green scum that clung to the sides. A ceramic mountain peak intended for a far larger aquarium thrust from the murky waters where snails crawled and the half-poisoned goldfish swam. Its lower reaches were imprisoned, like the fish, like the myriads of tiny snails, within the glass walls of the bowl; but its point, lifted in an island above the green water, was in air and free;

yet it was without life, as dry and sterile as a bone: Death Island.

There was no difference between the ornament and the hospital in which he had worked but size. Like the ornament, the hospital had its lower six-sevenths thrust in the teeming life of the prison. Only its highest floor, Margotte's ward, higher than all the surrounding buildings, was free to look out over the countryside, across the neatly tilled fields of the prison's farm to woods and free farms and roads and houses; but the highest floor was the abode of Death, and the wind that breathed through its open windows carried away men.

Was he there now? He could not be sure. If there were, as the woman said there was, a cure that provided an unending health, what need would the prison have for a ward for incurables? No incurables would exist; no one need ever die.

No one need ever die.

Alvard found that his fingers were reaching for the steel mesh, seeking its support. It was not there, and for a moment it seemed that his arms would drag his body behind them, out the window. He drew back. The sill was no higher than his hips, and he had been leaning a long way out, with the veering wind tugging at his stiff white hospital gown. A question formed in his mind; and with it, an irrational need to shout it, to fling it on the wind. He tried to phrase it; but the words would not come. At last, feeling his legs weakening beneath him, he leaned out again, hoping that the thing he must ask would form itself in his mouth by its own energy.

He gasped for breath; then heard from somewhere nearby another voice shouting to the night. It, too, was a question; he could not make out the words (though he thought he heard *instead)* but the rising inflection of the last was unmistakable.

The young woman (her name is Megan Carstensen), comes the next day, bringing Alvard a Bible. She asks why he smiles, and he says, "It seems so old-fashioned." But he takes it.

"We have a library here that trades books with libraries on the outside, so I ordered it for you. I thought you might like it—that it might remind you of your original period."

"You said you were a trained counselor. Is that what they teach you?"

"More or less. I hope you didn't think, though, that when I said that I meant I was trained in counseling cryogenic cases like yours. There aren't that many of you. I *am* a counselor, though, and trained in psychology."

"I suppose it's different now," Alvard said.

"Psychology? I suppose so. You were frozen before Kinglake's *The Death of Love* was published, I think. So it ought to be quite different."

"No more Freud."

"Of course not. Did people really believe those things?"

"Sometimes."

Idly, Alvard opened the pebble-grained black cover of the book she had given him. A voice said, "Who is the Son of Man?" and he slammed it closed at once.

"I suppose you're not used to those. It's a speaking book. There's . . . . a little person in the binding who'll talk to you. If you don't want to hear him, just don't open to the endpapers—that's where he lives."

"I'm used to them. I developed them."

"Really?"

"Yes, really. We—Barry Seigle and I—called it Speaking Pages Corporation. That was our company. Didn't they give you some sort of case data on me?"

"It didn't have that kind of information," Megan told him. She looked, somehow, as if the small, square room had become a cage to her, her eyes straying toward the always-open door and the empty cream-and-green corridor outside.

"What *do* you know about me, then?"

"All of it? I don't have time—I'm supposed to be seeing other patients, you know. If you want, I can lend you the file and let you read it over. You can give it back the next time I come."

"My own file?"

She nodded, eager to placate him and go.

"Yes," he said slowly. "I'd like to see it. We didn't do things like that. Allow people to see their files."

"Here." From underneath her chair, she drew an object that seemed midway between a hatbox and a bureau, and took out a slender folder. "Before you start on that," she said reluctantly, "I'd like to ask what happened last night. An orderly found you on the floor, under the window. The window was open."

"I wasn't trying to commit suicide. After coming all this way—"

"Pardon?"

So he had internalized what she had said earlier about a journey—time had become some vast voyage through the dark; and he an astronaut without ship or suit. "All this *time*," he said. "I meant all this *time*. To kill myself. I wouldn't do that now."

"The doctor says you shouldn't have gotten out of bed at all. You might have died from that alone. The cells of your body are regenerating themselves now; but it will take six weeks, at least, for the process to be complete. Your heart deteriorated to some extent during suspension."

"I understand," he said.

She smiled and stood up, leaning over his bed. "Then be careful," she said. "If forever means a long, long time, then you're going to live forever. There are a lot of things to do—even here."

He managed to say, "They used to believe you'd get bored with it."

"Nobody has yet."

She turned to go, and he heard the tiny sound her trouser legs made as one thigh whisked against the other. He asked, "Do you have to go now?"

"I want you to talk to that case record. I'll be back—tomorrow—it will give me a chance to catch up with my schedule."

She was gone before Alvard noticed the peculiarity of her phrasing. He put down the file; it slid from his lap and fell open on the floor, spilling papers.

A voice very like his own recorded voice, as he had sometimes heard it at the office when he played back his own dictation, murmured, "Good afternoon. I am Alan Alvard, number one eight three two eight. What may I tell you about myself?"

It was even in the files now. To have found it in the Bible did not, in retrospect, so much surprise him—the temptation to chat with Christ would be irresistible. But file folders? He wondered how they read the information in now, and where the microchips and the speaker were. When he had designed the first ones, he had had to make the covers twice the normal thickness.

"Would you like a straightforward account of my life?"

"No," Alvard said involuntarily.

"Then you have questions to ask?"

"I suppose if I say no again, you'll ask me to close you. I remember having programmed a routine something like that."

"You'll have to admit there isn't much use in having me open if you're not interested in my life experience."

"Do you know where you are now?"

"Yes. I am a patient in the hospital of Greyhame Prison. Room six seventeen. Six seventeen is a private room."

He was not on Death Island then; still down in the water. He tried to recall what side of the building six seventeen was on. At last he asked, "Is there a window in six seventeen? Do you know that kind of thing?"

"One window. The room is three meters by two hundred and fifty centimeters, roughly."

"Which way does the window face?"

"West."

He glanced at the window. "And what time is it now?"

"I cannot provide that information."

"You said, 'Good afternoon.' "

"My time sense is not precise."

"There's supposed to be a switch near the head of my bed somewhere. If I call the nurse, will she tell me what time it is?"

"I can't provide that information either."

Alvard fumbled at the headboard, remembering visits to his mother's hospital room, so many years ago. A cord with a button at the end. There was nothing.

From a concealed speaker somewhere, a man's voice asked, "What do you want, six seventeen?"

"What time is it?"

"Is that all? Eighteen thirty-one."

Half past six in the evening, then. Again he looked toward the window. No light from the setting sun penetrated it.

The file folder on the floor asked, "Is there anything more I can tell you?" The voice was slightly muffled; no doubt the speaker was face down. Alvard leaned out of the bed painfully until he could pick the folder up, leaving the papers where they had fallen.

There was a disc of what looked like aluminum foil inside the front cover. "Is that your speaker?" he asked.

"I can't provide that information."

"Then you can talk only about . . ." He found that it was more difficult than he had expected to pronounce his own name as though it were that of a stranger. "About Alvard— I suppose. Is that right?"

"I can tell you anything you want to know about myself."

"Have you talked to Megan?"

"You mean my counselor. Yes, I've spoken to her."

"Has she . . ." Alvard hesitated. He had been going to say, Read the papers in you, but that would only have led to further fencing. He substituted: "Read your case record?"

"No."

"You're certain?"

"A log is kept on every prisoner, listing everyone who reads the file."

It would be futile to ask the folder why she had not. Instead, Alvard said, "Was she well informed already when she talked to you?"

"About me? She knew nothing about me."

"How long did you talk?"

From the doorway, an orderly asked, "All right if I bring your supper in now?"

"I suppose so," Alvard said, and closed the folder.

"Want me to pick up that stuff on the floor for you?"

Alvard nodded, flattening his lap to receive the tray. "Thank you very much."

"No trouble. You'll be able to do for yourself pretty soon. I went by here with your slum once before, but the yap was in here."

"Thank you for waiting."

"I just wanted to tell you what happened. The nurse said you called and asked what time it was, so I figured you wanted to eat." The orderly picked up the folder, thrust papers into it, and put it beside Alvard's tray. "Anything else I can do for you?"

"You can tell me why the sun doesn't come in the window," Alvard said.

The orderly stared at him.

"I used to work here in the hospital. We're high up, and unless I'm mistaken, that window looks west. Even if the sun is too low now, the light should have been coming through it a little earlier."

"I'm not so damn sure this is the west side," the orderly said.

"I am."

"Well, I don't know about the sun—I'm no astronomer, you know what I mean? I don't spend my time sticking my head out of windows to see where the sun is or where the light falls. When I get out of this place, *then* I'll look at the sun." The orderly glanced around the room as if to see if he had for-gotten anything, and wiped the palms of his hands on his tunic. "You get sunshine in here earlier, don't you?"

"Much earlier," Alvard said, "yes."

"Then be happy with what you got. I have to go now." He was out the door before Alvard could think of some remark that might have stopped him.

The room's artificial lights were brighter now than they had been the last time Alvard had noticed them. For a time he sat with the folder closed in his hands; his shoulders hurt where their protuberant bones had pressed the mattress too long.

"Good evening. I am Alan Alvard, number one eight three two eight. What can I tell you about myself?"

"You can tell me about the way you're built—the design of this file folder that talks to me."

"I can't provide that information."

"What was Alan Alvard's profession before his arrest? How did he make his living?"

"I was vice president and research director of a specialty publishing company."

"How did you get that position?"

"I invented a device I called the Genre Jinn. It consisted of a micro-miniaturized computer implanted in the binding of a book. The computer was programmed at assembly to discuss the content of the book with the readers."

Alvard closed the folder, and after a time a shudder passed through his thin body. There was no one there to see it, but the springs of the bed gave witness with a low creaking and rattling that continued even after he thought his emotions were under control. When he opened the folder again, he asked, "Was the invention a commercial success?"

"Yes, it approximately tripled the cost of each book, but volumes of my design largely replaced the expensive, illustrated 'coffee table' books that had been popular gift items previously. The idea was expanded and improved to include textbooks and books of other kinds."

"Is it still in use?"

"Yes, but my patent was effectively broken in . . ." (The voice—his own—droned on for a long time.)

When an hour or more had passed, the orderly returned and found Alvard still sitting up in bed with the file folder and the Bible on his lap. "Want me to take those?" he asked, and when Alvard nodded, he laid them on the table beside the bed. "I thought you might want me to dial you down for the night."

"Thank you," Alvard said.

✳

Morning brings a new orderly, a stout woman, with his breakfast. She spins the control until Alvard sits again. Her hands are rough; her hair, when she bends to put the tray on Alvard's legs, smells of disinfectant.

"Megan is waiting to see you. You want me to tell her to come back when you've finished?"

"I'll talk to her now," Alvard said.

The orderly shook her head. "You ought to wait until you've had something. It's just morning squares and tea."

"Then I can eat while I talk to her. Perhaps she'd like some."

"She already ate. It's oh nine five three. I'll tell her you'll talk to her."

Alvard picked up a pink-frosted square and bit into it. It was rich and chewy, but not actually very good; he sipped the cooling tea.

"Hello, Alan. Sleep well?"

He nodded. "You're prettier than I remembered."

"And I poisoned a young man who was much prettier than I am." She drew the room's one chair up to his bed. "So how do you like having me sit beside you while you eat?"

"Fine," Alvard said. "But aren't you afraid I might push you out the window?"

"You couldn't, which brings me to one of the things I wanted to talk to you about today. You're going to have visitors, which means that you're going to have to go down to the visiting rooms in a wheelchair—they won't allow them up here. Think you can stand it?"

"Who?"

Megan produced a slip of paper. "Jessica Alvard, Lisa Stewart, Jerome Glazer."

When she had gone, the three names continued to repeat themselves in his mind. Jessica Alvard would be Jessie; she had had to use his name to see him. His lawyer's name had been Glazer, but the first name was not Jerome. He could not recall it, but not Jerome. Lisa Stewart (a false, would-be stage name, surely) he could not remember at all. He wanted to review his file to see if there was some mention of Lisa Stewart there, but Megan had taken it with her. The Bible remained; he opened the cover, and heard: "He makes his angels spirits, and his ministers a flame of fire." It seemed to have no application to him—was Lisa Stewart a spirit, or a flame of fire? He put the book aside, reflecting that his behavior was being shaped by Megan's expectations; he had not looked into the Bible since he was a child.

✳

He wakes. It is dark but there is someone in the room, a pale presence. "Who's there?"

"Just making sure you're all right. Go back to sleep." Alvard could see the man's teeth, dimly shining, when he spoke.

"I'm not sleepy." He moved his right hand in the way that kindled the lights. A long knife-scar split the brown skin of the orderly's face; he appeared to be middle-aged. "What time is it?"

"Twenty till twenty-four hundred."

"I was supposed to have visitors."

"Doctor prob'ly said for you to sleep."

"They wouldn't wake me up?"

"You been sick. If you can sleep without taking anything, that's better. That's the good way."

"What about the people who were coming?" Alvard felt furious, knowing it for weak, foolish anger even while it gripped him.

"Told them to come back some other day, I suppose. Listen, I have to look in on the others, but I'll tell you something about tomorrow that will be good for you to know. Before breakfast, if you're awake then, call Nurse and tell him you'd like some sun. Then I'll come and take you up on the roof. Wouldn't you like to get out for a little? They're supposed to do it, but they won't unless you ask. I'm on till eight."

When the gray light of dawn was in the window, Alvard told the remote and invisible nurse that he would like to go up to the roof, and in half an hour the orderly with the scarred face returned with a wheelchair. "How old are you?" Alvard asked him.

"Old enough. When they iced you down, I wasn't even born yet. Is that what you're thinking about?" On silent tires Alvard glided through the hospital halls. He tried to recall the color of the walls when he had worked here. Whatever it had been, they were mostly pinkish green now.

"You are thinking," the orderly began with the stilted formality of the uneducated, "if I am curious about those old times you come from and want to hear about them? No, I am not. If you wish to talk of it, I'll listen; but I already know all I want to about those old days."

"Then why did you want me to come up on the roof with you?" The elevator seemed to be the one he remembered. It was slower and noisier now.

"Because I like to my own self—why do you suppose? You know how I grew up? In a little bit of a apartment, with a old granny that was always wanting to talk about those old times. Mr. Kennedy and all that. She was so great on Mr. Kennedy." Unexpectedly, the orderly laughed; it was a warm laugh, as though recalling the grandmother who had bored him as a child made him happy now.

"That was before my time—Kennedy," Alvard said.

"Always *Mister* Kennedy. Don't no one use that now, that *Mister*."

The elevator jolted to a stop, and the doors slid back. The first thing Alvard was conscious of was the rush of cool air, fresh, with the undying newness of sunrise. Then of the fog, circling the roof until he could scarcely see the parapet. The light of day had not yet reached the rooftop. "They've made me immortal," he said. "Do you know that?"

"Me too."

"I didn't know. No wonder you wanted to come up here."

"Sure." The roof's surface was tar, slightly uneven. The orderly began to push Alvard's chair slowly across it. Small, hard tar-bubbles shattered under the wheels.

"When I smelled the air—just a minute ago, when the elevator doors opened—I understood what it meant. I don't think I did before. A hundred thousand dawns. A million. Research for five hundred years, then rest and read for another five hundred. Only I think I'll do the resting first."

The orderly chuckled. "That's good. This is a good place to do it."

"They'll release me, won't they? What's it like outside?"

"Won't do you no good to know. They won't let you out. What do you think? They want us running around loose now that they're all going to live for always?"

The orderly had laid a blanket over Alvard's legs before they started up. Alvard tucked it tighter now. He felt cold—yet he knew that what the orderly had said could not be the whole truth. A life sentence could not mean forever.

"Not so many people out there now," the orderly told him. "Not like in your day, I guess. There's a lots of houses and apartments vacant. That company that rented to us—when I was a kid, you know? They could have let us have a bigger space. Two apartments together. Only they wouldn't." His breath smelled of oatmeal, heavy and a trifle scorched.

"How many people in the United States?"

"That isn't what they call it anymore. It's the Unified States and Kingdoms. I don't know for sure how many there is. Not as many as it used to be. You ever been out in the country?"

"Yes," Alvard told him, remembering boyhood.

"I was, one time. What it was," the orderly gave the wheelchair a little shake to express a smile Alvard could not see, "was, we went to hide out—you know? And there was all kinds of places. Old farms and buildings and even little towns where nobody lived. You know, in town sometimes there will be blocks where nobody lives except maybe winos at night? Out there, it's whole towns."

"I see," Alvard said. After he had spoken, he realized that he really was beginning to see; the fog was thinning now, the daylight had grown brighter and warmer. And what he saw was a band of night that would not fade. It seemed to be a half mile away, and it rose far (he could not be sure yet how far) above the roof where the orderly slowly pushed his chair.

"They are always yellin' at the women to have children; but it don't do no good. A woman that has a child is riskin' her life, you know? And now they can always put it off."

"I see," Alvard said again. He pointed. "What is that?"

"In the haze there? You mean the walls?"

"Is that what they are?"

"The walls to keep us in. Didn't they have them when you were here?"

Alvard tried to remember. "Not as big," he said, "and closer. Those must be—I couldn't say how high. And this place is bigger than it was."

"I suppose. I'm goin' to have to take you down now. My shift's about over."

Back in his room, a nursing aide gave him a recorder and a box of tiny tapes and told him to write letters. He began one to Jessica ("Dear Jessie: I know you tried to see me the other day. I fell asleep. I am sorry . . .") but he found himself paralyzed with embarrassment time after time, and eventu-ally erased it all, telling himself that Jessie would no longer be at the old address, the apartment he had taken for her. (Had Glazer continued to pay the rent?)

In the now-familiar room, the walls he had seen from the rooftop seemed to hem him round. He had only to shut his eyes for them to appear again, distant, frowning, built of some dark material that could not be concrete. Perhaps it was stone. If the world were running out of people, it might be running out of concrete too. In his own time he had seen plastic give way and wood and metal return again as the supply of petroleum was exhausted. Outside, now, it might be that sidewalks were being laid of brick and stone once more—if any sidewalks at all were being built in the dwindling cities.

The thought of those diminishing cities, he found, did not sadden him. For a time, there had been too many people; everyone had known it. Now there was no longer that urge to achieve immortality through children. Real immortality was at hand. Possibly that was why Catholic priests and nuns, for so many hundreds of years, had

not cared about having children—they had felt immortality already,
believing in the survival of the soul after death. Now everyone must
feel like that, knowing of the survival of the body. The forests would
be coming alive once more; growing. The deer, the wolves and the
bears and the foxes, could have more children now.

The walls circled him round again, reminding him that his own
eternity was to be only here, in some long gray building filled with
the sound of clanging steel. Atop them walked the tiny, white-coated
figure of Dr. Margotte. He forced himself to stare at the real walls
of painted plaster.

What of art and literature and science? Perhaps (though he found
he did not think so) they were only snatches at immortality too.
Gone now, if that were so, or perhaps only drowned in unending
procrastination. No more Great Expectations, no more great works
of any kind? Alvard did not, would not, believe it.

*Despite all the clichés of fiction, the gates do not slam shut
behind visitors on visiting days. Several guards stand by. There are
more guards in the towers, isolated behind crystal windows. Trus-
ties in gray uniform walk, apparently aimlessly, across the courtyard stretching between the gate and the administration building.
Visitors arriving by bus are herded through the gates, like geese
being driven to the market of a walled French town. Like geese they
talk to themselves more than to others; like geese they try to stray
and are driven back; like geese they are mostly gray, and smaller
than a man.*

*In the administration building, trusty clerks—nearly all of them
women too—ask whom they wish to see, and what their relationship to the prisoner may be, and the nature of their business. If the
prisoner is being disciplined, he or she will not be permitted visitors
One of the deputy wardens will be available if the matter seems
urgent. If the visit is merely social, close relatives will be given
preference—an hour a day is allotted, but only on Fridays, Satur-
days, and Sundays. Unsuccessful visitors are invited to wait until
the next visiting day in the Lodge—technically a commercial*

enterprise, but in practice a part of the prison administration. The Lodge is twenty-two kilometers from the prison gate.

"Next. Name?"

"Jessica Bonner Alvard."

"Uh-huh. I had you yesterday." The trusty was a heavy, dark-haired woman, puffy-faced. "And you want to see . . .?"

"My husband. Alan Alvard."

"You know the case number?"

Jessie shook her head.

"You ought to learn it. It would save you a couple of minutes here." The trusty went to the rear of the room to ask a computer terminal, and after five minutes or so returned. "You had a girl with you last time."

"Yes," Jessie said. "She had to go back to the city."

"Your daughter?"

Jessie thinks about it. "In a way."

Alan Alvard moves his hand in the way that summons the nurse's voice. The hand is heavy as lead, and for a time he understands, though he could not explain, that it is in some way the wrong kind of hand, one that will not activate the proximity switch that controls the speaker and (someplace far off) the microphone and signal light on the nurse's desk.

"What do you want, six seventeen?"

It is not the nurse's voice, nor does it come from the speaker. Dr. Margotte is standing, just out of sight, beside the door. Beyond him, on silent rubber wheels, is the dead-cart with its folded sheet.

"What do you want?"

Afraid to reply, Alvard waits.

The orderly with the scar wakes him, balancing his breakfast tray while he shakes him by the shoulder.

"Did you want me before?"

Alvard stared at him.

"I thought maybe you did. Nurse said you called, but then you didn't answer."

"Didn't they send someone?"

"They were too busy. To tell the truth, a patient doesn't get too much attention here unless he asks for it."

Alvard nodded. "It was the same way before."

"Sure. They don't want too many of us pokin' around, gettin' into trouble, stealin' the medications. You want to go up on the roof again after you eat? It'll be sunny up there now."

Alvard looked at the window. Clear light was pouring in. "What time is it?"

" 'Bout ten-thirty."

"I thought you were on nights."

"I was, but we change around every couple of weeks. I'm on days now. I could leave you up there awhile. A lot of them like that. Maybe you would like to push yourself around in the chair a little. You strong enough for that?"

"I think so," Alvard said.

"I'll come back when you finish your breakfast."

Alvard watched the orderly as he left. His neck was as wide as his head, his shoulders bulky and bunchy under the white uniform tunic. He might have been an iron pumper, a weight lifter.

There was a mirror on the little table. He slid out of bed and stood in front of it for a few seconds, supporting himself by clenching the tabletop with both hands. He had been as big as the scarred man. In college he had wrestled and boxed, and even played two years of football, though he had always felt out of place; the only engineer on a team of future high-school coaches, unable to share its arrogance and clannishness.

He would be no match for the scarred man now, even when his legs had strengthened. The face that stared from the mirror was hollow-cheeked and livid with bruises; the hospital gown below it looked as though it hung on the back of a wooden chair. A corpse alive.

When he was a boy he had gone to church with his father. It was only long afterward that he had understood that his father's devotion was of the kind that had been new in his young manhood in the seventies—the newly old Jesus-people almost indistinguishable now from the ancient tradition of Pentecostalism. His mother had died when he was too young to recall the details, and lay in the crowded yard west of the little building, under a chaste white stone with an Egyptian cross cut into the top. A place among friends in the country— a commune—had been the dream of her generation.

At first his father had him wait on the steps while he visited his wife before going in. But when he was nine, he made him come with him, and stand under the drooping branches of the willows. It had reminded Alan, then, of the death of Little Nell. One autumn he had wanted to brush the leaves away, and his father had prevented him. Perhaps he had felt they would keep her warm somehow, all those little leaves shaped like the blades of knives. His father had burned most of his mother's pictures, but one that had remained showed her with long fair hair—no doubt it was from her that he had inherited his own blondness—falling over her shoulders. His father had told him once that that had been the style when they were married—long hair, straight, worn down. He had said that women sometimes ironed their hair to keep it straight; but somehow the picture reinforced his belief that his mother (her name had been Ellen) and Little Nell were one and the same. Perhaps there had been an illustration in *The Old Curiosity Shop,* and his father had let him see it; perhaps the two faces were something alike.

That was why he had done it, of course. Made books talk. He thought: "I should have known it before—but then I suppose I wouldn't have done what I did." Little Nell could speak now, thanks to him; all the others too, thanks to Little Nell.

Sentimental slop for sure. Even the people who liked that book did not like Little Nell. But they had had their mothers for as long as they wanted them—not had to remember a girl-mother who was only a picture, not listened to Dad reading books in the evening because only books could comfort him for long, not heard the guitar music played over and over in the front room at night because she had taped it for Dad. Still, it wasn't Little Nell who played the guitar; it was Dora, with a Ta ra la! Ta ra la!

No wonder he had seen old Doc Margotte and his meat wagon waiting outside through the solid wall. He was morbid. Well, who wouldn't be, forty years dead—that was it, that was right, *dead,* as dead as poor Ellen Alvard, as Dad-dead as Raymund Alvard her husband, now.

Not frozen, not sleeping, not hibernating. Dead.

They had drugged him and let the cancer kill him, and frozen his corpse before it had time to rot. Dead, indubitably dead.

What was death? The cessation of breath? They had waited for that. The end of heart action? They had that too. The termination of cellular processes? That had occurred on freezing.

Where had *he* been then? Or was he only a wind-up toy, equipped now with the near miraculous battery (originally intended for wristwatches) with which he had equipped his books? If only a toy, did it matter—even to him—if he was wound up or not, if there was no child to see?

A book then. He was a book, of course. (He laughed aloud, then held his hand over his mouth for fear someone might come in.) And this, this was a bookcase. This prison. How could it have taken so long for him to understand? Not a gold-fish bowl, not a cage, not even a jail. A bookcase. Not open shelves either—a cabinet with solid doors of dark wood, doors that closed.

He got out of bed and tottered to the window to look out, and there they were, half a mile away, the towering, dark doors. And he could see across the roofs of the surrounding buildings—so this was the seventh floor after all. What was it the orderly had said the country was called now? The Unified States and Kingdoms. The U.S.K. They must have adopted the British system for numbering the floors of buildings.

Death Island—here he was. Looking carefully now, out into the sunlight, he could even see the old walls, the brick walls he remembered, much nearer than the new, dark ones. They had expanded the place then—built the new prison in a ring around the old one. No wonder the grille had been done away with—who, climbing from that window, could escape through all the maze of walls and cell-block buildings? It was a city, and it seemed a bigger city than any he had known.

But it was only a bookcase. The trick was to get off the shelf, to get into circulation. He looked up at the cerulean sky, and the white clouds, still symbols of freedom, unchanged since his own time. From forty years since. And then . . .

Leviathan!

It was as though in looking up he had looked down instead, and beheld a planet turning beneath him. Too big—oh, far too large a thing to be in air. High up, but so large, still, that even so it seemed to fill the sky. As he watched, its shadow came, dyeing the prison inky black. It was a . . . what? Not an airplane. Not like a ship either—a thing of the air surely, or of the space above the atmosphere, a thing of heights. Not silver; steely metal splashed with brown. As a dam massive; ruined, crazily aslant, and drifting, with the sun shining through rents where the hull plates and internal fittings had been torn away and only the great, curved beams of the skeleton remained.

Antigravity. They had antigravity then. But in what struggle had that billion-ton ghost ship been ruined? Why didn't they board and salvage it? Was it radioactive? Was there a nuclear device aboard? Was it, perhaps, simply too big for them—for anyone—to handle? The shadow reached his window, plunging it in darkness.

A new orderly comes and finds him in his bed. His legs are shaking from his exertions and his body is bathed in sweat, but the orderly seems to notice nothing. The shadow is still at the window.

"Visitors," the orderly said. He too had a folding wheelchair.

The elevator thumped to a stop, and the doors grated back as they had when he was taken to the roof. The orderly muttered, "We got our own visiting area here. So you patients don't have to go out in the bad weather to see them. Right over here. The screw will tell you the rules."

The guard was already watching them. He was a heavy, middle-aged man. His uniform was blue gray, and he carried no weapon. "You got a hour," he said, "if you want it all. Only you already lost ten minutes because you were late. If you don't want to talk anymore, snap your fingers behind your back and I'll come in and tell you your time is up. I'll be listening to everything you both say—that's the rule. She's brought you something, and she'll have to leave it with me to be checked out before you can have it; but if there's nothing wrong with it, I'll give it to you if you'll wait around a little. Tomorrow's a visiting day too; after that, no more until Friday. She'll probably ask you."

Alvard said, "Who is it?"

"You'll see her in a minute." The guard pulled open a metal door, and took the handles of the chair from the orderly. The floor changed from lumpy tile squares of uneven wood. They turned a corner, and Alvard found himself looking across a battered countertop.

✳

Behind another guard, Jessie walks the wide streets of the prison. The wrecked ship floats above her, casting everything into deepest shadow; but she pays no heed to it. From time to time she appears about to speak—not to the guard, but to an invisible presence to her left. Her head turns. Her lips twitch. Then she faces straight again and pats the leather bag she carries.

"In here. You been here before?"

Jessie shook her head.

"You look like you been coming here for years."

"I used to come—a long time ago. It was a lot smaller then. We went to a different building."

"He did a stretch before, huh?"

Jessie was looking away, and pretended not to hear him. Age had its uses. The television and most of the magazines she read said that people like her—people who had not received C.T. until they had already aged—would stay old, stay as they were. But last week she had read (in a small, square magazine she had gotten at the market) that a few doctors disagreed. Even old bodies, the magazine quoted them as saying, would gradually regenerate themselves. At any rate, no one knew for sure. The magazine was nestling in her purse now, next to the other present she had brought for him. She would give it to him too. Not tell him, but let him read the article himself. Meantime there was Lisa. No, that wouldn't be fair—the article. What if it was wrong?

"Sit down. If you have any object you want to give the prisoner, you have to let me have it. If it's okay, I'll pass it on to him. You can ask him if he got it next time you come."

"I have a book."

"You'll have to let me see it when you're finished."

"All right." A narrow line of black ran down the center of the counter. She reached out to touch it, and her hand struck an invisible substance. "They used to have wire," she said.

"This way we don't have to worry about your passing anything through. You'll be able to hear each other fine."

"All right," she said again. The guard left. A minute ticked away, then two, before she heard someone coming, the shuffle of feet and the soft whirring of wheels. Then he came. He was in a wheelchair and looked terrible, yet still it was he, immediately recognizable. She had been twenty-five.

He said, "Hello, Mrs. Alvard." It was a joke of his.

"You knew me. I didn't think you would." He had known her, but she had seen the shock in his face. She said, "I'm old now. Sixty-five. Time to retire if I were working, according to the old way of thinking."

"Did you have to work?"

"No. Thanks to you."

"They broke my patent. Somebody here told me."

"Not until after twenty-five years. I had saved some from what the lawyer was giving me; by then I was too old to work anyway. Fifty."

He nodded, the shock still lingering in his face.

"I know to you it seems like no time at all; but for me it's been most of my life. You're someone I remember from when I was young."

For a moment, neither said anything. There was a fly in the room, on Jessie's side. It buzzed and occasionally crashed into the invisible partition. He said, "It was good of you to come, Jessie; I know you didn't have to, with the money gone."

"I felt I owed it to you; it's good that it happened now. Twenty years ago I was so worried about it. I was afraid they'd bring you back, and we'd both feel . . . that we ought to be together again. But I'd be too old for you; I was forty-five then."

"I'm thirty-seven physiologically," he said. "Remember? I was too old for you."

"Yes, but you were intelligent. So brilliant, Al." She sounded as though that had made a difference, had balanced her youth. "Now there's no question about it. So we can both relax. I'll write you sometimes, and send you things. Cookies and things."

He smiled. "Don't tell me you bake now."

"I'll get them from the store. They'll still be better than what they give you here. No, I never learned to cook—it always seemed . . . you know."

"Yes, I know."

"One of those second-class things that women did. I ate out. Or thawed freezer dinners in the oven. I guess the real second-class thing women do is live off men."

He said, "Jessie, I *wanted* you to have the money," very softly.

"I know, and I thought that was my chance. I could live on it until I got into acting, or dancing. And I had some parts. Really, Al, I got some parts. I just never went over." He nodded, and she relaxed her grip on the edge of the counter. Her purse had fallen to the floor.

"I hope there were some other men," he said.

"Oh, yes."

"That's good. I wouldn't want to think of you waiting alone for forty years."

"There were others." She laughed, and it sounded almost like her old, happy laugh. "You weren't even the first, Al. It was Barry, remember? But you were the only one that left me with anything when he was gone. If you're worried that you owe me something for waiting . . ."

"I'm not," Alvard said.

"Good. Don't be. I'm the one who owes you." She bent to fumble in her purse. Her eyes were wet, and she blinked back the tears as though she were afraid they would make her mascara run, though she wore none. "I'm the one. It's me." Because her head was below the level of the counter, the words were muffled.

When she straightened up again, she was holding a brown paper envelope. She said, "She's going to come. For you." And pressed a picture flat against the invisible wall between them.

It was a young woman lying on a chaise longue on what appeared to be the terrace of a small apartment. Billowing smoke-black hair above an expressionless face, clear, pale skin touched with pink at the cheeks, narrow waist, swelling hips, long, straight legs.

"She looks like you," Alvard said. "Exactly like you. The way you used to be."

"Her name is Lisa."

"Pretty name."

"She was here with me yesterday, but they said you couldn't come, and she had to go back last night. They're casting a play. I already signed up for her, so she can get in. They still have the visiting thing like they used to—you know, the cottages—even though there's women in here too now."

He teased her in the old way. "What will she call herself? Jessica Alvard or Lisa Alvard?"

"She won't have to pretend; they've dropped all that."

"Don't cry, Jessie."

She shook her head, blindly and helplessly. The first tear had overflowed her tiny handkerchief. "I won't be jealous of Lisa, Al. Do you remember how jealous I used to be?"

Alvard said, "We really should have been married before I went in. It would have made everything easier."

"I wanted to, Al."

"I know you did; but what would it have been for you, being chained—" He paused, as if suddenly conscious of the banality of what he was saying.

"Maybe it would have been better for me. I don't think the men I lived with after you did me much good." Outside, the shadow of the great derelict, slowly drifting over the expanse of the prison, came at last to an end. A ray of sunlight as sudden as the glare from a flashbulb darted through the window and transformed the invisible partition between them into something that reflected almost as much light as it transmitted. As though some tormentor had thrust a mirror at her face, Jessie saw herself as she sat in the worn wooden prison chair. Her hands, too small for her body and dotted with reddish brown, were clenched in her lap; her shoulders were rounded and bent; her face, beneath her gray hair, was rounded too, and bent away from the image of the face she recalled from only a few years before—the corners of the eyes twisted down, the nose pulled out and coarsened. She looked like every old woman she had known and despised while she herself had been young: like the wardrobe mistress at the Theater in the Park, like that woman in Paris who took care of the apartment building, like the one who came to clean when she was living at the Towers; most of all, like her mother.

And through her own aged image she could see Al; still young, but looking (the phrase came to her mind and was accepted before she realized how appropriate it was) as if he were dead and buried—his cheeks sunken, and his face livid with bruises. Worse, she saw him seeing himself. He raised his right arm, and it was half a second before she understood that he was trying to cover his face. It should have been comic, the old melodramatic vampire gesture; but it was not. It was so not-funny, that high, knobbed forehead with the skull showing so plainly through the tightened skin, those haunted blue eyes in nests of dark flesh, so not-funny that she forgot her own anger and the hatred she had directed against herself, against the old woman in the wooden chair.

Her lips were moving, but she seemed to stop and listen to discover what it was she was saying: "Poor Count. Poor Count." He was wheeling the chair clumsily around. "I brought you something, Al," she called. "I'll leave it with the guard. He'll give it to you." He was nearly through the door now. "Next time Lisa will come. She'll come, Al, I promise."

The guard was beside her chair already. "You folks finished?"

"Thank God," she said, "Lisa didn't see him this time. He'll look better in a week, won't he?" She stood up, holding the edge of the counter. Other fingers had worn depressions in it there. "You were brought up on a farm, weren't you?"

The guard smiled. "That's right, ma'am. How did you know?"

"The way you talk. He was too. I was raised in Queens."

Is that so? Mostly city people in here. We don't get country people very often."

"Murder," she said. She sounded as though she wanted to lay everything out at once.

"It usually is, for country. Farm people don't steal." He seemed proud of it. "But they'll kill you if they get mad enough."

"That's what Al did—got mad and killed his friend."

"It figures. Cain was a stockman, you know, and Abel was a farmer. You talk to your Bible, ma'am?"

Jessie shook her head, but the question seemed to remind her of her gift. She drew it out of her bag and handed it to the guard. "I brought something for him. Would you look it over, like you said, and give it to him?"

On the way back to the city, on the bus, her eyes were obstructed by tears, and she could not read. She held the magazine from the market open in her lap instead, and let the little voice Al had put there so long ago tell her of the sunken continent of Mu, and of women who held communion with the joyful spirits of the dead, and how C.T. would—in time—make even old, round, bent faces young again. Provided the degenerative diseases did not kill their owners first.

Alvard lies with his hands behind his head, while a doctor—his name is Porter—looks him over. " 'What we've got to do, is to keep up our spirits, and be neighborly,' " Alvard quotes to him. " 'We shall come out right in the end, never fear.' "

"You must be feeling better today."

"I don't look bad, do I? For something brought back from the crypt?"

"For someone brought back from the crypt, you're in very good condition indeed. So good that we should have you out of the hospital in another week or two."

"I won't be sorry to go," Alvard told him.

"Most patients are. The food is better here, and there's less crowding."

"I don't like being on this floor. I'll still be able to use the library, won't I, when I've left the hospital?"

The doctor glanced at the stack of books on the night stand beside the bed. Their dark bindings and faded gold stampings looked out of place against the white enamel of the stand and the white paint of the wall, but shadowy and comfortable. "You like to talk to books, don't you?" he said.

"I like to read. I have all my life."

"So do I." The doctor was looking at the dim titles on the books' spines. *"Elements of Economic Statistics; Transitory Currents in Semiconductors; The Autobiography of Preceptor Neal; A Military History of the Union of South Africa; Selections from the Novels of Charles Dickens.* Have you read all these?"

"Not yet. The Dickens book is mine—a woman I used to know brought it to me. The rest are from the library here."

"You have varied tastes."

"Something for everyone," Alvard said.

The doctor nodded. "Now that we're finished, you've another visitor, I'm afraid, waiting outside."

A guard—a tall, hawk-faced woman—stepped into the room. The sound of her boots seemed incongruous in this building, dominated by the noises of patients' soft slippers and the staff's crepe-soled shoes. "Your tray from lunch—it had a knife, a fork, and a spoon on it. Is that right?" Her voice was hard, but without emotion.

"I think so," Alvard said.

"You think so. Okay. It was supposed to, and the kitchen says only the fork and spoon came back. You want to give me the knife now?"

Alvard held out empty hands. "You think it's here?"

The doctor said, "I doubt that he's strong enough yet to stab anyone."

"Probably the orderly took it," the guard said, "but I've got to look."

"Don't be rough with him. That's an order."

"I wouldn't anyway."

When the doctor was gone, the guard began a methodical search, looking first in the drawers of the night table, then removing them to look behind them and under them. "You're the person who invented talking books, aren't you?" she said.

Alvard nodded, looking at the hawk face.

"I thought so. I'm glad I finally got to meet you. You're one of the people who helped to make my girhood happy, although of course I never thought of it that way at the time. Do you know what I liked? Those old Nancy Drew mysteries. They reissued all those old books as talkers, and I used to fall asleep gossiping with Nancy about footprints and mysterious lights." (All this while the dark, sharp features never relaxed, and the sunken eyes, pretending to look under the night stand, behind the books, beneath the high bed, were on Alvard's face.) "You know, sir, I wouldn't much blame you if you did take that knife."

"I didn't," Alvard said, "so it's no use watching me while you look. I can't tell you where anything is hidden."

"It's a jungle out there."

"It was in my time too," Alvard said.

"I suppose it was blacks then, wasn't it?"

"Mostly. If you were white it was blacks."

"And if you were black it was the whites." The guard laughed softly. "I can imagine. But at least you'd know what side everyone was on. That's pretty well over with now—that black and white thing. It's women now, if you're a man. Ah, you didn't know that, did you?"

"You're a psychologist," Alvard said.

"I try. In my little way." The guard straightened up, running her hands down her thin body as though she were wiping her palms. "I'm married, myself. My husband and I get along. God knows why they do it; but they get the men who aren't strong—boys and old men, mostly. Or the ones who are sick." She paused, watching Alvard. "And of course some of the men have gone over to them— you know what they get. Then too there's ganging up, and a certain amount of ambushing. There's more of them now than there are men in here."

"I see," Alvard said. "I haven't noticed many women guards."

"There's a few of us. Not many. The province thinks it's a man's job, mostly—and then they've got seniority. Seniority's a great thing. Would you mind rising up? I've got to make sure you're not lying on it. It would be good if you got out of that bed altogether. You're here for murder, aren't you?"

That night, when the hospital was quiet, Alvard drew the knife up, pulling gently at the thread he had raveled from his sheets, and began to whet the edge on the stone sill of the window.

*

Alvard walks to the battered counter in the visiting room. It is his first full day on his feet, and he is proud of the newly regained ability. His face is beginning to fill out again; his shoulders are no longer so sharply boned as they were.

"I can't give you my card," the nervous young man seated across from him said, and held it up for him to read. "Jerome Glazer. You were a client of my father's, and the firm has looked after your estate."

"Is there any?" Alvard asked.

"Technically there is always an estate—certain property, certain interests—even though it's often too small to bother with. In your case, your estate—which was considerable—is largely exhausted. Your patent was successfully circumvented about twenty-five years ago; did you know that?"

"I've heard."

"When you were frozen you were legally dead, so the company . . . " The nervous young man searched for a few seconds among the papers in the attaché case in his lap, then gave up. "The company went to your partner's heirs. What was his name?"

"Barry Seigle."

"Right. So your estate consisted of the accumulating royalties from the patent, which—fortunately—was in your name rather than the company's. Could I ask why you killed him, by the way? I've always wondered."

"Sooner or later," Alvard told him, "the time comes when the man with the money wants to get rid of the man with the ideas. I was the man with the ideas."

"He was trying to crowd you out? Listen, I'm sorry if I upset you—it was a long time ago now."

"Not for me," Alvard said.

"I understand. It's just that I more or less grew up with the case—my father used to talk about the various court fights over the patent, and the cost of keeping you cryogenically preserved, and so on. Your life has been the background of my life, in a way."

"Your father's dead?"

The young man shrugged.

It was a helpless, hopeless kind of shrug, and Alvard asked again, "Your father's dead?"

"He's gone. It used—when C.T. was newer—to happen a lot. A man, you have to realize, like Dad . . . "

"Yes?"

"A man like Dad would work, as he thought, all his life . . . in something. Dad had his law practice. He never took in partners, never tried to be big. He just tried to be the best. Some rich clients to carry the office; a few poor ones so he could feel good about himself; some cases that were out in front of the current state of the law, cases that would set precedents for the future. He tried to be the best." Glazer had a pimple on the underside of his chin, and he picked at it with the nails of his forefinger and thumb as he spoke. "When the C.T. came in, he had already spent—I don't know, thirty years, a little less. On his practice. Some criminal cases. Civil suits by individuals, mostly ones with some criminal angle, where it was alleged somebody had forged documents, something of that kind. And the C.T. he got wouldn't make him young again; just keep him like he was. His digestion was bad, you know, but he played handball twice or three times a week. He was still sexually potent, I think."

"If he killed himself, you don't have to tell me," Alvard said.

"He didn't—at least, I don't think he did. As far as we know he just—went away. I think he had the idea that he was going to bum around the continent. A lot of them thought that, you know. I went into his room that night, as it happened, and he had a kind of canvas suitcase-shaped bag, and he was putting a checkered shirt in it. I asked if he was going fishing, because every two or three years one of the rich clients would insist on his going with him, up in Maine. We've lost him now—he went to another firm. Anyway, Dad said yes, he was. That was the last time I ever saw him."

"I understand."

"I'll see him again, of course. If he hasn't been hurt, he'll come back sooner or later. The ones who set out to travel like that—they don't usually do it for long. A few years. Sometimes only a few months. Then they settle someplace to spend another thirty years doing something else. I'll run into him somewhere, perhaps."

"You're carrying on with the firm, though."

"Yes, I'm an attorney. I was going to be Dad's first partner; now I'm running the show. You don't retain us anymore because the money's gone. But I feel we owe you something. I wanted to give you an accounting—I have the papers here—and to tell you I'll act for you should the occasion arise."

"It will arise," Alvard said.

Glazer nodded. "I've been thinking of something. You know, I suppose, that just having had C.T. won't get you out? That was a big issue some years back—whether or not the life imprisonment of an immortal prisoner constituted cruel and unusual punishment. It was decided that the term *life* was to be construed as five hundred years. But no one has ever ruled on cryogenic preservation. You were legally dead while you were frozen; and we can argue that your imprisonment now exceeds the term prescribed by law. If we win, we might even get you damages in addition to your release. I'd be willing to pursue that on a contingency basis."

"I see," Alvard said.

"So it's much to early to give up hope. That's what I wanted to tell you."

"I expect to be released a long time before the action you're proposing comes to trial," Alvard said. "But go ahead with it anyway."

"You expect to be released?"

"I said so, didn't I? They'll be looking for some legal way to get me out. Probably a pardon—but they might come to you, and if they do, you could suggest this business about exceeding the term. It might help someone else later on."

"Do you mind telling me—"

"Yes, I do," Alvard said. "In fact I won't tell you. But if everything goes as planned, I ought to be out in a few months."

"A few months?"

"Or a few weeks. The thing is already done, actually. I'm just waiting for it to cook."

"Anything you say to me is a privileged communication."

"I understand that," Alvard said. He stood up. "Are you the only visitor?"

"As far as I know."

"There's a motel outside the gates. I can't think of the name of it."

"The Lodge."

"Are you staying there?"

Glazer nodded.

"A dark-haired girl, very pretty. A voluptuous figure."

"I didn't see her."

"How about a gray-haired woman? Round face. Kind of a large nose?"

"A lot of those. But there aren't any other visitors for you—not that I know of."

✳

Megan Carstensen, fresh and cool and virginal as an asphodel in an ash can, is waiting for him in his room. The wind from the open window tosses her golden hair. "I've got good news for you. It's unofficial still—but good news."

He said: "They're turning me loose."

"Not quite that good." She laughed. "But the hospital is turning you loose, yes. You're going to be discharged."

"Uh-huh." She was sitting on his bed, so he took the chair.

"That means you'll be going into a cell in one of the blocks. You'll still come in every day for an hour or so—outpatient status. I've been trying to persuade them that the best way to handle that is to give you a job here. After all, that was what you did before you were frozen. You were an orderly, weren't you?"

"Yes," Alvard said. "I was an orderly."

"I wanted to talk to you about your cell assignment. Do you know how it works now?"

Alvard shook his head.

"You get to pick cellmates. If there's an empty cell, and you and some other people want to have it, you get it. Everyone has to agree, of course. Or if a cell has an empty bunk, you can go into it if you want to, and the people who are already there are willing to have you."

"It wasn't like that," Alvard said, "before I was frozen."

"It's a relatively new thing. And of course, it's only for good behavior. If you act up, they'll take you out and put you in a punishment cell."

"I don't know who I could stay with anyway."

"How about me?"

He stared at her.

"I'm not too bad, am I? We don't have many cosmetics in here, so you may smell a little sweat from time to time, but I do what I can, and I shave under my arms. Naturally, if you don't want to . . ."

"I do, certainly," Alvard said. "You took me by surprise."

"I know. Your mouth was open there for a while. I forget sometimes that you date from the period before birth-control drugs made this kind of prison possible."

"It was possible," Alvard said. "It was just that no one did it."

"Anyway, it's not exactly a honeymoon cottage. There are two other men there now—you don't have to raise your eyebrows at me like that—but there are four bunks. If you want number four, say so."

"I'd think that the other men would rather have a second woman."

"If I say it's all right, they'll go along with it."

"I want to come, certainly. It's just that this is a bit of a surprise."

Megan smiled, and the smile made her look even younger—almost like a child. "That's good. That's fine." She patted the bed beside her. "Come here and sit with me. Want a hand up?"

"I can manage," Alvard said. He stood up with little more effort than he had given to the same act before the cancer had struck, and seated himself beside her. "I have a . . . friend outside. Will she know?"

"Only if she finds out through the grapevine—but it's a pretty good grapevine. Inmates tell visitors, and the visitors tell each other, down at the Lodge."

"She used to be jealous—so did I. But it doesn't make sense now; she's too old." Alvard might almost have been talking to himself. "Barry said she pulled a gun on him once."

"They picked up most of the guns years ago," Megan told him.

"She had other men after I was gone. She said so."

"Did it bother you? Knowing that?"

Alvard shook his head.

"Then you'd probably get along with us all right. I trade around, you understand. But you'll get yours, as soon as you're strong enough. In fact, you'll get more than yours."

"I'm strong enough now."

She put a hand in his lap. "Not quite, but soon. You just tell them when they ask you. It's Two C Sixteen B. Here, write it down." She gave him the pen she carried clipped in the opening of her tunic, looked around for paper, and finding none, handed him a book from the pile beside the bed. "You can put it in here. They'll be around in a day or so."

The book was Thomas Wolfe's *You Can't Go Home Again,* and when Alvard opened it to write on the flyleaf, Wolfe's voice said: "Mrs. Jack crossed the room and stood before the mirror looking at herself. First she bent forward a little and stared at her face long and earnestly with an expression of childlike innocence. Then she began to turn about, regarding herself from first one angle, then another. She put her hand to her temple and smoothed her brow." A second voice interrupted, cockney and reverent, filled with an inexhaustible sincerity: "She's Color-Sergeant of the Nonpareil battalion, and there's not such another. But I never own to it before her. Discipline must be maintained."

Megan noticed nothing; Alvard wrote *2C16B* and closed the book.

The warden's office contrives, without bars or wire or even rumpled gray cloth, to remain an organic part of the prison whole. Her desk, her couch, her private cabinet of mementos, even the scent from the bowl of violets on her small table belong to the official community that yet controls North America; but they are here as ambassadors, feigning a settled luxury in the alien country of steel and concrete.

"This is him," the guard announced as he led Alvard in.

The warden said, "Good morning, Alan." And then, "You may go, Sergeant Bonilla. Alan's behavior has been exemplary—I'm sure we'll have no trouble."

Alvard stood in front of her desk, glad that he wore the pressed whites of the hospital. A stranger, a silent man who looked thirty or thirty-five, sat to her left in an armchair; the warden seemed to be pretending he was not present.

"I'm sorry," she said, "that we haven't had an opportunity to meet sooner. I've been talking to your file, and yours is an interesting case."

"I always thought so," Alvard said.

The warden laughed throatily. "Will you shake hands? I've found that some prisoners don't want to shake hands with me." She rose and extended her hand, which Alvard took. "Good. It isn't often that we have a person of your abilities here—though I suppose we've had you for forty-three years, come to think of it. I've got to set up a tickler system to remind me to initiate personal contact with the really extraordinary inmates. I have the feeling we're wasting you on hospital work."

"I enjoy it."

"But you might enjoy other things more. Alan, I'd like you to meet Lon."

The silent man stood up and thrust out his hand. "Lon Matluck."

"Lon is from the District President's office." The warden looked toward him. "What is the precise title of your board, Lon?"

"The Advisory Commission on Technological Development."

"Yes. Lon has an offer to make you, Alan. A very attractive one, I think. I'll let him explain it to you; but I should say in advance that it has the full backing of the administration here."

Matluck said, "It's nothing complicated. We want you to do research in your old field—applied cybernetics—for the District. Bernice assures me that her office will see that you are given a space suitable for laboratory use, and that you will be released from any other duties. I'll coordinate with you, and with her people here, to get you the equipment you'll require."

Alvard said, "No."

"Aren't you being a little hasty?"

The warden smiled at both of them—she had the beautiful, even teeth of an actress. "I think we have to remember that Alan's previous work led—at least indirectly—to his imprisonment. It's natural for him to feel that he wants nothing more to do with it. What he has to realize, however—what we all have to realize—is that that kind of emotion is actually only a form of aversive conditioning. We use the same thing in our rehabilitation programs; but this is *accidental* conditioning—the research actually had nothing to do with the imprisonment. At some point, a functioning human being has to rise above her—or his—emotions."

"I won't do it," Alvard said, "unless I'm out. Fully out. Set free by a new trial or pardoned. You can talk to my attorney."

The warden and the man from the District President's office exchanged glances. Then he said, "Has it occurred to you that you owe something to society? You were the inventor of speaking records—"

"Books," Alvard told him. "Barry and I applied it to books. You sound as if you're talking about recordings. And the courts have ruled that I did not invent them; I've read the transcript."

"Nevertheless, you did invent them. You know it and we know it. Your patent was set aside on a technicality."

"Nice of you to say so."

"Our country is locked in a paradox. It is necessary that the people believe that they have the right of ownership of property, ideas, and so on—you have to understand that. Yet at the same time, it is vital that the government and the extra-governmental corporations—those whose assets exceed half a billion, let us say—have access to the actual real estate, inventions, or whatever. Thus we have laws of eminent domain, and so on. You have been victim of that essential system—from time to time someone has to be if our civilization is to continue. All right; we admit it and we're willing to make it up to you now. But not to the extent of condoning murder."

Alvard asked, "May I sit down?"

The warden said, "Of course. I've been very remiss," and gestured toward a chair.

Alvard sat. "Do you know why I killed Barry Seigle?"

Matluck shook his head and said, "You did kill him, then. I believe you pleaded innocent."

"By reason of insanity. Yes, I killed him. When I was developing the Genre Jinn—that's what we called it, and since you're admitting I originated it, we might as well use the name—Barry Seigle made a suggestion. A technical suggestion. Do you follow me? I had been talking to him about the problem of hard-wiring that much specialized logic into the space provided by a book cover; even with microminiaturized circuit chips to work with, it wasn't easy. And he made his technical suggestion."

"I understand." Matluck nodded.

"Barry handled the financial end. He raised money for us, got the backers, set up our distribution system, handled sales and advertising."

"I understand," Matluck said again.

"I did the research and oversaw our production facility. Also, I chose the books we would do. Each book, at first, was a new problem. Eventually I worked out some generalized hardware, but we still had to write a new assembler language program for each. I did that."

"And that," the warden began, "is exactly—"

Matluck silenced her with a gesture, and Alvard knew (he had been fairly sure before) who was in charge.

"Later—a long time later, when we were a success and on our way, perhaps, to being one of those extragovernmental corporations you talk about—Barry reminded me of that suggestion he had made. Please understand that it wasn't a new idea—I had been working in that area before. And in the terms he made it, it was so general as to be valueless. But I questioned him further—it wasn't the first time he had brought it up—and I found that he actually thought that he was the real inventor. He had let me take the patent out for legal reasons, he said, and because I had a plausible technical background."

The warden asked, "And you killed him for that?"

"He didn't know, you see. He didn't know what had gone into the development. He thought that his stupid, actually useless suggestion had been the key. And I couldn't take it. I was trying to beat his thick head against the wall, and it was the window instead, and it broke. We were eighty-three floors up, and the windows weren't supposed to break. All that glass falling—it might have killed a hundred people."

"And he—this Barry Seigle—went through?"

"I pushed him through. The air was rushing out all around us, and Barry was screaming." Alvard paused. "Have either of you ever really invented anything? Done anything creative?"

The warden only stared at him. Matluck shook his head.

"There's a moment when you know what to do. You *know* it. Or the machine suddenly works the way it should, and you *know* why. Barry wore those big, old-fashioned belts. Nostalgia for the eighties. A big buckle with the Australian Army insignia and a U.N. motto. You've probably forgotten it. But I looked down and saw that buckle, and I *knew* what to do. I got my right hand under the belt, and heaved up as if I was pressing a weight. You ought to have seen his eyes pop."

"I'm glad I didn't," Matluck said.

"I don't think I owe society a damn thing. Or Barry's family either—all he had was a wife, and when he was dead she owned Speaking Pages, and she was glad he was gone. I owe Barry himself; but there's no way I can pay him, ever. Does it stand to reason that after killing my best friend, to hold on to the only thing in my life that's really mine, I'd put that thing at your disposal for the sake of a prison job? For anything at all less than freedom and wealth?"

Despair is the oldest inhabitant of the punishment cells. She is there, sitting in her corner, when the prisoner arrives; when he leaves she will be there still, with her limp, useless hands clasping one another—though he may not leave her behind.

The cells were small rooms without windows. The floor was three meters long and a trifle under two meters wide. The ceiling was two meters high. Walls and ceiling were concrete, painted a faded brown; the room contained a bunk, a small basin with a cold water tap, and a slop jar. The light in the center of the ceiling could not be turned off.

The door was solid metal, unlike the doors of ordinary cells, which were barred. It was also unlike them in being always shut. About a hundred and seventy centimeters up, there was a small window fitted with thick glass, opaque from the prisoner's side.

The walls were not scratched with names, dates, or clever sayings, because the prisoners had nothing to scratch them with. They wore gray prison shirts, gray trousers without belts, and stockings. They had nothing to look at, and nothing to read; they did not send one another tapped messages, because they had nothing to tap with, and no tunneling fellow prisoner ever came up through the floor. They marked the passage of time by counting their meals, which were unvarying, and served once a day. They were supposed to have no one to talk to, but occasionally a guard came (they were never sure if the guards were violating regulations, or had been sent to report on them) and once a week they were permitted to leave their cells for a shower.

For the first two days, Alvard waited patiently. He knew, or thought he knew, what was happening outside the prison, and he felt sure that he would spend no more than a few weeks at most in his punishment cell. On the third day, he grew bored with waiting, and began to amuse himself with fantasies. He wrote programs in his head and dwelled lovingly on his memory of the binding of *Selections from the Novels of Charles Dickens*. How sweetly and cleanly it had curled back when the blade of his knife, as sharp as a scalpel, ran alone its edge. The chips within had glittered like the windows of a city by night; and a city they had been, throbbing with a thousand voices.

He heard the click as the bolt of the door retracted under the prodding of a coded card. The guard who entered was male and muscular, with a broad, inexpressive Slavic face. "Dinner already?" Alvard asked. It was not a meal—the guard had no tray.

"Right. Sorry I'm late with your chow." Deadpan, he extended two envelopes.

The tops had been slit by the censor. "Thanks," Alvard said. By an effort of will he did not look at the return addresses.

"Nice view. Nice place you have here."

"Sure."

"We have mail service like this every day. I'm your friendly mail carrier, and if you're not getting anything I write something for you myself. I got what you call a nice hand. Like you see in the ads for hotels. You get a letter signed *Regency,* why, that's me. You want to read what I wrote you now, or you got time to blow air?"

"I'll have a lot of time to look at these," Alvard said.

"That's the spirit. When I was in independent command of the Big Sandy, my woman was Nina Paynter. The star—you know? She used to send me tapes, just whispering on those little ones that only hold an hour. I used to play them over the bullhorn until I found out the crew was starting to tap-dance. Just the same, I think hearing the voice is better than looking at all those chicken scratches."

"You can't read."

"I'm the fastest in the world. Got the best memory for it too.

Want to hear the names of all the cities in the U.S. and K.? Listen."
The guard's mouth opened and closed without a sound, leaving the
wide face as impassive as before. "Backwards." His lips opened and
shut again. "Now I'll slow 'em down for you." An elaborate yawn.

"Okay, you didn't read my letters," Alvard said. "Great.
Thanks."

"I got to be moving. I'll ask her majesty if I can come back
tomorrow. You get some of the other guys in, and we'll play soccer."

"It's a date. You bring the ball."

When he was nearly out the door, the guard paused. "I almost
forgot to tell you. Up at the hospital, everybody's askin' if we killed
you yet. Especially one guy, the brain surgeon." He held up a thick
hand, with the first and second fingers bent out of sight.

For an hour afterward, the letters lay unread on the foot of
Alvard's bunk while he paced the room. From time to time, he
stooped and touched their envelopes—one of common white paper,
the other rough and tinged with cream.

He went to the door, tried to peer through the glass, and pounded
on it with his fist. No one came. "Margotte is dead," he called. "He
was an old man. He must have been dead for years before the
discovery of C.T."

No one replied.

"You were only waving, right? You just happened to hold your
hand that way."

He waited for an answer, but none came, and at last he stepped
back from the door. "Maybe there are a whole line of them—the
doctors with blasted hands. Maybe they don't know themselves."
For the first time since childhood, tears welled in his eyes.

✳

*After hours have gone by, he sleeps; and after hours more, wakes
and sits up, and rubs his face with his fingers, and picks up the two
letters and juggles them in his hand.*

He smiled as if the juggling were a conscious prolongation of
pleasure.

The cream envelope:

My friend:

I hope you understood, during our talk in Nancy's office, that the arrangement I outlined to you then was the most generous authorized at that time. Since returning here to the Capital, I have discussed your case with the District President himself. Soon I will be visiting you again, with a still more generous offer. Meanwhile, I hope that you will give consideration not only to the profound advantages such an arrangement offers you but also to the service you can render your District, and your fellow citizens.

With respect,

Lon Matluck
Chairman, Advisory Commission
on Technological Development

Alvard nodded to himself, then read the letter over a second time. He chuckled.

The second envelope contained a folded sheet of plain paper, and what seemed to be a greeting card, its exterior reddish and pebbled in imitation of crushed morocco, and stamped in gold: I'M SENDING YOU A BIT OF MYSELF.

The letter first:

Dearest Al,

I tried to come and see you again, did they tell you? Somebody in the lobby said you were sleeping with a woman—in her cell; but you know I don't believe it. Anyway, at the office they said you were in punishment.

Lisa was going to come too, but at the last minute something came up for her, so she could not make it. I don't know what you did, but I hope you will be out of punishment soon because we both want to see you. Lisa wants to meet you.

Lisa sends a greeting for you. To say high is the way she puts it. You'll like her—she is fantastically cute and has such a sweet disposition and such a sweet way about her. (She's watching over my shoulder when I write this, Al, but I'd say it anyway!) We'll be back next weekend, hoping you are out of p. See you then!!

Much, much love

Lisa and Jessie

ps. Al, a man came around to talk to me and he asked a lot of questions about you. Lisa was gone. He wouldn't say what it was for, and I didn't tell him anymore than everybody knows already—except I said I thought you had already suffered enough, too much for something you did when anybody would be crazy mad. What's happening, Al? But if it's true about the woman there, don't tell me.

The card opened stiffly—the paper was thicker and harder than that of the Christmas and birthday cards he had been accustomed to. The picture inside seemed to leap out in startling three-dimensionality: a room—or perhaps a small stage—decorated with white Louis XVI furniture, and tapestries of aristocratic shepherdesses and swains bearing lutes. A young woman's voice, high-pitched and plaintive, began to speak.

"Hello. My name is Lisa. Here's what I look like."

A slender, black-haired girl walked out onto the tiny stage. Megan had said they could clone individuals now; this was surely Jessie's clone duplicate—graceful, yet with an amateurish quality to her motions that was at once appealing and unsettling.

"I can sing, dance, act for you. Anything you like. I am a fashion model, and I've experience distributing literature at trade shows and conventions."

The miniature girl was taking off her clothing, one filmy piece after another.

"I *might* fill in if your receptionist is ill, but I don't want a full-time job doing that. And I won't wait on tables, or serve cocktails—it's bad for your legs, and you wouldn't want to ruin legs like mine, would you? I *will* pose in the nude for real artists and photographers, but I don't want to be intimate with a male model."

A new voice, not radically dissimilar, ingenuesque and theatrical, asked: "I beg your pardon, but did you ever play at Canterbury? I recollect meeting a gentleman at Canterbury, only for a few moments, for I was leaving the company as he joined it, so like you that I felt almost certain it was the same."

Alvard's lips twitched, and he whispered, "Miss Snevellicci." He dropped the card, which closed as it fell. "Miss Snevellicci, from *Nicholas Nickleby*. They have gone out, even though I have been in here. My own army. I feel like Mephistopheles." For a time he paced the room.

"Hello. My name is Lisa."

"Will you talk to me, Lisa?"

"Of course, if you like. But I am not just a pictured figure in this card. There is a real Lisa. Would You like to know how to reach her?"

"No, I'd rather just talk. You see, I'm in prison. I will live forever, but I am imprisioned. And it isn't really you I want to chat with—it's your guest, Miss Snevellicci. Could you let her speak, please?"

"I'll see," the Lisa voice said.

But when the new whisper came, it had neither Miss Snevellicci's archness nor Lisa Stewart's strained sensuosness. It was an old man's voice, foolish and quavering: "Will you go and see if Bob is on the lock? Send for Bob."

✳

Moored by a gracefully curving stem of crystal lift tubes, the Presidential Center floats six kilometers above the city. One hundred thousand metric tons of materials has gone into its construction—it weighs exactly nothing. Only the need for frequent communication with the surface, the crystal tubes and their shuttling free-dropping, free-rising cars, holds it bound at all. It makes its own power, purifies its own wastes. Though bound still to a stone ziggurat of stairs leading to the base of the tubes, it no longer requires those roots as it nods in the jet stream like a tulip.

The jewel in the center of the flower is the thousand-faceted dome cupping the President's Conference Garden. The center of its arch is three hundred meters above the floor, and it holds royal palms as readily as orchids, ferns, seven fountains, and the four people talking.

"Pardon me," Alvard said, twisting in his chair. "I'm not used to the suit yet." It had been expensive, and was well cut in the new style, with the coat loose at the waist and buttoning at the side.

The President smiled. "I understand you haven't worn a suit for some time."

"I think it comes to forty-four years."

"Well, we're glad you came out now to help us with this problem."

Alvard shrugged. "I hardly know what it is yet."

The thin woman, Dr. Pomme, snapped, "Dickens."

"Dickens?" Alvard swiveled his chair to face her.

The other woman (she was blonde and soft-looking, with large, intelligent eyes, and her name was Yarwood) murmured, "Yes, Dickens . . . Alan? After nearly fifty years of operation of the speech-active book and record system, it would appear that . . . some barrier . . . some kind of insulation . . . has broken down. The-. . . personalities generated in the cover circuitry are . . ."

The President interrupted. "Are able to travel from one dossier, report, or whatever to another. Things are already in a hell of a mess, and they're getting worse."

"Only Dickens," Dr. Pomme said. She had a narrow chest, close-set eyes, and a little nose as sharp and shining as the blade of a penknife.

"Edith has investigated all the instances we have been able to produce for her; Edith holds the chair of modern English literature at Yale. She tells me that in her opinion all the misplaced personae are major or minor characters from the works of Charles Dickens."

"The Question," the Yarwood woman began in her soft voice, "is whether this was done purposefully or accidentally, and whether it is a continuing or a singular phenomenon. The fact that all of them are from one book . . ."

"Dr. Pomme shook her head, a gesture that might have pared an apple. "Not all from one book. Thus far we have identified characters from every one of Dickens's major works, and quite a few of his minor efforts—Augustus Minns from 'A Dinner at Poplar Walk,' for example."

"Edith and I disagree on terms, you see . . . she is a student of literature; I am a physicist. When I say all are from one book, you, as the inventor of that kind of book . . ."

Alvard said, "The law has decided that I was not the inventor."

"The credit was stolen from you. We know that now. Even President Sanderson . . . he's going to do something for you, if you can help us with this. I was going to say that physically, there might be only one book involved. Edith and Sandy seem to feel that sabotage of some kind is indicated.... I think it may be a circuit failure ... an accident occurring in a single volume."

The President said, "But they move about; they actually go from one file to another."

"If the gain were shorted ... so that these personalities were conceived, so to speak, at maximum amplitude, they would remain so when inductive forces impressed them on the circuitry of another book ..." To Alvard, the blonde woman added, "They must be cover-to-cover. I've duplicated the effect in the lab ... it's a social disease of books, if you want to look at it that way. I destroyed my experimental materials."

For a moment, no one said anything more. The sound of the fountains filled the silence.

The President cleared his throat. "Your invention, Alan, has made it possible for my administration—and those that preceded it—to employ a great number of persons who, quite frankly, are close to functional illiteracy. Reading today, you understand, is something of a specialty. I don't even do much myself. We can't go back, now, to the enormous effort that was made for hundreds of years to implant in every citizen what is fundamentally a freakish communications skill. We can't afford to have the present system destroyed."

The elevators are small rooms, with comfortable chairs. The three of them sit facing one another, ignoring the unequaled view through the translucent walls.

"You'll want some of the infected books to work with," Dr. Pomme said. "I brought you this." She fumbled in her attaché case for it, then handed Alvard a small volume. "A modern novel. Just junk, but there are several of them in there."

"Thank you," Alvard said.

The other woman touched his shoulder confidentially. "You're going to need someone to show you around. The world ... it's changed. You'll work with me? We have nice facilities. In Chestertown, across from Baltimore."

"Some people are meeting me outside," Alvard said, "but I'd be delighted if you'd come with us. Jessie and Lisa, and I'm sure that Jessie, at least, will be there. She's supposed to rent us a car."

"My name is Brenda," the blonde woman said. "I've never heard you use it."

"You look a lot like Megan—that's a woman I knew—"

"In the prison? You shouldn't . . . be ashamed of it. Or her. Naturally you knew women there. Was she beautiful?"

Dr. Pomme swiveled her seat until she faced the serene clouds.

"Very," Alvard said.

When the elevator stopped at last, she hung on his arm. Edith Pomme ignored them as they made their way down the long flight of broad steps. Alvard could see Jessie sitting alone in a vehicle that looked like a matchbox on wheels. "I doubt that you two are going to like each other," Alvard said. "She may even think you're the woman I knew in prison, but what does it matter? We're going to live forever and be free."

Brenda Yarwood squeezed his arm.

"Ten thousand years from now, the three of us will take a picnic basket and come looking through the ruins of this city for these stairs."

Someone (an elderly man, white hair flying in the wind) is running up the steps toward them. His hand is extended, and Alvard recognizes the hand before the face. "Remember me?" Dr. Margotte asks. "We used to work together." Alvard hears his own voice saying, "I thought you were dead."

"I was frozen. Like you. I heard you were going to be here today, and I've been waiting for you. I came to the prison once, but you were in solitary. I beg your pardon, madame." Old-fashioned word, old-fashioned courtesy; he wants to be introduced to the lady. Alvard turns instinctively until he half-faces each, and only then, despite all his aversion to Margotte, learns why he fears him. His eyes are precisely the protuberant eyes of Barry Seigle, going over the edge, going down to the pavement eighty-three floors below. Jessie is steadying (a gun?) on the top of the car door, and the thought of jealousy on Lisa's behalf flickers in Alvard's mind. Edith Pomme's book slips from under his arm, and at his feet he

hears a tiny voice: "Wine-stains, fruit-stains, beer-stains, water-stains, paint-stains, pitch-stains, mud-stains, blood-stains!"

It is the peddler pursuing Bill Sikes.

But Jessie has a camera, Alvard thinks, not a gun. He has seen the flash. The book is near his head now. "Mud-stain or blood-stain—"

THE RENEWAL

PAMELA SARGENT

"A pig cannot fly, and however conscientiously he may diet, however he may direct his mind to lofty thoughts, he just isn't going to get off the ground—as long as he remains a pig; and neither is his swinish temperament going to become angelic, or even human, however firmly or tenderly we teach him. Man, also, is both limited and confused in his fundamental nature; the confusion of poorly reconciled instincts and emotions amounts to racial psychosis, a kind of built-in schizophrenia. The evidence is very strong that there is no cure—as long as we remain human."

> —R. C. W. ETTINGER,
> *Man into Superman*

"Beware of the pursuit of the Superhuman: it leads to an indiscriminate contempt for the Human."

> —GEORGE BERNARD SHAW,
> *Man and Superman*

"They will move easily and gracefully, as one does who has no conflicting nervous impulses . . . They will be much more *alive to things* . . . immensely amused . . . They will be busy, laughing people."

> —H. G. WELLS,
> *Star-Begotten*

"Any viable modification must preserve human versatility, human flexibility, the capacity to adapt both physically and mentally to changes in environment. Excessive specialization through biological experimentation on the human form would always be a dead end."

> —MERRIPEN ALLEN, Preface to
> *Guidelines for Biological
> Modification of Human
> Subjects*

i

As she gazed over the field, Josepha Ryba saw the maple tree. It dominated the clearing in front of her small house and marked the boundary between the trimmed lawn and the overgrown field. The tree was old, perhaps as old as she was. It had been there when she cleared the land and moved into her home.

The other trees, the hundreds along the creek in back of the house and the thousands on the slopes of the nearby hills, had to struggle. She and the gardeners had cleared away the deadwood and cut down dying trees many times. Gradually, she had become aware of changes. The pine trees across the creek flourished; the young oaks near the flat stones she had placed in a circle were gone.

Thirty paces from the maple a young apple tree grew. She had planted it a year ago—or was it two years? Two gardeners, directed by her computer, had planted the tree, holding it carefully in their pincerlike metal limbs. She did not know if it would survive. A low wire fence circled it to protect the tree from the small animals that would gnaw at its bark. The fence had been knocked over a few times.

Josepha looked past the clearing to the dirt road which wound through the wooded hills. A white hovercraft hugged the road, moving silently toward the field. The vehicle was a large insect with a clear bubble over its top. Small clouds of dust billowed around it as it moved. The craft stopped near the tangled bushes along the road, the bubble disappeared, and a man leaped gracefully out onto the road.

Merripen Allen had arrived a day late.

Josepha waved as he jogged toward her. He looked up and raised an arm. She wondered again why she had asked him to come. They had said everything and she had made her decision.

But she wanted to see him anyway. There was a difference between seeing someone in the flesh and using the holo, even if an image appeared as substantial as a body, at least until one reached out to it and clutched air.

He looked, as she expected, exactly like his image. His wavy black hair curled around his collar, framing his olive-skinned face. A thick moustache drooped around his mouth. But he seemed smaller than the amplified image, less imposing.

She was still holding her cigarette as he came up to her. She had been living alone too long and had forgotten how some felt about such filthy habits. She concealed it in her palm, hoping Merripen had not seen it, then dropped it, grinding it into the ground with her foot. She entered the house, motioning for him to follow.

Josepha disliked thinking about her life before the Transition. But her mind had become a network of involuntary associations, a mire of memories. She had been living in her isolated house for almost thirty years and would not have realized it without checking the dates. She had not believed it at first.

It was time to pack up and leave, go somewhere else, do something she had not tried. Her mind resonated here. The sight of an object would evoke a memory; an odor would be followed by the image of a past experience; an event, even viewed at a distance, would touch off a recollection until it seemed she could barely get through the day without succumbing to reveries.

Josepha was more than three hundred years old but she could still feel startled by the fact. She looked twenty-two—except that when she had actually been twenty-two she had been overweight, myopic, and had dyed her hair auburn. She had become, in what would have been her old age in another time, a slim woman with black hair and good vision. She was no longer plagued by asthma and migraine headaches and could not remember how they felt.

But she remembered other things. The events of her youth sprang into her mind, often in greater detail than more recent happenings. She had thought of clearing out the memories; RNA doses, some rest, and the reverberations would be gone, the world would be fresh and new. But that was too much like dying. Her memories made her life, uneventful and pacific as it was, more meaningful.

But now Merripen was here and the peace would soon end.

Merripen Allen slouched in the dark blue chair near the window. His dark brown eyes surveyed the room restlessly. He seemed weary, yet alert and decisive. All the biologists were like that, Josepha thought. They were the ones who had made the world, who kept it alive, who had banished death. They held the power no one else wanted.

Merripen was the descendant of English gypsies. His clipped speech was punctuated by his expressive arm gestures. Josepha suspected that he deliberately cultivated the contrast.

They had spent several minutes engaging in courtesies; exchanging compliments, describing the weather to each other, asking after people they each knew, making an elaborate ceremony of dialing for refreshments. Now they sat across the room from each other silently sipping their white wine.

Josepha wanted to speak but knew that would be rude; Merripen was still savoring the Chablis. He might want another glass and after that there would be more ceremonial banter, perhaps a flirtation. He would pay her compliments, embellishing them with quotations from Catullus, his trademark, and she would fence with him. She had gone through all this in abbreviated form with his image. A seduction, at least in theory, could last forever. Sex, however inventive, and however long it went on in all its permutations, grew duller. It was too much a reminder that other things still lived and died.

Merripen finished the wine, then gazed out her window at the clearing, twirling the glass in his fingers. At last he turned back to her.

"Delicious," he said. "Perhaps I'll have another." He rose to his feet. She motioned him to sit, got up, and walked slowly to the oak cabinent in the corner where the opened bottle stood. She brought it to him and poured the wine carefully, place the bottle on the table under the window, then sat down again.

Merripen sipped. His visage blurred as she focused on the red rose in the slender silver vase on the low table in front of her. As she leaned back, the rose obscured Merripen's body. The redness dominated her vision; she saw a red bedspread over a double bed in the center of a yellow room. She was back in her old room, in the house of her parents, long ago.

She was fourteen and it was time to die. She locked her door.

She gazed at the small bottle, fumbling with the cap, suspended in time past, vividly conscious of the red capsules, the red bedspread, the cheerful flowered curtains over her window. The pain these sights usually brought receded for a moment. A voice called to her, the same soft voice that had called to her before, the disembodied voice she had never located.

She had been dying all along. The black void inside her had grown while the pain at its edges quivered. It would end now. As she swallowed the capsules, she was being captured by eternity, where she would live at last . . .

She had emerged from a coma bewildered, uncomprehending, connected to tubes and catheters, realizing dimly that she still breathed. She tried to cry out and heard only a sighing whistle. She reached with her left hand for her throat, touched the hollow at the base of her neck and felt an open hole. They had cut her open and forced her to live as they lived.

At night, as she lay in the hospital bed trying not to disturb the needle in her right wrist, she remembered a kind voice and its promise. Someone had spoken to her while she lay dying, while she hovered over her drugged body watching a tube forced into her failing lungs. The voice had not frightened her like the voice she had been hearing for months. It had been gentle, promising her that she would live on, that she would one day join it, and then had forced her to return. She was again trapped in her body.

Perhaps her illness or the barbiturates had induced the vision. Yet it had seemed too real for that. She knew dimly that she could not discuss it, could not make anyone understand it, could not even be sure it was real. She felt she had lost something without even being sure of what it was. But the promise remained: *not now, but another time.*

Josepha touched the rose and a petal fell. Her death was still denied her. She had lived, coming to believe she should not seek death actively, that three hundred, or a thousand, or a million years did not matter if the promise had been real.

Merripen spoke. She looked away from the rose.

✳

The evening light bathed the room in a rosy glow. Merripen's skin was coppery and his tight white shirt was pinkish. "You are still with us," he said.

"Yes."

"You still want to be a parent to these children."

"Certainly." Josepha had decided to become a parent two years earlier and had registered her wish. Her request had been granted— few people were raising children now. Her genes would be analyzed and an ectogenetic chamber would be licensed for the fetus. She had been surprised when Merripen Allen contacted her, saying that before she went ahead with her plans he had a proposal to make.

He and a few other biologists wanted to create a new variant of humanity. They had been consulting for years, using computer minds to help them decide what sort of redesigned person might be viable. Painstakingly, they had constructed a model of such a being and its capacities, not wanting to alter the human form too radically for fear of the unknown consequences, yet seeking more than minor changes.

Merripen sighed, looking relieved. "I expected you wouldn't back out now, almost no one has, but two people changed their minds last week. When you asked me here I thought you had also."

She smiled and shook her head. It was Merripen's motives she wished to consider. She had worried that she might change her mind after seeing the child, but that was unlikely. There were no guarantees even with a normal child, since the biologists, afraid of too much tampering with human versatility, simply insured that flawed genes were not passed on rather than actively creating a certain type of child.

Even so, she had wondered when Merripen first made his offer. They had argued, he saying that human society was becoming stagnant while she countered by mentioning the diversity of human communities both on Earth and in space.

"We need new blood," he said now, apparently thinking along similar lines. "Oh, we have diversity, but it's all on the surface. I've seen a hundred different cultures and at bottom they're the same, a way of passing time. Even the death cults ..."

She recoiled from the obscenity. "In Japan," he went on, "it's *seppuku* over any insult or failure, in India it's slow starvation and extreme asceticism, in England it's trial by combat, and here you play with guns. For every person we bring back from death, another dies, and the people we bring back try again or become murderers so that we're forced to allow them to die for the benefit of others." He glanced apologetically at her, apparently aware he was repeating old arguments.

Josepha did not want to think about death cults and the sudden flare-ups of violence that had reminded her of the Transition and had made her retreat to this house. She looked down at the small blue stone set into a gold bracelet on the Bond which linked everyone through a central system. The micro-computer link lit up and rang softly when someone called her; she could respond over her holo or touch her finger to the stone, indicating that she was unavailable and that a message should be left. More important, the Bond protected her and could summon aid. But even the blue stone could not guard her from everything; many knew how to circumvent the mechanism.

"But matters must be different in space," she replied, thinking of the huge, cylindrical dwellings that hovered in space at the Trojan points equidistant from Earth and Moon.

Merripen shrugged. "Not as much as you might think. The space dwellers were more innovative when they first left Earth, but now ... you know, they pride themselves on being safe from the vicissitudes of life here, the storms, the quakes, the natural disasters. They make endless plans for space exploration and carry out none of them. Their cult is a cult of life with no risks."

"But there are the people on Mars, the ones out near Saturn, or the scientists who left our solar system a century ago. Surely they're not stagnating."

"They are so few, Josepha. And as for the ones who left, we have heard nothing. They may be dead or they may have found something, but in any event, it'll have no effect on us."

"I think you're too pessimistic," she argued, wanting to believe her own words. "How long have we had our extended lives? A little more than two hundred years. That's hardly long enough for a fair test. People change, they need time."

"I'm afraid the only thing time does for most people is to confirm them in their habits. Oh, some change, those who have cultivated flexibility. But they are so few. The others are a heavy weight holding us back. In the past, it took great deprivation and a strong leader to make such people change. There is no deprivation now and no leader. Perhaps these new children will open our eyes."

She found this turn in the conversation distasteful, but she had to expect such views from Merripen. He was too young to remember the surge of creativity, the high hopes that had existed for a short time after the difficulties of the Transition, but he knew of them and must sometimes long for them. She tried not to think of her own placid life and how hard it had been to force herself to consider being a parent. Stability, serenity, the eternal present—she would forsake them for something less sure. She thought of the ones who had left the solar system and wondered how they had brought themselves to do it.

"The children," she murmured. "I'd rather discuss them for a bit, settle some of my questions, I still don't understand completely." She was trying to draw Merripen away from his disturbing speculations.

"You've heard it all before."

"I didn't really listen, though. I didn't want to confront the details, I guess."

Merripen frowned. "If you're still ambivalent, you'd better back out now."

"But I'm not ambivalent. I agree with your general goal at least. And maybe part of it is that I'm afraid if I don't try something different now, I may never be able to . . . that's not the best motive, but . . . " She was silent.

"I understand."

"You said the children won't have our hormones. Won't that limit them?"

"That's not accurate," he replied. "Certain hormonal or glandular secretions are needed to insure their growth. But they won't be subject to something like the sudden rush of adrenaline we feel when disturbed or under stress."

"That could be dangerous. They might not react quickly enough."

"We've allowed for that. Refinements in the nervous system, quicker reflexes, will allow them to respond as quickly as we do, perhaps even a bit more quickly. The difference is that they won't act inappropriately. Our behavior is often the result of feelings, which are in turn rooted in our instincts and our survival biology. Their behavior will be based on rational decisions as much as on that."

"Our instincts have served us well enough in the past," Josepha murmured.

"They may not serve us well any longer. We don't have inevitable physical death anymore, yet our instincts probably go on preparing us for one. The rationality of these children will take the place of instinct and complement the instincts that remain."

Merripen paused as Josepha considered what he had told her before. The children would look human, but would have stronger muscles and bones less vulnerable to injury. They would have the ability to synthesize certain amino acids and vitamins, such as C and B_{12}; they would be able to live on a limited vegetable diet.

But the most extreme change, she knew, involved their gender. Merripen had explained that thoroughly, although she was aware that she had only a general understanding of it. They would have no gender—or maybe it was more appropriate to say they would have two genders. They would bear both male and female reproductive organs. They could reproduce naturally, each one able to be either father or mother, or by using the same techniques human beings now used. But they would lack sexuality. Their desires and ability to reproduce would become actualized only when they decided to have offspring; they would have conscious control of the process. Merripen had outlined this too in detail, but she recalled it only vaguely.

Josepha imagined that this radical alteration had probably alienated prospective parents who might otherwise have participated in the project. They must have thought it too much; sex had been separated from reproduction for ages and androgynous behavior was commonplace for men and women. Physically androgynous beings seemed unnecessary; the lack of sexuality, such a major part of human life, repellent.

Josepha was not bothered by it because sex, she thought sadly, thinking of the few men she had loved, had never been very important to her. But Merripen was reputed to be a compulsive sexual adventurer. She wondered if that was why he asserted that the children would be more rational without such an intense diversion. He might be fooling himself; the children might develop sexual desires of their own once they started to reproduce.

"We don't really know what they'll be like in the end," she said.

"We've done the projections," he answered. "We have a pretty good idea. But it *is* an experiment. Nothing is guaranteed." He picked up the empty wine bottle and turned it in his hands. "This entire society is an experiment. The results are not yet in. All of us crossed that line a long time ago."

The room had grown dark. Josepha reached over and touched the globular lamp on the table near her. It glowed, bathing the room in a soft blue light. "It's late," she said. "You're probably hungry."

He nodded.

"Let's have some supper."

✳

Later, alone in her room, Josepha mused. She could not hear Merripen, who was in the bedroom at the end of the hall, but she sensed his presence. She had been alone in the house for so long that the presence of anyone impinged on her; her mind could no longer expand to fill up the house's empty space. She drew her coverlet over her.

Merripen had once discussed what he called the "natural selection" of immortality, his belief that certain mechanisms still operated, that those unsuited to extended life would fall by the wayside. He believed this even as he tried to prevent death. The Transition had weeded out many. The passing centuries would dispose of many more.

Ironically, she had survived. Nothing in her previous life had prepared her for this, yet here she was. She had been a student, a file clerk, a wife, a divorcée, a saleswoman, a sales manager, a wife again, a widow. She had been a passive graduate student who thought knowledge would give her a direction; she had succeeded only in gaining some small expertise on the pottery of Periclean Athens and in avoiding the real world. She had always worked because her first husband had been a student and her second an attorney paying child support and alimony to his first wife. Her purse had been snatched once, her home had been burglarized once, she had undergone two abortions. In this ordinary fashion, while the world lurched toward the greatest historical discontinuity it had ever experienced, Josepha had survived to witness the Transition. Only now did she feel, after so long, that she was even approaching an understanding of the world and her place in it.

She had been in her fifties when the techniques for extended life became available. The treatment had seemed simple enough; it consisted of shots which would remove the collagen formed by the cross-linkage of proteins and thus halt or retard the physical manifestations of aging. Even this technique, which could make one no younger but only keep one from aging as rapidly, had created controversy, raising the specter of millions of old citizens lingering past their time. Many chose to die anyway. Others had themselves frozen cryonically after death, hoping they would be revived when medical science could heal them and make them live forever. Cryonics became big business. Some concerns were legitimate. Many were fraudulent, consigning their customers to an expensive, cold, permanent death.

Josepha, retired but in need of extra money, became a maintenance worker for a cryonic interment service. She walked among the stacks of frozen dead, peering at dials. By chance, she found that several of her fellow workers dealt illegally in anticollagen shots, selling them to people under the mandatory age of sixty-five for recipients. Knowing that penalties for selling the shots were severe, she was too frightened to become a pusher. But she bought a few shots.

Soon after, work on the mechanisms which caused cancers to multiply, along with genetic research, had yielded a way of restoring youth. Research papers had been presented tentatively; most people had waited cautiously, until at last impatience outran caution and the world entered the Transition in bits and pieces, one country after another.

There were failures, although few wanted to remember them now; people who were victims of virulent cancers, those who could not be made younger, a few who grew younger and then died suddenly. Some theorized that the mechanisms of death could not be held in check forever; that in the future, death might come rapidly and wipe out millions. Testing the new technique thoroughly would have taken hundreds of years, and people would not go on living and dying while potential immortals were being sustained in their midst.

Everyone knew about the Transition, the upheavals, the collapsing governments, the deaths, the demands. There were some facts not fully known, that were still strangely absent from computer banks and information centers; exact figures on suicides, records of how many were killed by the treatments themselves, who the first subjects had been and what had happened to them. Josepha had searched, and found only unpleasant hints; one small town with a thirty percent mortality rate after treatment, prisoner-subjects who had mysteriously disappeared, an increase in "accidental" deaths. She had lived through it, surviving a bullet wound as a bystander at a demonstration of older citizens, hiding out in a small out-of-the-way village, and yet any present-day historian knew more than she could remember. She suspected that the only people who knew almost everything were a few old biologists and any political leaders who were still alive.

In her nineties, half-blinded by cataracts, hands distorted into claws by arthritis, Josepha had at last been treated and begun her extended life. She had survived Peter Beaulieu, her first husband, and Gene Kolodny, her second. She had outlived her brother and her parents and her few close friends. And until now, she often thought, she had done little to justify that survival.

She could not accept that so many had died for the world as it was now. The vigor and liveliness had gone out of human life, or so it seemed. Perhaps those who would have provided it were gone and the meek had inherited the Earth after all.

But she could change. She was changing. Either the death cultists were right and their lives were meaningless or their extended lives were an opportunity which must be seized. She recalled her own near-death and the promise of another life; even that possibility did not change things. She had to earn that life, if there was such a thing, with a meaningful life here, and if there was no other life, then this one was all she had.

More than three hundred years to discover that—it was absurd. There were no more excuses for failure, which explained the suicides and death cults at least in part. Merripen's project would force the issue. She remembered how his enthusiasm for his dream had been conveyed to her during their first discussion, in spite of her doubts. She thought: maybe most of us are slow learners, that's all, well, we'll learn or be supplanted.

She refused to think of another possibility; that the world might not accept the children, that any future beyond the present was unthinkable.

✳

Josepha arrived at the village where the parents and children were to live a month after her visit with Merripen. Three houses, resembling chalets, stood on one side of a clearing. Four others, with enclosed front porches, sat almost two hundred meters away on the other side of the clearing. Behind them, on a hill, she saw a red brick structure which was large enough for several people.

A bulldozer, a heavy lumbering metallic beast, excavated land doggedly while two men watched. She assumed that the two were involved in the project, although they might be only curious bystanders.

Josepha walked through the clearing, which would be transformed into a park. A tall African man stood on the porch of one house, his back to her. She saw no one else. She came to a stone path and followed it, passing the unoccupied houses. Each was surrounded by a plot of ground which would become a garden. The park would eventually contain two large buildings; a hall where everyone could gather for meals, recreation, or meetings, and a hostel for the children. One part of the recreation hall would be used as a school.

The path ended at a low stone wall. Josepha stood in front of an open metal gate and looked past a small courtyard at a two-story stone house. She approached the gray structure and peered through a window. She saw sturdy walls instead of movable panels, a stairway instead of a ramp, and decided this was where she would live. The house was too large for only one parent and child, but she could find someone to share it with her.

She heard footsteps and turned. The tall African man stood at the gate. He adjusted his gold-trimmed blue robe and bowed slightly. She returned the bow and moved toward him, stopping about half a meter away. His black hair was short and his beard closely trimmed. "Chane Maggio," he said in a deep voice as he extended his right hand.

She was puzzled, startled by the lack of ceremony. She suddenly realized that he was telling her his name. He continued to hold out his hand and at last she took it, shook hands, and released it. "I'm Josepha Ryba."

"You are startled by my informality." He folded his slender arms over his chest. "Perhaps I am being rude, but we have little time to become acquainted, only a few months before gestation begins and then only nine months to the birth of the children. I am afraid we cannot stand on ceremony in our salutations."

She smiled. "How long have you been here?"

"I arrived this morning. I believe we are the only prospective parents here." He offered his arm and she took it. They began to amble along the stone path.

She sensed that Chane Maggio remembered the Transition. She was not sure how she knew; perhaps it was the informality of his greeting, the sense of contingency in his voice, or his silence now as they strolled. Younger people always wanted to fill the silences with words or games or actions of some kind. The Transition was only history to them. To Josepha, and those like herself, it would forever be the most important time of their lives, however long they lived. It had made them survivors with the guilt of survivors. The simplest sensation meant both more and less to them than to those born later. Josepha, acutely conscious of Chane's arm, the clatter of their sandals on the stones, the warm breeze which brushed her hair, remembered that she was alive and that others were not and that she was somehow coarsened by this. A younger person, caught in the timeless present, would accept the sensations for themselves.

"This venture promises to be most interesting," Chane said softly in his deep voice. "I have raised children before—I had a son and daughter long ago—a rewarding task, watching a child grow, trying to—" he paused.

Josepha waited, not wanting to be rude by interrupting. "There are problems, of course," he continued, and she caught an undercurrent of bitterness and disappointment. "There is always the unexpected." His voice changed again, becoming lighter and more casual. "They live on Asgard now, at least they did fifty years ago. They claim it's too dangerous to live here."

"I once wanted to visit a space community," Josepha said. "For years I kept intending to go, but I never did."

"More people live in space than on Earth, but of course you know that."

"I didn't know."

Chane raised an eyebrow. "I was a statistician for many years. There are approximately two billion people on Earth and almost twice as many in space."

"That many," Josepha murmured, inwardly chastising herself for not knowing. She could have asked her Bond.

"Of course, there has been a small but noticeable decline in the population." The man paused again, having strayed too near an unpleasant topic. "Tell me," he went on, "did you ever make pottery? I believe I own a vase you made, it was a gift from a friend."

"That was a long time ago. I had a shop with a friend, Hisa Onoda. Hisa made jewelry and I did pottery, that was a little while after the Transition, when we all still had to credit purchases to our accounts."

"This was later, after accounts."

"Well, we stayed in business after that just for our amusement. We'd trade our items for things we liked, paintings, sculptures, but the Whatfor finally ruined it for us. We refused to duplicate anything we made, but others duped the items anyway."

"Even so," he said, "what is important about a thing is its beauty or utility, not its scarcity."

"I know that," she replied. "I don't think Hisa understood it, though. She'd always made jewelry, things like that. It was important to her that each item be unique, she used to tell me that everything she made was only for a certain individual, was right for that person and wrong for anyone else. Sometimes she would refuse to sell a particular object to a customer, she would insist that he look at something else. What's strange is that the customer would always like the item she would pick out more." An image of Hisa's small body crossed her mind: Hisa in her sunken tub, wrists slashed, lips pale, red blood in swirls on the water, her Bond detached and resting helplessly on the floor. *Too late.* Josepha quickly buried the image. "I'd been a salesperson before the Transition, but Hisa made it an art."

"I was a politician," Chane said. He stopped walking and released her arm. "Does that startle you?"

She thought: what must you have done? She did not reply; she could not judge him.

"I was fortunate. I survived because I saw clearly where things were going and knew when to relinquish my power and wait. I saw that those in power could not hold the tide back indefinitely, and that those who tried to hang on would suffer—as they did."

She listened, only too conscious of her own past sins of omission. She had heard the stories of powerful people who had gained access to the treatments, then given up their positions to go into hiding. Not all had survived. Others had kept their power, many hoping to restrict the gift of extended life to themselves. Both groups bore responsibility for the collapse of civil order at the beginning of the Transition.

"I have changed," he was saying. "I have little interest in such things now." She nodded, almost hearing his unspoken challenge: would it be better if I had died?

The mood of their meeting had been destroyed. Chane bowed, murmured a few courteous phrases, and departed.

The other parents had arrived, one at a time, for the past few months. Construction was finished; the machines had moved to a nearby lake, where three lodges would be built.

Josepha, unused to groups, had grown more reticent. She was quiet at the frequent parties for the thirty prospective parents and at the meetings with the biologists and psychologists who lived nearby.

The parties were usually formal; word games were played, objects and sensations were exhaustively described or put into short poems in various languages by the literarily gifted. Direct questions were never asked.

Most of the villagers had remained only names to her. She saw Chane Maggio fairly often, although even he seemed more reserved. Wanting to know more about her companions, she had resorted to the public records in her computer.

She had discovered what she had suspected; most of them were veterans of the Transition. Had Merripen wanted older people, or were older people the only ones willing to volunteer for the project?

Her other discoveries were more intimidating. She reviewed them now as she sat in her living room knitting a sleeve for a sweater. The villagers included Amarisa Drew, who had been both an agronomist and a well-known athlete, Dawud al-Ahmad, former poet and chief engineer of the Asgard life support systems, and Chen Li Hua, a clothing designer and geologist.

She looked up from the blue wool and saw Merripen Allen entering her courtyard. She called to him, telling him to enter. Her door slid open; Merripen stamped his feet in the small foyer, then entered the living room.

He settled in a high-backed gray chair in the corner across from her. "What can I do for you?" she asked.

"I've been visiting each person here individually, I want to be sure there aren't any problems and that everybody's settling in. I hope you'll all start loosening up soon, get to know each other better."

"That takes time," she said, "especially if you're used to solitude. And I have to . . ."

"Yes?"

"I don't quite know how to put it. Everyone else seems so accomplished."

"It's difficult to live a long time without that being the case."

"No it's not," she replied. "I haven't done much."

Merripen chuckled. "Almost everyone I've seen has told me that. So I'll have to tell you what I told them. First of all, I wouldn't have asked any of you to become involved unless I had a good opinion of you. Second, although I've always admired modesty, I don't like meekness, especially in prospective parents who need strength for any problems they may face. You should all be more at ease when you become better acquainted."

"I guess," she responded, as if accepting his exhortation. He was not deceiving her. Almost no one wanted to be a parent now; of the few who did, most had probably rejected Merripen's offer. He had probably taken those he could get, rejecting only those obviously unsuitable.

Merripen seemed worried. He was pulling at his moustache. Josepha resumed her knitting. "I hope," she said, "that you're not having doubts." She said it lightly.

"Of course I am," he replied, startling her with his harsh tone.

"But then why—"

"Not about you people, not about whether we should go ahead, that's settled." She sat up stiffly, clutching her needles, shocked at the way he had interrupted her in midsentence.

"I'm terribly sorry, please forgive me," he said more quietly. "At any rate, I didn't come here to discuss my worries. I wanted to talk about your child. Have you decided on who the second parent will be, or do you intend to form a liaison with one of the people here?" Each child, she knew, was to have two parents, as that would provide each with more links to other human beings and avoid possible emotional problems for a parent whose child was his or hers alone. It was hoped that the children would regard all of the people in the village as members of a family. "We need time to make tests, as you know," he went on. "We have to check for possible incompatibilities or flaws that need correcting."

"I've decided. I made up my mind a while ago and just didn't realize it till now." She put the knitting aside. "Nicholas Krol."

"Excuse me?"

"Nicholas Krol," she repeated. "The other parent. He was a composer, maybe you've heard the name."

"Did you know him?"

"Yes, I knew him, I knew him well. I was in love with him." As she spoke, Josepha saw Nicholas Krol's steady gray eyes and his ash brown hair, but she could not remember his face clearly. Something inside her seemed to break at the realization. "I met him after my divorce, we lived together for a couple of years. He was ambitious, he wanted me to be ambitious too, accomplish something, but I was afraid to try, too afraid of failing. We broke up finally, he didn't want to, but I—" For a moment, she recalled his face. She tried desperately to hold it in her mind, and lost it.

"Why?" Merripen asked. "Why Krol?"

"I don't know if I can explain it. He challenged me, he encouraged me. Everyone else just accepted me the way I was. I shouldn't have left him."

"Then why did you leave?"

"Because it was easier to give up."

Merripen seemed puzzled. "It seems a strange motive for picking him, you having regrets."

"It isn't only regrets. He was the most important person in my life, although it took me much too long to see that." She realized she sounded shrill. "I was self-destructive when I was in my twenties, always acting against my own self-interest. That's why I left Nick. Later I changed, and acquired a sort of stubborn passivity." She closed her eyes for a moment, waiting for her sorrow and bitterness to pass.

"May I be frank?" the biologist asked. She nodded. "You want the child of a man you loved long ago, so perhaps you're trying to recapture that love. Is Krol still alive?"

She shook her head.

"So guilt enters the picture as well. You're alive and he isn't. Do you even know whether we can acquire his genetic material?"

"He would have had his sperm frozen, I know it. You don't know what he was like. He would have made sure of it. He had a bit of vanity, I used to tease him about it."

"I'm sorry, Josepha. I think you're making a mistake."

"If you have another suggestion, please offer it. I'm willing to listen. But I don't think I'll change my mind."

"I would like your child to be mine as well."

She stiffened in surprise. She was sure that the man had no romantic interest in her. "Why?"

"I'm in charge of this project, it was really my idea in the beginning. I'll be living here most of the time, it seems only suitable that I should also be a parent and share this role with you people. If you wish, I can become your lover, if you feel that would strengthen our bond as parents."

The proposal repelled her. She picked up her knitting. Her needles clicked. She heard a few Chinese phrases as two people passed the gate outside. At last she put down the needles and looked at Merripen.

"I must say no." She could not leave it at that. "I think it would be a mistake for you to have your own child here. If you're going to be in charge, you shouldn't be in a position where you might favor one child over the others. And you should try to preserve some objectivity."

"You think it's possible for anyone to be completely objective?"

"Of course not. I do think you can get so personally involved that you don't notice certain things, that emotional considerations become more important. And anyway, I think you want this child out of some misplaced desire to be like all of us here—you can feel noble, not asking us to do something you wouldn't do yourself, and . . ." She paused. "There's only one reason for having a child, Merripen."

"And what is that?"

"Because you want to help another human being learn and grow. You should regard all the children here as yours. Isn't that enough for you? You don't have to prove anything to the parents here, and you might ruin what you're working for by trying."

"You won't reconsider?"

"No. I suppose, if you wanted to, you could prevent me from having a child at all as well as barring me from the project."

"What do you think I am?" Merripen replied in injured tones. "We don't force our desires on others, our work is for everyone's benefit. You should know that by now."

"You have power whether you want it or not and whether you want to recognize it or not. Everyone knows it. It's just nicer not to mention it."

"Are my wishes more irrational than yours?" He smiled lopsidedly. "You want a dead lover as the father."

"I knew him. Krol's child will have intelligence and strength. And if we really do value life as much as we profess to, then what is so irrational about wanting some part of a dead man to live again?"

He slouched in his chair. For a moment, Josepha thought she saw conflicting emotions in his dark eyes, disappointment warring with relief. He had made his noble gesture without having to follow it up.

"You have to remember," the biologist said softly, "that these children will not be quite like us. You may be disappointed if you're trying to recapture something you've lost."

Josepha sighed. "I suppose you'll ask someone else to be a parent with you."

"No. The others have already made their choices."

She felt relieved by the answer, but remained disturbed. She worried again about Merripen's reasons for beginning the project.

Josepha had gradually become better acquainted with the other village residents. She felt most at ease with the three now sitting at her round mahogany table sipping brandy; Vladislav Pascal, a small, wiry man who had been a painter, Warner Chavez, a tall, slender woman with impossibly large black eyes who was once an architect, and Chane Maggio.

Warner and Vladislav were going to raise a child together. Many of the villagers had already paired off or formed groups, but Josepha was still alone.

She had gone that afternoon to the nearby laboratory where the embryos were gestating. She had peered at the glassy womb enclosing her child, Krol's child—it had looked like all the others. Feeling vaguely uneasy, she had left quickly.

Looking around the table at her guests, Josepha saw Warner gaze sleepily at Vladislav. Chane had said little all evening as the three reminisced about their second youth, during the Transition, everyone's favorite topic lately; even the hardships of the period had acquired a benign glow in retrospect. The shabbiness of the towns and decay of the cities had not mattered to any of them. With their newly youthful bodies and restored health, anything had seemed possible.

Josepha had migrated to the nearest large city after her treatments, with hordes of others. She had lived in a decrepit hotel, sharing a bathroom with ten people and had not minded. Surrounded by people constantly meeting to plan new cities, new machines, new arts, new ventures and experiments, she had known that the hardships would be temporary. They were all high on dreams, sure the worst was over, too busy to remember the dead. Now she sat, like the others, amid what they had built and looked backward to the building and dreaming while awaiting a new beginning.

Warner smoothed back her thick red hair and rose. Vladislav got up also. "No, don't show us out," he said to Josepha before she could stand. "Lovely meal, lovely. Don't forget tomorrow, we're expecting you both. Most of the village will probably be there and we'll all try to forget that it's a party for the psychologists." He bowed to Chane and the couple left.

Chane seemed abstracted. He toyed with his snifter. She said nothing, sensing that he wanted silence.

She did not know Chane that well in spite of his frequent visits. The public record of his life had told her little. He had been his African nation's ambassador to China, then its foreign minister during the years before the Transition. His grandfather had been an Italian. His life during the Transition was a mystery. But somehow she was at ease with him. She could sit there pursuing her own thoughts while he was lost in his own. Occasionally they looked at each other and smiled; they did not have to fill the silences with words.

Tonight he seemed more apprehensive than usual. She lit a cigarette and pushed the ivory cigarette box to him across the table; Chane too was a secret smoker. He shook his head. "I must ask you something, Josepha. I've been putting it off. May I be open with you?" His deep voice was subdued.

"Of course."

He put his hands in front of him, palms down on the dark wood. "I must tell you something first. As you know, I was married in my previous life and had a family. You have undoubtedly guessed that my relations with them left something to be desired."

She nodded, not knowing what to say.

"My wife was an intelligent, educated woman and I thought enough of her to make her one of my advisors. We married late in life, in our thirties. We agreed on everything, almost never fighting. After our children were born, I began to feel that she became more demanding, that instead of helping me, she was distracting me. I began to blame her for everything that went wrong. Eventually, I took to spending more time away from her. It probably seems a familiar story. Eventually, we separated. I was very bitter about it."

"Chane, why are you telling me this? You don't have to justify yourself to me, I made plenty of mistakes too."

"But I want you to understand this before I make my request. It took a long time for me to see that much of this was my fault. I was telling myself how important my ministry was, my country was in a very difficult period then and I couldn't take the time for personal problems."

"Wasn't it true?"

"Of course it was," he replied. "It's no excuse. Work is a wonderful thing, especially demanding work. It means you have a good excuse for not trying to solve your personal problems, for avoiding them, for taking and not giving because the work is more important than anything."

"Well, sometimes it is, isn't it?" She stubbed out her cigarette, spilling some ashes on the table.

"Oh, sometimes. Very rarely. The world is moved by historical forces, by certain developments, by things we don't control."

"The Transition changed things, and that was the result of scientific research by a few people."

Chane finished his brandy and lit a cigarette. "A transition of some sort was bound to happen anyway, events were moving toward one. It was a more complex situation than you imply. The world was already changing and the biologists only hastened it. Look at them now. What can they really do?"

Josepha shook her head. "You're wrong, Chane. Here we are with this project. You're saying it won't make any difference at all, but you're here just the same. You're contradicting—"

"No, you don't hear what I'm saying." His voice was firm. "There is only one way people can influence the future and that is by the quality of their relationships with others, the ways in which they treat people, caring about them and showing it constructively. Sharing what you might learn with someone, loving someone, raising a child to be both inquisitive and compassionate. There is no one more powerless than a person who has the power to intervene, you either become driven by it and by forces you don't understand, holding it at whatever cost, or you realize that all you can do is be a moral and rational example, a symbol perhaps of something better. Or you run away in the end, as I did."

Chane paused. A pale blue wisp of smoke circled his head. "Merripen believes," he continued, "that the children here will change the world, in other words, that he himself will. It's a deception. Yes, they may make a difference, but not because of a peculiar physiological makeup. It will be our relationships with them as parents, our personal attention, how we act toward them, that will make them what they might be. If we raised a group of children like ourselves and tried to give them a creative and open view, the results might very well be similar. Except that it may be easier for these children."

"Yet you agreed."

He smiled. "Oh, yes. I wanted to be part of it, I don't want to run away as I did before."

Josepha considered Chane's arguments. She was not sure that she agreed; it seemed that the combination of heredity and environment was needed. But she did not feel like arguing about it now. "Who is to be your child's other parent?" she asked.

"My wife, of course. You're surprised. She's still alive and she agreed. I've been lucky, able to patch things up instead of living with guilt and ghosts." The statement seemed forced. Josepha looked down as he spoke. "She's a stranger now," he went on. "I suppose I am too."

"What did you want to ask me before, Chane?"

"I . . . it's hard to know how to phrase it. I'd like you to consider sharing your life here with me, raising our children together."

She looked up, startled. He lowered his eyes and put out his cigarette. She knew that she found Chane attractive, although neither of them had nourished the attraction with the usual romantic games and ploys. She liked him. It seemed a rather weak foundation for a relationship.

"Why?" she asked gently.

"I feel at ease with you, that's the main reason. Let's try it at least, if it doesn't work out I can move again after the children are born." Something in the tone of his voice reminded her of Merripen Allen. Again, she worried about the reasons for the project. She thought: it's a mistake, it may hurt the children in the end, it will change all of us here forever.

But that was false. If it failed, it would change nothing and would be forgotten by the parents as everything was when one had enough time. She shook her head.

"You're refusing me, then," Chane said.

"Oh, no, I was thinking of something else. I'd like you to stay, this house is really too big for one parent and child." That sounded too cold, too pragmatic. "I think we'll get along," she added.

She wished that she could feel happier about the decision.

Josepha adjusted easily to Chane's presence. Their life together was marred only by an occasional gentle argument. But Chane remained impenetrable. Josepha imagined that she must appear the same way to him. Even their lovemaking did not bridge the gap.

It was probably just as well, she thought. This way, at least, she could preserve some sense of privacy. Both could keep an emotional equilibrium that would conserve their strength, the strength they would need when the children were born.

She knew, however, that they could not remain on that peaceful plateau forever. Their shared lives would force them into confrontations sooner or later. But it was hard to break old habits, difficult to believe that there might not be time enough to let events happen and allow differences to be resolved. Better, she knew, to settle each issue as it came up, instead of trying to sort everything out now.

When she finally realized that there had been no time, only a few months, and that she and Chane were still far from understanding very much about each other, all the children were ready to leave their wombs and enter her world.

ii

Teno, her child, Krol's child, was with her at last. Teno had no surname; it was customary to let people choose their own last names.

She had been surprised at how ordinary, how normal, the child appeared. Teno had her dark hair, a face like a small bulldog, and olive skin. She could see nothing of Nicholas Krol in the child;

perhaps that resemblance would come with maturity.

Josepha often felt tired. She leaned against the courtyard gate, inhaling the mild spring air, grateful for a few moments to herself. The flow of time had fragmented into a million discrete segments which seemed to jostle against each other. The children had to be fed, washed, taken outside for a few minutes of air, played with, hugged, dressed, undressed, and put to bed. The village had shaken off its lassitude; the children were now the center of everything. It would have been easier to let the psychologists, with the aid of a few robots, assume many of the parental duties, but almost no one took much advantage of that. It was as if they all wanted to be sure nothing went wrong, that the children would not be damaged by neglect.

"Hey!" a woman's voice shouted. Warner Chavez was approaching her along the stone path. Josepha put a finger to her lips as she opened the gate.

"Everyone's asleep," she exclaimed as her friend entered the courtyard. "Even Chane, he's exhausted. He was up at dawn with Teno and Ramli." Ramli was Chane's child.

Warner smiled. "So's Vlad, he and Nenum are probably both stacking deltas by now." Josepha found herself thinking: men don't have as much stamina. She was mildly ashamed of the thought.

Warner sat down on the grass, folding her trousered legs in a half lotus. There were pale blue shadows under her black eyes. Josepha sat down with her back against the stone wall, wrapping her arms around her legs. She too was tired, not fatigued enough to sleep, but too weary to concentrate. A part of her always seemed removed, watchful, listening in case the children should need her. Chane was like that too. Neither of them could sit for more than a few minutes lately without listening for sounds or getting up now and then to check things.

Warner was gazing at the red tulips blooming in a row next to the house. She looked away quickly, probably wondering why Josepha planted such short-lived flowers. "Tell me, Jo, have you talked to Chane much about the children?"

Josepha shrugged. "We haven't had that many conversations lately. It's hard to keep talking when you're tired all the time, I can't even watch the holo without feeling sleepy. I guess I didn't think looking after them would take so much out of me."

"What I meant was, has Chane said anything to you about the kids. He was a parent once, wasn't he?"

"What do you expect him to say about them?"

"What they're like compared to normal . . . compared to other kids. Maybe I'm being silly, but there's something unnerving about them."

"Is there?" Josepha rested her chin on her knees. "Teno's really not much of a problem, all things considered. I was expecting all kinds of little crises."

"Think about the way they cry, for instance. Doesn't it seem strange to you?"

"Is it strange?" Josepha asked. "I wouldn't know, I suppose, I was never around children that much. My brother Charlie was older than I was, and I didn't have a younger brother or sister."

"Well," Warner replied, "it's not that awful squalling I remember, the kind of crying that sounds like a cat in heat and you know the poor kid is colicky or damp or maybe hungry. With these kids, it's more of a steady cry, I don't know how to describe it. It's- . . . calm, steady and calm. Sometimes I'll hear a real howl, but it's as if they're only exercising their lungs. That's what my Nenum does anyway, and others too. Aren't Teno and Ramli like that?"

Josepha nodded. "That isn't normal?"

"No." A breeze ruffled Warner's long red hair. "All right, they're not quite like us, with their immunities and their modified neurons and reflexes, they weren't meant to be, but they look so much like ordinary kids that . . . I picked up Nenum yesterday, after a nap, just to hug my child, you know the feeling. You just want to let them know you're there and you care. Nenum just sort of put up with it, that's all. It's always like that. I can't describe it any other way. There's just no response at all."

"Maybe you're making too much of it, Warner. You said it yourself, they weren't meant to be like us, that's the point of the project. Anyway, things don't look right when you're tired most of the time, you make more of them or think something's the matter when it isn't."

"I know that."

"They're still our children."

"Of course. They made sure of that, genetic bonds as well as emotional ones." Warner's fine-featured face contorted. "I don't know what they'll be. I don't know what they are or what they'll become. I don't even know whether Nenum is my son or daughter, am I supposed to call my child 'it'?" Her slender body drooped.

"Does that really matter? It wouldn't change how you act toward Nenum. And you didn't know what your other children would be like, or what kinds of adults they would become."

"I knew they were human," her friend said harshly. "I can't even look at Nenum without remembering that, I keep seeing . . . maybe I wasn't ready for this, Jo."

Josepha felt at a loss. She tried to look reassuringly at Warner. "Yes, you were," she said as firmly as possible. She got up and sat near her friend, putting an arm over the red-haired woman's shoulders. "Look, Merripen wouldn't have had you come here if he thought otherwise." She tried to sound convincing, recalling her doubts about how Merripen had selected the parents. "It's normal to have doubts. Maybe when you feel this way you should just go and hold Nenum and put those thoughts out of your mind. It doesn't matter. You and Vladislav have to take care of your child, that's all. Think of things that way."

Warner smoothed back her hair with the chubby hands that seemed unmatched to her slim arms. "You're right. Maybe I'm just disoriented. I'm not used to anything different after all this time."

Josepha, hearing a cry, suddenly sat up. The cry was steady, punctuated by short stops, a smooth cry without any variation in pitch. A second cry, slightly lower, joined the first. Teno and Ramli were awake.

Teno and Ramli were toddlers, trying to walk.

Only a short time ago, it seemed, the children had been unable to sit up. Now Josepha and Chane watched as the two struggled across the floor.

She and Chane had preserved their quiet and reserved relationship. Much of their conversation concerned the children. Their lovemaking was partly a formality, partly a friendly and often humorous way of reassuring each other during moments of loneliness. Most of the time it was easier for each of them to wire up and live out a fantasy encounter.

Chane sat at one end of the sofa, Josepha at another. Ramli

toddled unsteadily toward Chane and stretched out small brown hands to him. Teno moved to Josepha, grabbing for her arms almost before she held them out.

"Very good!" she said brightly. Teno, solemn-faced, held her hands for a moment, then sat on the floor. Chane picked up Ramli, seating the baby on his lap. He held up a hand, holding out one finger, and Ramli began to pull at the other fingers Chane had concealed. The child studied them intently for a moment, then quietly looked away, as if losing interest.

The children were always like that. If she or Chane wanted to play a game, they would respond in a serious, quiet way. If she wanted to show them some affection, they put up with it, with expressions that almost seemed to say: I can do without this, but obviously you need it.

What did they need? She watched as Chane placed Ramli on the floor. The two children crawled over the rug, peering intently at its gold and blue pattern. Did they require something they were not receiving from the adults around them? An observant person could tell if an ordinary child might be having a serious problem. Even given the wide variations in normal behavior, abnormal responses became obvious in time. But they did not know what normal behavior would be for these children.

She sighed, thinking of old stories; children raised by wolves who could never learn to speak, could never really be human. She watched as Teno and Ramli poked at the bright spot where a beam of sunlight struck the rug.

Teno looked like her, with black hair, olive skin, high cheek-bones—but the eyes were not her brown ones. One could look at dark eyes and read expressions too easily. Knowing this, Josepha had always had difficulty gazing directly at people, wondering if they could read her thoughts. Teno's eyes were Krol's gray ones, impossible to read, always distant. She saw the quiet, mildly curious expression on her child's face and was suddenly frightened.

But that was foolish. She had been listening to Warner too often. She must stop giving credence to Warner's recurring doubts and worrisome hypotheses.

She realized that Chane was staring at her. Her worries must be showing on her face. She smiled reassuringly. His sad eyes met hers;

he did not smile back. Then he turned his head toward the window.

She felt like reaching out to him, holding him, and the force of her desire surprised her. But she restrained herself, and the moment passed.

When the children were two and a half years old, it became customary to take them to the recreation hall and let them play together under the supervision of a few parents and psychologists. Kelii Morgan, who had once been a teacher and was now a parent, was often with them.

The children responded to him in their restrained fashion. They were patient when the affectionate Kelii laughed or hugged them impulsively, but they enjoyed the folk stories and myths he had learned from his Welsh and Hawaiian forebears. They responded most to tales of a quest for some great piece of knowledge. They heard the humorous stories too, but never laughed.

Josepha came often to see them at play. The children were already used to each other, having visited each other's homes frequently. They liked new places and had never clung to a parent in fear. But their play seemed to her a solemn affair. She had expected rivalries, fussing over toys, laughter, teasing, a few tears.

Instead, she saw red-headed Nenum taking apart a toy space city, peering at the different levels and at the tiny painted lake and trees at its center while Ramli looked on. When Ramli grabbed one level, Josepha expected Nenum to become possessive. But the two began to reassemble it together, whispering all the while.

She saw Teno play with a set of Russian dolls, removing each wooden doll from a larger one until the smallest doll was discovered. When Dawli, the frail-looking child of Teofilo Schmidt, came to Teno's side, Teno willingly yielded the dolls and crawled off in search of another toy.

It was all strange to her. If one played alone, it was because the child wanted to be alone, not because the others left the child out. Josepha searched for tears or the formation of childish cliques, and saw only inquisitiveness and cooperation. Even the muscular, big-boned Kelii, who seemed to be their favorite adult, got no special affection. If he held a picture book on his spacious lap, a child might climb up and sit there, but only to see the illustrations more clearly.

They never misbehaved, at least not in the normal way. If a child wandered off, pursued shortly by a worried parent or psychologist, the young one was usually found investigating a plant or a toy or how a toilet worked. If they were told not to play with the computers until they were shown how to push the buttons, they listened, asked questions, and tried to understand the machines.

On one occasion, Ramli had punched Teno in the stomach. Teno had retaliated with a blow to the arm. Each cried out in pain as Josepha, worried and at the same time almost relieved by the show of normality, rose to her feet to stop it. But the battle was over. The two had learned that violence caused pain.

Although she tried to ignore it, she often felt frustrated. Chane had become more withdrawn, making frequent calls to old friends late at night behind the closed doors of his study. The children could not reward her love with spontaneous displays of affection. She wondered how long it would be before a parent, bewildered by the lack of any real emotional contact with a child, might lash out at one of them.

Josepha and Chane sat in the park with their children. The spring day was unseasonably warm, the blue sky cloudless. A week ago, a third birthday celebration had been held for all the children. The adults had been sociable and gregarious, the young ones solemn and bemused.

Teno and Ramli knelt on the grass, playing an elaborate game with marbles and pebbles; only they knew its rules. Twenty meters away, under an elm, Edwin Joreme lay on a brown blanket with his head on Gurit Stern's lap. Edwin's child Linsay poked at the grass with a stick. Gurit had apparently left Aleph, her child, at home.

Edwin was a thin man with ash blond hair who looked almost adolescent. Gurit, auburn-haired, green-eyed, and stocky, was one of the few in the village who still intimidated Josepha. Gurit had been a soldier before the Transition. Although she seemed a friendly, hearty sort, there was something hard in her, a toughness, a competence that made Josepha ill at ease. Watching Gurit, she thought of what the woman must have seen and imagined that she was one who probably savored her extended life instead of simply accepting it.

Edwin sat up and moved closer to Linsay. He spoke to the child; Linsay listened, then returned to probing the ground. Josepha thought that Gurit might have passed as the mother of both. Lines creased her face at eyes and mouth, and in the bright afternoon sunlight one clearly saw the gray hairs framing her face. Chane had once asked Gurit why she had not wanted a more youthful appearance. She had laughed, saying she got tired of seeing young faces all the time.

Edwin was still trying to distract Linsay, murmuring to the child intently. Josepha turned to Chane. He had brought some notes with him, but she did not know what they were about. He was ignoring them, gazing absently in the children's direction.

"Is something wrong?" she asked.

He shook his head.

"What are the notes for?" They were written in Italian and Swahili, two languages she did not know.

He was silent for a few moments before replying. "Just some reminiscences, personal things, incidents I might otherwise forget."

"Can't you just consult the computer records?"

"Those are public records, Josepha. They tell nothing of subjective attitudes or personal reactions. And several incidents aren't recorded." His lowered eyelids hid his dark eyes from her.

Impulsively, she touched his arm. Then she heard a cry, a thin, piercing wail.

Edwin was shaking Linsay, muttering under his breath at the child. Linsay wailed. Josepha froze, not understanding what was happening. Chane jumped to his feet, his red caftan swirling around his ankles.

Gurit quickly grabbed Edwin's arms. "Stop it," she said firmly. "What's the matter with you?" He pushed her away violently. Trembling, he stared at his child and then, shockingly, slapped Linsay.

Josepha tensed at the sound. "Why can't you respond?" Edwin was shouting. "I'm sick to death of it, you're as bad as a robot, not the slightest human feeling—"

Gurit again seized Edwin, holding him tightly, and this time he was unable to break away from her strong arms. He crumpled against her. Linsay sat calmly, blond head tilted to one side.

Josepha got up. "I think we should go," she murmured to Chane, feeling that Edwin would not want them to witness any more. Teno and Ramli had stopped playing and were staring at Edwin, fascinated. Josepha thought wearily of all the questions she and Chane would have to answer later.

"We're going home," she said to the children.

iii

A small death had entered their lives. Josepha and the children were burying the cat.

They had walked to the woods north of the village and stopped at a weedy clearing. Josepha wore a silvery lifesuit under her gray tunic; she always wore the protective garment when in the forest. She stood under a maple tree, shaded from the summer heat, while Teno and Ramli placed the small furry body in the grave they had dug. The children were dressed only in sleeveless yellow shirts and green shorts. Their stronger bones and muscles did not need lifesuit protection.

The children were seven now. Their rapid growth and the cat's death made Josepha feel she was aging. She could no longer suspend time by living in a permanent eternal stability. Her child had been a toddler so recently. Now Teno was a student, learning to read and calculate or going off with Kelii and a few parents to the lake for a day or two to learn about the outdoors.

Teno was more of a companion to her as well. The child would ask questions about the desk computer, a sandwich, the lilac tree outside, about Ramli and Chane, about what parents were, and after Josepha had explained about Krol, questions about death. The child never smiled, never frowned. Josepha would see only expressions of thoughtfulness, concentration, curiosity, puzzlement.

Ramli and Teno began to cover the cat with dirt and leaves. They had kept the animal for three years; Chane felt that having pets was good for children. They had named the orange and white cat Pericles. Josepha loved animals but had never kept a dog or cat before, knowing that eventually the creature would die. It had been easier, when she lived alone, to watch the robins return to the trees, or the geese fly back to her pond after their migration. She could imagine that the same birds were returning.

The children got along with Pericles in their solemn way. They had learned that tweaking his tail caused him pain and that he would repay any affront to his feline dignity with a baleful stare and the swipe of a paw. They had cleaned out his box, scratched him behind the ears so he would purr, and protected him from the forays of Kaveri Dananda's cocker spaniel Kali, although Josepha had always felt that Kali, despite the ferocity of her name, was frightened of the cat.

But they had also learned that Pericles would kill. Josepha had not always been able to hide the small birds who were victims from the children. It had been hard for her to explain the cruelties of nature and the instincts of animals that even humankind had not fully escaped. The children had listened and absorbed the information, but she did not know if they were reconciled to it.

Now Pericles was dead. He had disappeared for a few days, to be discovered by Chane near the woods outside the village this morning. The small furry body he had carried home had been unmarked. Josepha, seeing it, had wanted to cry. The children did not cry. Heartlessly, it seemed, they had the computer link sensor scan the body to determine the cause of death, which had been, oddly enough, kidney failure. Then Ramli had kindly suggested that they bury the creature in the woods he had loved.

The children had finished. Josepha went to them and they stood by the grave silently for a few minutes, then began to walk slowly back toward the village.

"Do cats always die?" Teno asked.

"All animals do sooner or later."

"From accidents?"

"Sometimes. Other times it's disease, or getting old." She did not like discussing these matters, but there was no point in shielding the children from them.

"Some people die from accidents too," Teno said emphatically.

"They don't have to," she replied quickly. "If the medical robots get to them in time they don't, and usually they reach them in time because of the Bond, that's why we all wear them."

"Some people want to die," Ramli said loftily. Josepha was too startled to reply. "I saw about it. They kill themselves or sometimes they kill somebody else or ask somebody to do it and they fix their Bonds so they don't find them in time."

"I know that," Teno replied. "I saw a dead guy on the holo, he shot himself and there was blood all over, he put a bullet right in his head and they couldn't bring him back."

Josepha felt sick. She wanted to tell them not to use words like kill, but that would only turn it into a potent obscenity for them. She wished Chane were here instead of home getting dinner ready. "Where did you see such a thing?" she said, trying to keep her voice steady. "You couldn't have seen it at home or at school."

"Over at Nenum's," Teno said.

"Don't lie to me," she answered harshly, stopping along the narrow path and turning to confront them. "Warner and Vladislav wouldn't allow it."

"Nenum knows how to override."

She could read no expression in Teno's gray eyes or Ramli's black ones. She wanted to get angry, be firm, forbid them to look at such things again, but knew it would do no good. It would only make them more curious.

"Why do they want to die?" Ramli asked.

Josepha shook her head. "It's hard to explain. Sometimes they're unhappy or just tired of everything or . . . people like us used to die, you know that. Many of us still don't know how to handle long lives."

"That's dumb," Ramli said tonelessly. "I want to find out everything and it'll take forever. I don't want to die."

She smiled at them. "Of course you don't." She motioned to them and they resumed walking.

"Is Pericles a ghost?" Teno inquired.

"Where did you hear about ghosts?"

"Kelii told us stories about them. They're dead people except they're ghosts, and you can't see them except sometimes."

She recalled the voice that had spoken to her years ago and was silent. "Are there ghosts, Josepha?" her child said.

"What do you think?"

"I don't think there are any."

"Kelii says it's made-up stuff," Ramli said. "He says people made it up because they didn't know anything. I said if I didn't know I'd find out, I wouldn't make it up."

"Did you ever see a ghost, Josepha?" Teno asked.

"How can she see one if there aren't any," Ramli muttered.

"She can think she did."

"No," she responded, feeling that she was being honest only technically. She could not explain her own experience and conviction until they were older, though she doubted they would understand her even then.

She thought of all the deaths she had seen and suddenly felt very old, too old to be raising children. The responsibility weighed heavily on her. The decisions were too difficult, the mistakes too frequent. She remembered her own father and mother and the problems they had encountered with her and her brother Charles. Her parents had died in an auto accident a few years after she had married Gene Kolodny. But she had been estranged from them long before, deeply resenting them for reasons never fully understood, knowing she had failed them in some undefined manner but afraid to find out how. After their deaths, filled with guilt and regrets about things left unsaid and undone, she had been forced to put them out of her mind.

They reached the edge of the forest and looked out at the village. The paths were filled with strollers; others sat on the front porches sipping cool drinks. Josepha looked down at Teno and realized that now she could think about her mother and father without the old feelings. It was as if she had a bond with them through the child, as if she was no longer cut off from them even by death.

"It's fair," Teno said suddenly, interrupting her reverie.

"What's fair?"

"Pericles dying. He killed things and now he's dead."

More visitors now came to the village. They had been arriving ever since the children's birth.

There had once been talk of raising the young ones with other, "normal" children, but nothing had come of it. Josepha supposed that it was too late to do anything about it. The visiting children from outside, however curious they might be at first, soon learned that the children here were uninterested in their games, pranks, emotional displays, and rivalries. The visits ended with each group of children keeping to itself.

A few biologists and psychologists came, but most of the visitors were simply curious. Now that the children were older, and the differences between them and the rest of humankind were more obvious, more outsiders arrived. They peered into the recreation hall at Kelii and the children. They went down to the lake where the young ones were being taught to swim. The children bore up well under this inquisitiveness, being even more courteous and well behaved while under observation. Josepha sensed, however, that the visitors might have preferred seeing the children scream or yell or laugh or cry or gang up on someone.

She saw Chane standing with Edwin Joreme and a group of visitors, ten tall Tartars who had congregated in front of Merripen Allen's small cottage. They had just arrived; Chane had accompanied them to the village.

He had been visiting old friends. She had urged him to get away for a few weeks, remembering how refreshed she had felt after a solitary sojourn at her old home. But he looked weary to her. She waved at him and bowed to the Tartars, who bowed back.

Chane seemed surprised to see her. He made his farewells to the visitors and came toward her, greeting her with a light kiss on her forehead. "I didn't expect you to meet me," he said.

"We missed you." She took his arm and they began to walk through the park toward their house. The dark gray sky seemed to hang over them and the brown grass, scattered with red and yellow leaves, was desolate. Chane shivered slightly in his long gray coat. Edwin had taken charge of the visitors, leading them over toward the recreation hall. Josepha recalled the day he had struck Linsay; since then, he had become one of the gentlest and most patient parents here. She could only wonder at what it cost him. His hazel eyes were often doubt-filled and distant.

"Were there many visitors here while I was away?" Chane asked.

"Indeed there were. Didn't I mention it to you when you called? Maybe I didn't."

"I don't think you did."

"Well, don't worry about them, Chane, everyone pretty much ignores them now."

"I have good reason for worrying. I'm even more concerned after being outside. Before, when I called my friends, I was sure they were exaggerating the suspicion and hostility of others toward this community. Now I know they weren't."

She felt a slight prickle of fear. "What are they upset about? What can possibly happen here?"

"They're afraid of the children, of what they might become."

"But that's so silly. What could they do? If anything, the kids should be afraid of us. That is, if they could feel fear. I don't know if they can."

"Granted, it's foolish," Chane replied. "But you've seen the visitors here. They all act a bit apprehensive. The group I came back here with did. I don't understand Russian or Tartar, but I saw that much. And that's nothing compared to what I've seen elsewhere. Those who come here at least give us the benefit of a doubt." He sighed. "People don't want things to change," he murmured, as if speaking to himself.

She was silent. They approached the house and stopped at the gate. "Are Teno and Ramli home?" Chane asked apprehensively.

"They're over at the hall."

They entered the house, hanging their coats in the hallway. Chane went to the living room and sat on the sofa; he sprawled, head forward, feet out. "I heard one rather interesting proposal," he said as she came into the room and sat next to him. "Some believe that the children should be taken away from here."

"Taken away!" She clasped his hand tightly.

"There was talk of exile, putting them on a colony out by Saturn or some such place."

Josepha was stunned. Recently various groups had started to send murderers and other very disturbed people out to small space colonies under robotic guards. Eventually, it was hoped, they would be aided by new biological or psychological techniques. In reality, they were usually forgotten. Josepha doubted that anything much would ever be done for them. It was small wonder so many murderers attempted suicide rather than risking such an exile.

"But the children aren't criminals," she said. "They've done nothing. Sending them away would only guarantee their bitterness. How are they going to feel about people who would do that to them? They might, in their reasonable way, decide that they have to defend themselves."

"I said that. If they're exiled now, though, so the idea goes, there's not much they can do, they're only children. And once they're gone, there's nothing they can do anyway if they're guarded. I argued with a lot of people, Josepha. I didn't get far." He withdrew his hand and looked away.

She suddenly wanted to hurry to the hall and make sure Teno and Ramli were safe. Instead, she leaned back and closed her eyes. The village had become a fortress, a settlement surrounded by danger, uncertainty, hostility. The visitors were members of reconnaissance missions, spies, enemies.

✳

Teno sat on the floor, placing furniture inside a small doll house. Josepha sprawled on Teno's bed, watching the solemn eight-year-old arrange the tiny sofa and chairs Chane had carved. Little figurines lay next to the child—a small mahogany Chane in a red robe, a tiny Josepha with waist-length black hair, and two smaller dolls.

"Two kids from outside were at the hall today," Teno said. "I don't think they liked me." The child's tones were quiet and measured.

"Why do you say that?"

"I could tell when I talked to them."

Josepha peered at Teno. The child's eyes were hidden by long dark lashes. "Did you like them?"

Teno shrugged. "I don't know. Kelii told me I could show them the garden so we went outside, but then the boy said to go around the side of the hall, so I did, and then the girl said for me to take down my pants."

"She said what?" Josepha said, trying not to look too shocked.

"Take down my pants. She said they wanted to see me there and I said I would if they would, so they showed me theirs and I showed them mine and they said I was a freak."

She wanted to reach over and hug the child, but Teno seemed calm and undisturbed. "What happened then, dear?" she managed to ask.

"I said I wasn't and I liked having a penis and vagina and they only had half of what I had and I don't think they liked that. Then the boy said a lot of people didn't like us because we were different from them and I said that was stupid because everybody's a little different from everybody else. I think he was going to hit me but he didn't, and we went back inside."

Josepha sat up on the bed, folding her legs under her. "Do things like that bother you, Teno?"

"No, it's just dumb." The child picked up the Chane doll and put it inside the house.

"Listen," she said quickly, "maybe all of us can go down to the lake this weekend and take out the sailboat. Would you like that?"

"You forgot, we have a camping test then." The children were going to be set loose in the forests beneath the nearby mountains for three days, with only a knife, compass, and poncho each. The young ones were well prepared; they were all skilled campers and robots in the area would be alert to any danger. But Josepha found herself worrying anyway.

"Tell me," she murmured, "why are you so interested in campcraft?"

"We all are."

"I know that." It was one of their peculiarities. Although the children varied in their interests and aptitudes—Teno enjoyed mathematics while Ramli preferred botany—they always remained interested in what all the others were doing. It was as if they thought that if one was interested in something, it might be worthwhile for all of them. "I didn't ask that," Josepha went on. "I asked why *you* were interested."

"It's fun. I like to go and watch the deer, but you have to sneak up on them or they run away. I like to watch the campfire when we sit around. Anyway, we need to know that stuff."

"Why?"

"I might have to live in the woods. Lucky we don't need as much food as you, so we wouldn't have to hunt anything. We could stay a long time."

"Why would you have to live in the woods that way?"

"Maybe they won't let us live anywhere else and we'll have to hide."

"Who won't?"

"The people that don't like us." Teno picked up the Josepha doll and held it.

"Teno," Josepha said quietly, "do you mind it, being different?"

The gray eyes gazed steadily at her. "No. I'm the way I am, I'm me," the child said calmly.

✳

Josepha saw the woman before Alf Heldstrom did.

She and Alf were designing a history course for the children. Even with the computer's aid, the project was more difficult than they had expected. They were arguing over how to present the history of the Transition when Josepha noticed that a woman, an outsider, was watching them.

The visitor was standing under a nearby weeping willow. She was thin, almost emaciated. Her pale platinum hair was clipped short.

"Have you seen that woman before?" Josepha whispered to Alf.

"Never." Alf brushed a wavy lock of long golden hair off his delicate face. "She seems to be alone, usually visitors come in groups."

"It may be silly, but I don't like the way she's looking at us."

The woman walked toward them. Josepha felt apprehensive. She nodded and the blonde woman nodded back. She stood in front of them, nervously pulling at the sleeve of her blue jacket.

"Hello," the woman said softly. "Are you parents?"

Josepha was startled by the directness of the question. She glanced at Alf. He raised an eyebrow and stared back blankly with his blue eyes. She turned back to the visitor. "Yes," she replied.

Alf uncrossed his legs and sat up. He and the woman stared silently at each other while Josepha tried to keep from fidgeting. At last the woman looked away. "I'm Nola Reann," she said to the air, speaking so softly that Josepha had to lean forward to catch the name. "Where are the children?" She looked at Josepha.

"Camping."

"Camping. I can't imagine why."

"I'm Josepha Ryba. This is Alf Heldstrom. Won't you sit down?"

"Thank you. I'll stand." Nola Reann put her hands inside the pockets of the blue jacket she wore over her silver lifesuit.

"Most of the people who come here are biologists or psychologists," Alf said, in an obvious effort to relieve their discomfort. "We do, of course, get a cross-section of other types too."

"I'm a meteorologist. I'm in space most of the time."

"What did you do before that?"

"I didn't do anything before that. I'm only twenty."

Josepha glanced at Alf, who seemed as surprised as she was. It was easy to forget that there were young people in the world. She tried to recall what it felt like to be twenty.

"Are you here to study the weather?" Alf asked as Josepha attempted to decide if he was being courteous or sarcastic.

"No." Nola swayed on her feet as she surveyed the village. Her dark eyes betrayed her uneasiness. She seemed oddly impatient. She had not lived long enough, Josepha supposed, to be anything else. "What are you trying to do here?" the young woman said suddenly.

"I beg your pardon," Alf murmured.

"What are you trying to do here?"

"We're trying," Josepha answered calmly, "to raise our children."

"Why these children? They're not even normal, they're alien and soulless."

"I *beg* your *pardon*," Alf said harshly. "You have no right to say that. Do you know them? Have you seen them or talked to them?"

"I've seen them on the holo. That's all I need to see. You don't know what you're doing."

"You have no right to say that," Josepha replied. "You have no right to come here and discuss our children in such a hostile way."

Nola Reann stepped back. "Hostile! I'm not hostile. Your biologists are hostile, enemies of the human body and what it represents. They want to change it and mold it, it's only dead matter to them, meat, if you will. They want to change it because they hate it, which means they must hate themselves on some level."

Josepha thought of Merripen. "Tell me," Alf said, smiling slightly, "since you're a meteorologist, how you rationalize the implants I know you have, the ones that provide you with a direct link to the machines you need to do your work."

Nola glared. "That's not the same thing at all. Such devices merely amplify the potential of the human form and mind." She waved her right hand in a gesture of dismissal.

"And your human form could not even be standing here in front of us without the aid of an exoskeleton," Alf went on. Josepha squinted, noticing for the first time the slender silver wires on Nola's hand and the metal support around her neck, partially concealed by her high-collared blue jacket. The woman, she realized, had spent her life either on the moon or a low-gravity colony. For a moment, she felt sorry for her, but that was as patronizing and wrong as Nola's feelings about the children.

"Do you have any idea," Alf was saying, "what people three hundred years ago might have thought of you?"

Nola smiled, once again hiding her hands in her pockets. "I'm still a human being. I think like you, I feel like you. Everything I use simply aids me in achieving my full potential. I don't lack emotions or sexuality like your children do." She turned her head and looked at Josepha with conviction. "Extended life has at last made it possible for us to become fully human. We can be everything a human being can be. There is no other point to life. These children insult us by saying that we cannot succeed as we are."

"How strange," Josepha said. "If I reasoned the way you do, I might conclude that extended life denied us our humanity by denying us death." She forced out the words with difficulty. "Some people obviously do feel that way."

"You mean murderers and suicides," Nola said blatantly. "I quarrel only with the means they use. They anticipate death, that is all, reach for it prematurely instead of awaiting its eventual arrival. Of course, murder and suicide are at least human talents."

"So is rationality," Alf said.

"What is reason without the fuel of the emotions, the tension between the two that makes all achievement possible? A dead, soulless thing." Nola lowered her voice. "Your biologists are trying to cloak their despair by creating these new beings. They're not giving us a chance to succeed as we are."

"Are you a meteorologist or a missionary?" Alf asked, raising an eyebrow. "Do you think the human body is sacrosanct? It's only nature's set of compromises. People have been trying to alter it in small ways, either for aesthetic or practical reasons, for centuries."

"Not this drastically." Nola paused, as if at a loss. "It's a mistake."

Josepha thought: there's nothing more to say, we won't even know if we were right or wrong for a long time.

Nola Reann turned and strode away quickly, without a farewell. Josepha moved closer to Alf. "She's unusual, isn't she?" she said softly. "Others aren't like that."

"Do you talk with many people elsewhere?"

She shook her head.

"She may be extreme, but she's not all that unusual."

"What will they do?"

He sighed. "I don't know. There's not really much they can do."

Josepha looked up and gazed past the park. Behind the houses ahead, robot guards patrolled the grounds. There were more guards lately.

✳

Teno and Ramli were playing with four other children in the living room. Josepha could hear them from her study: Teno's inflections, Ramli's slight drawl, Nenum's murmur, Aleph's rasp, Yoshi's sing-song, Linsay's guttural throat noises. They had already passed their wilderness survival test, although it would hardly have mattered if they had not. Unobtrusive robots had been near them at all times. The village had held a celebration for the children when they returned, but the ceremony had meant more to the parents than to the young ones, who seemed content with success alone.

She did not mind the noise, although there was more of it than usual. She paid it little attention as she sat at her desk, watching the final history syllabus roll by on her reader screen. If neither she nor Alf had anything further to add, they would finalize it, show it to a teacher, then program the computer.

She tried to concentrate, not wanting to think of Chane. He and Warner Chavez had gone to one of the lodges for the day. She felt a pang at the thought. Vladislav, still living with Warner, had taken up with Chen Li Hua some time ago. Warner began seeing Chane a while later.

Chane had not tried to deceive her and she had made no objections. Yet even after two months of this, Josepha still felt twinges. At least Warner and Vladislav knew how they felt about each other. Josepha knew only that she would be hurt if she lost

Chane and that she missed him when he was not with her. But she did not know what he felt. Oddly enough, their lovemaking had improved. Jealousy was always a good aphrodisiac, but the price was too high.

She sighed. She and Chane had lived in isolation from each other since the very beginning. Except for the children and their upbringing, they shared very little of real substance. Their other obligations and pursuits had been carefully divided into equal portions, everything from rooms to housework to time alone to time with friends. There had been nothing strange about that; it seemed reasonable and practical.

But, looking back, she felt as if she had deceived herself. People grew closer, or changed, or grew apart; they were not capable of maintaining the same static arrangements day after day, year after year. Josepha, afraid to admit it to herself before, now knew that she was coming to love Chane.

She put her hands, palms down, on the reader's flat surface. She did not want to be alone anymore, surrounded by walls of sensible arrangements which protected only a solitary mind reflecting endlessly on itself and its own uniqueness. She had deluded herself by thinking that she could preserve those barriers in this village. The children had already penetrated them, binding her to the future and the past.

She recalled her pre-Transition life. It had not been that unusual in its isolation from family, demanding relationships, and any sense of continuity. The techniques guaranteeing personal immortality had preserved the individualistic society in which she had lived. Without that development, her fragmenting culture might well have been overrun by those who were unified and bound together in a common purpose. Only the attainment of the ancient dream of eternal life had been enough to save her culture and conquer the others as well. Small wonder, she thought, that Nola Reann and those like her felt threatened by the children, whose existence once more questioned everything.

The sound of a laugh startled her. She sat up and pushed the reader to one side. The laugh was hollow, devoid of merriment. She got up and walked softly out of the study, peering around the stairway into the living room.

The children were talking, lounging in various uncharacteristic attitudes around the room. Nenum stood slouching, hands on hips, looking quite pretty. A peculiar whine had crept into the child's voice that seemed familiar.

"I don't *know* why," Nenum was saying, tucking a short lock of reddish hair behind an ear. "I just feel depressed, you know, everything seems . . . " Josepha recognized the voice of Warner and the words of one of her common complaints.

Teno ambled over to Nenum. Her child's face was contorted in an odd expression, eyes wide, mouth pulled down. "Don't worry," Teno said, putting a hand on Nenum's shoulder. "Ah, you need a mood and you'll feel better. Uh, sometimes I feel that way myself. It'll go away."

"Why don't we have a party?" Aleph said, mimicking Gurit's tones. "I haven't tied one on in a while."

"I have a headache," Linsay growled, stomping fiercely around the room. Josepha recognized the tense but controlled voice of Edwin Joreme. "They get to me sometimes, they get to me."

"Oh, Edwin," Teno replied, "you don't mean that, ah, I know you. You *dote* on Linsay." Josepha heard herself, the pauses, the hesitation, the rising inflection at the end of sentences, and shrank back near the wall. Was that how she sounded, that silly mixture of meliorism and insecurity? Was that how they all sounded? She wanted to tiptoe back to the study, but puzzlement and curiosity held her as she listened:

RAMLI *(firmly):* Don't worry, I just have to make two calls, I won't be on long. Then we'll go. Why get there early?

TENO: I know I shouldn't, but, uh, I always feel so silly there. Li Hua's so intelligent she always makes me feel ignorant.

ALEPH: You know what I think? We could do with some tough times again. Builds character. Everyone's getting soft. If we had some hardships, a lot of people wouldn't make it.

NENUM *(whining):* I get depressed when I hear that. You're a hard person.

YOSHI *(gruffly):* The last time I was on Asgard, I noticed an interesting refinement in their holo transmissions.

LINSAY: Not *again.* Do we have to listen to that *again?*

TENO: Now don't be so rude.

Josepha peered around the staircase once more, still hidden in the shadows. She felt like a spy. Ramli was sitting on the sofa slouched over, feet extended. Teno fluttered around the room nervously, looking very pretty and very insecure. Nenum lounged in the corner, gazing seductively at Ramli. Pained by the too-familiar scene, Josepha closed her eyes for a moment.

When she opened them, the children were themselves, seated on the floor, arms folded, murmuring softly. "I don't understand it," Teno said clearly.

"It's the way they are," Aleph replied. "You know that. They're confused."

"That's not what I meant. They wanted us to be different from them, right?" Teno paused. "That means they wanted us to be better. So if they think we're better, then why don't they act more like us?"

"You know why," Linsay said. "They can't help it. Their bodies are different. They like feelings, but they lie about them too. They lie about sex the most."

"Well, I don't know why people like to think things that aren't true. When I touch myself or Ramli does, it feels nice and that's all, but they act as if it's the most important thing in the world."

"It must feel different to them," Nenum muttered.

"But they made us so we're different," Teno said. "I don't think they like themselves the way they are. And if they liked us, they'd try to be like us. They have minds, they can think. So if they aren't like us, it has to be because they can't help it and their feelings are stronger, or it's because they don't like the way we are either."

"But they made us this way," Ramli responded.

"We're an experiment. Experiments don't always work."

Josepha crept back to her study, knowing she had eavesdropped too long. She paused at her desk, remembering the calmness in the young voices as well as the eerie precision with which they had imitated the adults. The voices had lacked both humor and contempt. They had only been trying to make sense of their parents' behavior.

She wondered what else the children might be concluding about them.

✳

Josepha shivered slightly in her light jumpsuit and jacket. Gurit Stern stood with her. The weather was cooler; before them, the lake rippled. The water was calmer near the shore; farther out, the wind was whipping up whitecaps.

Aleph, Teno, and Ramli were on the dock, tying up the canoe they had taken out that morning. The young ones had wisely decided not to stay out on the lake. There was still time to have a meal inside one of the lodges before going back to the village.

Gurit, dressed only in a beige short-sleeved shirt and brown slacks, did not seem to feel cold. She smiled sympathetically at Josepha, then walked out onto the dock to make certain the canoe had been tied up properly. There was really no need to check. The children usually made only one mistake before learning a skill.

She was wondering idly whether they should turn the canoe over on the dock instead when she heard a voice. "Josepha!" She turned and saw Warner and Nenum scurrying down the hill toward the lake. She waved at them.

"I didn't think anyone would be out here today," Warner called as she came nearer.

Josepha smiled. "No one else is. Believe me, we wouldn't be either if we'd known it was going to be this cold."

Warner, dressed warmly in a red coat, smiled back. Nenum hurried down to the dock to greet the others. "We thought that as long as we've walked this far, we might as well eat before going home."

"We were just about to have lunch ourselves." Warner's eyes did not meet hers. "You must join us," Josepha continued. "I miss you, I don't see you as much lately."

"I wasn't sure if you wanted to."

"Oh, Warner. You're my friend." Josepha took Warner's arm as they began to climb the stone steps which led to the lodge, a large log cabin surrounded by evergreens.

"He loves you, Jo." Josepha, startled, let go of her friend.

"What do you mean?"

"I can tell. He hasn't said so, but it's obvious. I think he's afraid to tell you, I don't know why. Maybe he's not sure how you'll take it."

She was about to reply when she saw something move in the woods ahead. A man stepped from behind the trees. He was looking down toward the lake. He was dressed entirely in white; there were dirt and grass stains on his knees. He held his hands behind him, as if concealing something. Thick, dark, shoulder-length hair hung around his face.

He stood fifteen meters above them without moving. Josepha stopped and glanced quickly at Warner.

"Visitor?" Warner murmured.

"Alone? Out here?" Josepha looked back at the man. Farther up the hill behind him, a small robot moved swiftly toward the stranger on its treads. And then the man quickly raised his arm and she saw the weapon, a small silver cylinder.

He aimed. She heard Gurit scream: "Get down!" A beam of light flashed from the weapon.

Josepha turned numbly. Gurit had thrown herself over one child's body, two others lay near her, the fourth . . . something was wrong with the fourth. There was another flash of light, shocking her out of the paralysis that had settled over her. She looked back.

The man's headless torso toppled over into the foliage. For a moment she thought the robot had fired on him; then she realized the man had turned his weapon on himself. The robot reached his side and stood there helplessly, too late.

She turned to Warner. Her friend's head shook from side to side soundlessly. She held out her hands to Josepha, then spun around and began to run down to the children. Josepha followed her.

Gurit stood up, her hands on Ramli's shoulders. Teno, still lying on the ground, looked up. Josepha thought: they're safe, they're all right.

Gurit reached out to Aleph and pulled her child near her. But another small body did not move. Josepha suddenly realized that she could not see Nenum's red hair. Warner was running to the small body.

Josepha rushed to her friend, throwing her arms around Warner. "Don't," she managed to say. Warner pulled away and finally stood over her child.

Nenum too was beyond revival, head burned off by the visitor's weapon. Nenum's mother was silent, clenching and unclenching her fists, shaking her head, staring at Josepha with black, frightened eyes. Josepha opened her mouth and found she had no voice. Her knees buckled and she sat down hard on the ground, hugging her legs with her arms. Dimly, she saw Gurit go to Warner.

Warner began to wail. Gurit held her. Aleph observed them with pale green eyes. Josepha drew her legs closer to her chest.

Teno and Ramli were standing over her. She thought: we should go, I can't keep them here with this, what do I say, how can I explain it? Fear swept over her and she found herself shaking. Teno reached out and held her hands until she stopped.

Others, she knew, would be there soon. The robot had probably already signaled to them. The machine intelligence, having failed to protect them, waited on the hill, its head slowly spinning as it continued to survey the woods. It held the weapon in its metal fist. The children were silent, watching her with calm, questioning eyes.

Josepha wound her way past the cots and mats, trying not to disturb the children who lay on them. The young ones had been living here in the recreation hall for a week, always watched, never left alone nor allowed to wander. Two robots stood in the back of the room; another was posted near a doorway.

Kelii Morgan sat in a straight-backed chair near the mat where his child Alani was sleeping. He was unarmed; the robots would stun anyone entering the room with a weapon. She motioned to him. He did not move. The children slept, breathing rhythmically. They had not rebelled against the restrictions placed on them.

She moved closer to Kelii. "Should we go downstairs now?" she whispered. Alani stirred slightly. Kelii leaned over and adjusted the child's blanket.

"I'll stay here," he replied softly. "Go on, Josepha, you can tell me what happened later on."

"Sure you don't want company?"

"Go on, it's all right. I want to be here in case one of them wakes up."

She left the room and hurried down the ramp. Below, in the room

where the children usually played and studied, parents sat among
the desks, computer consoles, tables, and chairs. Most of them sat
on the floor. A few were on benches near the walls. Here three
robots also stood guard, and she knew that there were others
outside.

Chen Li Hua, who had taken it upon herself to call the parents
together, stood under the screen in the front of the room. "Where's
Kelii?" she asked in her flat, hoarse voice.

"He wants to stay upstairs."

"Then we might as well start, and I'll say what I have to say."

Josepha saw Chane near the doorway and made her way to him,
sitting down next to him on the floor. "Where's Merripen?" a man
asked, and she recognized the voice of Edwin Joreme.

"I didn't ask him," Li Hua replied. "I didn't ask anyone except
parents to come here tonight. If any of the others arrive, as I
suppose they might, that's fine, but I think any decisions we make
should be ours." She cleared her throat and squinted; her eyes
became slits. "Some of us have been asking for better security here
all along, for restrictions on visitors, for supervision of any stranger
who came here. We allowed ourselves to be talked out of it,
supposedly for the good of the children. You see where that got us.
It's time we insisted on whatever we think is right." The small
woman brushed a hand over her short cap of straight dark hair.

Chane, looking sad and pensive, reached for Josepha's hand and
held it. "They're gone," he murmured to her. "I went over to their
home and Li Hua told me. They left this morning, before anyone
was up."

"Where did they go?"

"I don't know. Vladislav went with two psychologists. Warner left
with a friend who came for her."

She was silent, thinking of what she could have done, what she
could have said to Warner and Vladislav, what she had been unable
to do. It had not been enough, holding Vladislav while he sobbed,
calming Warner, trying to figure out how to bury poor Nenum after
skin scrapings had been stored for possible cloning.

Josepha had aided Warner, a stunned almost catatonic Warner,
in arranging a small ceremony in the foothills beyond the nearby
woods. She, Chane, and Gurit had accompanied Warner and

Vladislav. As they stood, watching two robots place the small body in the ground, Josepha realized that the ceremony had been a terrible mistake. They were marking an irrational act, an insane act, completely outside the fabric of their society. They could gain nothing from Nenum's death. The death of any child would have been horrifying enough in former times; even during ages when such deaths were commonplace and expected, there had at least been the hope of a life beyond or the harsher view that the deaths of the weak might make future generations stronger. Their discovery that the murderer had been a man with two suicide attempts to his credit and a confused belief in some of the tenets espoused by people like Nola Reann only made the whole thing more absurd.

Josepha, standing with her friends, had found herself praying, clinging to the hope that the visions she had glimpsed so long ago were real. She wanted to speak of them to Warner and Vladislav, offer them something that would ease their pain. But she kept silent, thinking they would not understand or, worse yet, think she was mocking them with false hopes.

Warner had rejected the idea of raising Nenum's clone and had talked Vladislav out of it too. Instead, she had gone to Merripen, asking him to have the experience removed from her memory. He had called in a psychologist; at last they had agreed. It was a delicate business, this erasing of one's memory, and Josepha knew it would help Warner only in the short run. Her friend would lose the past nine years, but eventually she would become aware of discontinuities, of blank spots, and would attempt to fill them in; the memories, little by little, might return and have to be faced. And in the meantime, a black emptiness would exist in the back of her mind to bother her without her ever being quite sure of what it was until the recollections returned, perhaps wrenchingly, in dreams and disassociated fragments. Better to let time handle it, better to absorb it, face it, and let it fade. Merripen, she was sure, had agreed to the procedure only to assuage his own guilt and sense of failure in his responsibilities. The psychologist should have treated him.

But no psychologist would treat a biologist without the biologist's request. The biologists had created the society and sustained it with their techniques; to question the motivations of one would be to question the society. Eventually, of course, the children, these children of Merripen's mind, might question it and seek to change it, and then Merripen would be held to account, but not yet.

Li Hua was still speaking, apparently answering another question. She paused, and Josepha saw Gurit rise to her feet.

"Listen," the former soldier said firmly, "you have something to tell us and you've been beating around the bush. Make your point, Li Hua."

"Very well. You all know about those who want to exile the children. Now some think we should have raised them with other children from the beginning, but most of us thought that would be a hardship, that there might be animosity or a lack of understanding between the two groups. In any event, we thought it wiser to wait until the children were older, and we did encourage visitors, which was probably a mistake as I see it. The children are better off developing in their own way."

Gurit coughed. "The point, Li Hua, the point."

"I propose that we agree with the proponents of exile, and move to a space colony of our own as soon as possible."

Gurit sat down. Everyone absorbed the statement. A few shook their heads. Amarisa Drew, a tall Eurasian who was one of Yoshi's parents, waved an arm. "How is that going to solve anything?" she asked in her musical voice.

"It will ease the fears of those who distrust the children," Li Hua replied. "Security precautions will be simpler. The children won't have to face hostility. Any latent talents they have can develop more openly. Later, when they're older, they can return or lead out their lives wherever they choose."

"One moment, please," Dawud al-Ahmad called out. "Why should such a measure help? Why wouldn't those who fear the children grow more afraid in their absence? Ignorance is usually a greater spur to fear than knowledge." He tugged at his short beard. "Wisdom cannot grow in isolation."

"There's a practical problem," Kaveri Dananda said, "that you haven't mentioned either."

"And what is that?" Li Hua asked.

Kaveri stood, adjusting her green sari. "What is to prevent a group of the insane from attacking our little colony in space?"

The Chinese woman shook her head. "Such an action requires

planning and teamwork, something I hardly think fanatics would be able to do successfully."

"Nonsense," Kaveri replied.

"An isolated attack like the one Josepha and Gurit witnessed is one thing, a concerted attack quite another. Most people now have lost a good deal of the ability to work with others smoothly—we have been cultivating our individuality for too long. Disturbed people have this tendency to an even greater degree."

"But we would be vulnerable," Kaveri said. "And I think you underestimate the driving force of a mad idea deeply held."

"We would have ample warning, we could defend ourselves, and could station ourselves at such a distance from others that we would constitute no threat."

"But we could still be attacked," Dawud said. "Here, at worst, a few of us could survive. In space, we might all . . . " He held out his hands.

Josepha found herself rising to her feet. Nervously, she surveyed the room. Li Hua turned toward her.

"Josepha?"

She cleared her throat. "We're down here talking," Josepha began, "while the children are upstairs under guard. I don't know whether any of them actually feel fear or not, but they'll certainly acquire a good imitation of it if we go on this way. They'll learn to distrust and fear almost everyone if they haven't already. And if they turn into alienated adults as some fear they will, we'll have ourselves to blame, not the madman who shot poor Nenum. This exile will only make it worse for them. The only way we can help them is by returning to some semblance of normal life, here, in our homes, as soon as possible."

"A pretty set of sentiments," Li Hua muttered. "But how do we keep the same thing from happening again?"

"Don't you see?" Josepha focused first on Kaveri, then turned toward Amarisa Drew, hoping for support. "Don't you realize how many people will feel sympathy for us now? Distrust is one thing, murder quite another. If we communicate openly with others, we can win their trust."

"We tried that," Edwin Joreme said from across the room, "and you see what happened. My advice is to have the biologists tell everyone to leave us alone and let them know what might happen if they don't. They're the ones with power."

"You're wrong," Josepha answered. "They don't believe they have much power. Ask Merripen if you don't believe me. And even if they did, that would be no solution, it would create only more hostility." She glanced around. Amarisa, Kaveri, and Dawud were nodding their heads in agreement.

"Li Hua has suggested a specific course of action," Edwin went on. "You have offered only vague possibilities. Give us a course of action. What exactly would you have us do?"

It was a fair question. She did not know how to reply.

Then Chane spoke. "It's obvious," he said in his deep voice. "First, we must invite people to live here if they wish. I'm talking about welcoming them, not the sort of half-hearted tolerance of outsiders we have now. Second, some of us must leave the village for short periods to communicate with others, propagandize them, if you will. I have spoken to many people over the holo, but such a measure does not have the impact of personal, face-to-face communication."

"And who will go?" Lulee Bernard called out, looking like a small, auburn-haired, serious child herself. "Isn't it more important that we stay with our children?"

"Perhaps it is," Chane replied, "although I don't know how much good that'll do them if they have no place in our world."

Several parents nodded their heads, murmuring. "It might be dangerous for the ones who leave," Edwin objected. "Have you thought of that? You can't be protected as well, if at all."

"It's a risk we'll have to take," Chane responded. Josepha saw fear in his eyes. "We have little time to spare for once," he continued. "If we hadn't all grown so slow to act, we would have seen the wisdom of this course a long time ago. Since I brought this up, I'll volunteer my own services, if it's all right with the rest of you."

Josepha felt her muscles tighten. She could not look at Chane. He should have spoken with her before making such an offer. She could not object here in front of everyone and she could not stop him if he wanted to leave.

She thought: Warner was wrong, she was mistaken about Chane

loving me, and now I can't even ask her about it. Numbly she listened to the discussion go on, not really hearing any of it.

Josepha gave in; she had no choice. Chane had persuaded the villagers. He would be accompanied by Amarisa Drew and Timmi Akakse, a handsome Jamaican with the habit of changing her name every thirty years or so.

She wanted to argue with Chane, but she did not. Instead she tried to act calmly, explaining to the children why he was leaving them for a bit. They did not seem disturbed, asking only why they could not go as well. She had replied lamely that their studies were more important. But later she heard Teno tell Ramli that the parents were afraid they might be harmed by someone.

Whenever Chane glanced at her, she smiled, perhaps too brightly and reassuringly. The night before he left, he held her in bed and looked directly into her eyes and she knew she had not fooled him at all. She waited for him to ask her how she really felt, hoping she could stem the flow of angry and resentful words that would pour from her, but he did not speak, possibly afraid of what she might say.

She waited until he was ready to leave the next morning, off to join Timmi and Amarisa for a final session with Merripen before departure. Hating herself for speaking at such an awkward time, she heard her words: "You're leaving because of me."

Chane pulled back as if he had been struck. "No," he said finally, placing his hands on her shoulders. She wanted to twist away.

"Yes. First it was Warner and now this. You want to get away."

"You're wrong, Josepha, it has nothing to do with you. There's more to it than you think."

"It might be dangerous," she said, wishing she could stop the pointless argument. He took his hands away and she waited for him to walk out the door.

"I won't be gone that long. I wanted to bring you and the children along, but I know how hard it is for you to meet a lot of strangers. Anyway, you know we decided it just wasn't fair to ask young children, however rational, to defend their existence before people they don't even know."

She was beaten. She forced herself to smile again, to exercise the patience she should have learned during her long life. "I guess I'm being unfair," she murmured. "I'll miss you, but . . ."

"I'll be back before you know it."

He was gone.

She went to the window and watched him stride across the courtyard, closing the gate behind him.

iv

Teno was as tall as Josepha, Ramli somewhat taller. They had grown rapidly during the past years. They had retained their sexual ambiguity; slender bodies, slightly broad shoulders, a range of gestures that flowed from the delicate to the clumsy to the athletic. They were strangers.

They had not always been strangers. After Chane had left, Josepha had grown closer to them. She had taught them how to make pottery and how to sketch. She had been delighted when she found that they in turn were teaching these skills to the other children, though she was a bit disappointed with what they produced; accurate, photographically realistic drawings and simple utilitarian plates and vases. She had found at first that as she spent more time with Teno and Ramli, she missed Chane less.

Chane's first trip should have lasted two months. It had stretched into almost half a year. Had he been returning to her alone, it would not have mattered. But the children grew, the life of the village went on. She had consulted him during his calls and the children bantered pleasantly with his image, but Josepha had made the day-to-day decisions. Chane had returned to people who got along perfectly well without him.

He, Amarisa, and Timmi stayed away from the village for longer and longer periods of time. Estranged from their families while apparently having some success on the outside, Josepha knew they found their absences easier to rationalize as time passed. Perhaps they were also telling themselves that there would be time enough to renew their relationships with their children and their lovers after they had succeeded in their outside tasks.

Josepha sat in her favorite chair knitting while Teno and Ramli sprawled on the living room rug, poring over printouts and diagrams. She thought of Chane. She missed him more now, alone in this house with two increasingly impenetrable strangers. The hours she kept filled with new projects, friends, even a new intellectual challenge—she had decided to learn something about microbiology, equipping herself with a microscope and slides—only seemed to make her loneliness worse when she was alone with her thoughts.

She knitted and ruminated, remembering two encounters, realizing again how poorly she had handled both.

One had been with Chane during his first visit home. They had gone sailing on the lake with the children, then enjoyed a quiet dinner by themselves. She had filled him in on the events during his absence. He had told her about some of the understanding people with whom he had spoken.

"Have you become involved with anyone else yet?" he asked her as they sipped their after-dinner brandy.

"Why should I?"

"I don't expect you to deprive yourself simply because I'm away."

"Oh, Chane." She chuckled softly. "I'm used to being by myself, I used to like living that way, you know. You needn't worry about me. I don't need to be involved with another man."

She looked down at the pale green yarn, remembering that comment. She had fancied that she was reassuring Chane. But she had made the remark because of a dimly felt resentment, sure he had not missed the children or her that much; knowing also, since he had not tried to hide it, that he had enjoyed a few casual sexual adventures while away. She had spoken and told herself self-righteously that she would ease him. She had succeeded only in telling him bluntly that she could live alone and be happy about it while at the same time making him feel guilty about his own perfectly natural sexual involvements. She had hurt him, as she had unconsciously intended.

The second encounter had been with Merripen Allen. The biologist had taken to visiting her and the children while Chane was away. She had been sympathetic, knowing that Merripen had grown depressed about the project, feeling that it had escaped his control and that he no longer had anything to say about future events. He was an obsolete functionary wandering about the village, not needed by the children, unnecessary to the parents who had taken matters into their own hands. She knew the visits cheered him up and had been glad of it. But then she had hurt Merripen too.

He had come to her one night. The children were sleeping and she was alone. She offered him some wine but he refused it. Instead, he took her arm and led her to the sofa.

"Let me stay with you tonight, Josepha."

She drew back, surprised. "I can't, Merripen."

"Why not?"

"Well . . . there is . . ."

"Don't be silly. Chane's not denying himself, why should you?"

"I can't explain. It's different for me."

She had been foolish. Her needles clicked; the children chattered. It would have taken so little effort to give Merripen the human contact he had probably needed as much as the sex. And it would have been no sacrifice either; she had felt a sudden desire for the handsome biologist even as she refused him. Why did I do it? she asked herself silently, but she knew the answer. She did not want emotional risks. Merripen might have wanted a commitment of some kind; for sex alone he could easily have turned elsewhere.

She did not want things this way. She no longer wanted her self-imposed exile from life. She could not do anything about Merripen; she had turned him away for the last time. She wondered if it was too late to do anything about Chane.

Merripen, at least, had now found his way back into village life. All of the children sought him out. He was the only adult they did seek out. The rest of them, even Kelii, were ignored or tolerated.

It had started when the children were eleven. They were not overtly hostile or rebellious, simply more indifferent. Lulee Bernard spoke of not knowing where her child was much of the time; Edwin Joreme, even grumpier than usual, muttered about being told he didn't know much; Gurit Stern complained about being asked embarrassing questions and having her answers rejected out of hand.

The children were thirteen now. She watched them as they sat on the rug surveying diagrams and charts. They were adolescents. She should have expected it. They kept to themselves, cultivating a flat, inexpressive manner of speech, wearing short, clipped hair and simple clothing. All of these new young people were austere in appearance, as if criticizing the more flamboyant and varied garb of their parents.

"What are you looking at so intently?" she asked the children. Neither replied. "What is it?" she said again.

Finally Teno looked up. The child's short hair was curled at the ends, making the face seem almost pretty. "Ectogenesis chamber," the young one remarked.

"More biology? Is that all you think about?" They were silent. Josepha imagined that Merripen must be gratified by this recent obsession. "Whatever for?"

"See how it works."

"We have to use it someday," Ramli added.

"I know, but you don't seem to pay any attention to anything else," she responded, trying to sound lighthearted. "You spend so little time on your art now, or history, and you used to enjoy those things."

"This is more important," Ramli said tersely.

"I didn't say it wasn't, I just said there are other things."

They remained silent.

"You could at least reply."

"Aren't you supposed to see Gurit this afternoon?" Teno said blandly before turning back to the diagrams.

Josepha felt unaccountably depressed. Of course they were obsessed with biology; for all she knew, it was their substitute for the pair-bonding of normal adolescents. She did not know why they had not paired off; it might have little to do with their physiology. Having been raised together almost as siblings or relatives, the young people were following the pattern normal to such groups by not forming couples. Whether they would form such bonds outside the group remained to be seen.

There were, at any rate, good reasons for this interest in biological techniques. The young ones would not run the risk of natural childbirth even though, theoretically, they were capable of it. If they were to control their own reproduction, they would have to learn what the biologists knew. Perhaps they were also protecting themselves in case at some future time the biologists decided that this "experiment" was a failure.

She watched them, wondering what they might do if they began to think of themselves as an evolutionary dead end. In their rational way, they might simply design another kind of being, one better suited to life than either themselves or the human beings who had raised them.

Josepha thought: we're the dead end. Merripen believed that and he was the person they saw most often now. *We're the dead end.*

Josepha, standing near the gate, noticed the young visitors. There were four, two boys and two girls. They were dressed in shiny, copper-colored suits with high collars. One boy slouched; the other stood straight, hands on hips. One of the girls, tall and muscular, was speaking; she gestured with her arms, flinging them out from the shoulders. The other girl stood on one leg, flexing the other, pointing one foot toward the ground. Teno and Aleph stood listening; they were still as statues. Teno was in a worn brown corduroy jacket and pants and Aleph wore gray overalls.

"What are you staring at?" Chen Li Hua said in her hoarse voice. She sat with her back to the stone wall.

"Nothing. Some visitors, that's all." Josepha swung the gate gently. The hinges no longer squeaked, but the latch was still not working properly.

"As I was saying, Timmi was kind of discouraged about her trip to Madrid. There's a character there who's opposed to almost all biological modifications. Timmi couldn't understand his arguments, she suspects he may have doubts about extended life as well, but he has a following. Well, it just proves that if you use shit for fertilizer something always grows."

Josepha peered at the latch. "Why don't you have a robot fix it?" Li Hua asked.

"I guess I'll have to, this place needs work. One of the solar panels on the roof needs checking and one of my faucets keeps dripping."

"Your homeostat must need fixing too. This house always seemed poorly designed to me."

"Maybe, but I never liked the newer designs, they always seemed—"A movement caught her eye. She looked up and saw the tall, muscular girl pull back her arm. Suddenly she struck Teno. Teno staggered back.

Aleph leapt at the girl. The other copper-clothed outsiders moved in and Josepha could no longer see Aleph's stocky form. "They're fighting," she said uncertainly.

Li Hua got up and came to the gate. Josepha said, "We'd better stop it."

"Don't bother, I think they can take care of themselves. Look." Ramli and three others were running toward the battle. They reached the outsiders and pushed them away, dodging their punches. Teno and Aleph got to their feet. The tall girl and one of the boys moved back in, flailing wildly with their fists. Josepha saw that the village children were fighting defensively, blocking the blows, then pushing the others away.

The outcome, she realized, was not in doubt. There were six villagers to four visitors. Teno and the others also had quicker reflexes and sturdier muscles. They chopped and kicked efficiently. The visitors quickly retreated a few meters and stood together grumbling, nursing their injuries.

The violence sickened Josepha. She pushed the gate open and walked across the park with Li Hua close behind. She passed the outsiders, who seemed curiously unmarked by the fight in spite of their groaning. She reached Teno. One of her child's eyes was discolored. Aleph, Ramli, and the others were scratched and beaten; their clothes were torn. Yet they had won, or so it seemed.

"What was that all about?" she asked harshly. Teno stared back calmly.

"We had to defend ourselves." The child's voice sounded regretful. "They wouldn't have stopped trying to hurt us unless we did." Josepha spotted the scratches on Aleph's face and an ugly bruise on Ramli's arm. The visitors had tried their best to hurt them, yet the village children had responded only with defensive gestures.

"But how did it start?" she said.

"They don't like us and they're afraid."

Li Hua sighed. "What now?"

"We'd better talk to them," Ramli murmured. "We shouldn't just leave them there."

"It was hardly a fair fight anyway," Li Hua said. "Six against four, and you being stronger."

The young people seemed mystified. "What's fair about a fight?" Aleph asked. "The point is to stop it."

"Let's go," Teno said. They moved past Li Hua and Josepha toward the outsiders.

But the visitors were already leaving the park. Teno called to them; they did not answer. Josepha watched them get into a blue hovercraft parked near Warner's empty house and drive away.

❋

The children had gone camping in the foothills.

Josepha had seen Teno and Ramli off, helping them pack their gear, seeing them meet their friends outside the courtyard. As she watched them stride away in groups of two or three, hands clasped, packs on their slender backs, she had felt tired and old.

There had been no reason to worry. The young people wore Bonds and needed little food and water. But now a week and a half had passed and the children had not returned, nor had they transmitted a message. Josepha, somewhat uneasy, consulted her computer, which indicated that they were still in the foothills.

She called Alf Heldstrom. His image, seated behind a compositor, appeared. "Josepha! Haven't seen you since Lulee's party. Why don't you come over for lunch?"

"I'm worried about the children, Teno and Ramli haven't called in at all. Have you heard anything?"

"You shouldn't worry. They're in the foothills, I know the region, they can take care of themselves."

" I know where they are, I just found out."

"Look, if anything was wrong, an emergency signal would have come in by now."

"Does Merripen know what they're doing?"

Alf shook his head.

She noticed a light flashing on the console. "Alf, someone else is calling, can I get back to you?"

"Sure. Come on over if you like." Alf disappeared and was replaced by the image of Chane.

They exchanged their ritualized greetings. Josepha wanted to reach out to him, mend the rift, but she did not know how to do it. He asked about Ramli and Teno.

"They're not here now. The children all decided to go camping more than a week ago."

"I guess they're all right then."

"I'm sure they are, they haven't called in, but . . . well, I have to admit I'm a little worried."

"Did they say why there were going?"

"No, but . . ."

"Didn't anyone ask?"

"It's hard to ask them anything now, they seem to resent it, if they can resent anything. You'd know that if you . . ." Josepha caught herself in time. "They're older now, they aren't docile little children."

"So everyone just let them go off."

"Oh, Chane, it isn't as if they aren't prepared or hadn't gone before. If something was wrong, we would have had a signal."

He looked exasperated. "As if nothing could go wrong with their Bonds or they couldn't make a mistake or someone couldn't harm them."

"Who the hell are you to be so concerned?" she burst out at last. "You aren't even here most of the time." She stopped. This was no time to pick a fight with him. "Very well," she continued, "we'll go look for them. I imagine they'll be annoyed with us, or at least puzzled." They might have made an error, she thought. It was too easy to assume that because the young people were rational, they were infallible. "Chane, do you have any appointments today?"

"Late this afternoon."

"Break them. Please come home."

"What for?"

"I thought you were concerned about the kids." She paused. "That isn't the only reason. I miss you."

"I was just there."

"Almost five months ago."

"That's not so long."

"It is, it seems longer here. I miss you."

"You get along pretty well by yourself."

"Yes, I get along by myself, but I don't like it. I get along because, like you and everyone else, I think there'll be plenty of time to take care of things later on. It's a bad habit all of us have. And you see what happens. Later never gets here. I love you, Chane." Her face perspired. Her hands shook. She drew them under her desk where Chane could not see them. "Please come home." She waited, expecting him to smooth it all over while refusing."

"I'll be home tomorrow."

Startled, she gazed at his image silently, then held out a hand to it. "I'll go look for the children," she managed to say. "I'll let you know what's happened."

Josepha, accompanied by Alf and Gurit, glided swiftly over the treetops, surveying the ground below. The belt around her waist was constricting, the jet on her back heavy. But this way they had maneuverability; a vehicle would have restricted their movements. She steered herself carefully as they passed over a small clearing and saw the remains of a campfire, a blackened area surrounded by stones and covered with dirt.

Josepha was frightened now, trying desperately not to give in to panic, not wanting to suspect the worst. Immediately after the call from Chane, she had contacted a robot in the foothills and sent it to where the children should have been. Looking through the robot's eyes, her screen had shown only a deserted clearing while the computer told her that the young people were not there.

The signal she and the others were following, a low hum, grew louder. They were in the foothills. Josepha saw a glint of metal through the trees up ahead.

They came to another clearing and circled it, focusing on the signal. The robot Josepha had sent out waited there. The signal hummed in short bursts, telling her that the children were here. But they saw no one; only the signs, once again, of a campfire.

They dropped quickly to the ground. Josepha landed clumsily, stumbling onto her hands and knees. Alf helped her to her feet.

"I don't understand it," Gurit said as she strode around the clearing, peering at the trees, searching the ground for signs. Her middle-aged face was tense with worry; the lines near her lips were deep. Josepha waited unsteadily, still feeling unbalanced by the jet. Gurit stopped, bent over, then stood up. She held something in her hand.

She came back to Josepha and Alf, holding out the object. "Look, a Bond bracelet."

"I don't understand," Alf murmured.

"Very clever," Gurit said.

"But we should be getting signals from the other Bonds, shouldn't we?" Josepha shook her head, bewildered.

"This is a tricky business," Gurit replied. "Someone has relayed the signals through this one device and has managed to do it without triggering any emergency alert systems. I wouldn't know how to begin doing that."

"Then how," Alf said, his trembling voice betraying his fear, "are we going to find them?"

"The computer can track them if we turn off this Bond," Gurit said, "assuming, of course, that no one's fooled with the other Bonds."

"You think the children could have done this?"

Gurit looked from Alf to Josepha. "Possibly. I don't know why they would."

Josepha felt sick and cold, as if the weather had suddenly changed. "What should we do, Gurit?"

"We can go back home, put the computer to work, send robots out to search, and request a satellite scan of the entire area, but that might take days." She paused. "Or we can keep searching."

"But we don't know where . . . " Josepha began.

"I have an idea," Gurit interrupted. "Don't get scared when I tell you this. There was a landslide near here four days ago after that severe storm we had. My computer mentioned it after the storm was over, but I didn't think about it, I was sure the children had found shelter or else . . ." Gurit gazed guiltily down at her feet. Josepha knew what she was thinking: all of them had relied too much on the machines to guard the children. "They may be trapped," Gurit finished. She did not mention the other possibilities.

"That settles it, then," Alf said. "We must look for them near the landslide." His voice quavered.

A hill of dirt and rocks stood before them.

"There was a cave here, I think," Gurit murmured. "They might have gone inside during the storm." She removed her jet as she spoke, dropping it on the ground with a soft thud. She hurried to the mound and began to climb carefully.

Josepha reached for Alf's hand. She was numb, imagining Teno entombed inside, without food, without air. They could live without the food, but air . . . She thought: nature has killed them because they're mutants, travesties—and it wants to let us know that we can still die here, that nothing can protect us forever. She recalled the frequent trips of the young people from the village, their attempts to understand the natural world that was part of them and yet outside them.

Alf gripped her hand tightly, and she realized she would be hysterical if she gave in to her thoughts. Alf's hand was sweaty, his delicate face frozen. His blue eyes were filled with fear. He leaned against her heavily; she put her arms around him and his jet.

She watched quietly as Gurit scrambled over the rocks near the top of the mound. Gurit fell to her knees and did not move. Josepha waited, wondering what the woman had seen.

Then Gurit stood. "There's an opening here," she shouted down. Josepha sighed; the young people could not have suffocated. Gurit was bending over again.

"Do you hear something?" Josepha asked Alf, sure she was imagining the sound of another voice. Alf shook his head.

"They're inside," Gurit cried. She sat down suddenly at the top of the hill. "Call for help, they're inside."

Josepha had expected Chane to be angry, to reproach her and the other parents for their lack of supervision or to turn his wrath on the children. Instead, he had silently thrown his arms around Ramli, then Teno.

She had wanted to question the children about the reasons for their actions. But Teno and Ramli had been too tired to do more than bathe and eat a few raw vegetables before going to sleep. Chane's journey home had wearied him as well. The accounting would have to take place the next day.

She entered the living room. Chane was sitting on the sofa smoking a cigarette. She sat down next to him and touched his hand gently. He did not speak.

Most of the village had gathered near the cave that afternoon, waiting as the robots dug, sighing and crying when the young people finally emerged. Merripen, standing near Josepha, had unexpectedly hugged her when he saw the children.

The children were tired and dirty but seemed to have few injuries. Three medical robots had treated the cuts and bruises while protein tablets and water were distributed and adults hurried to the young people. Josepha had waited with Teno and Ramli for the hovercrafts that would take them all home.

Both children had been remarkably calm, describing some of their ordeal in steady voices. They had been trapped after taking shelter from the storm. After discovering that air could still reach them, they had parceled out the few provisions they had. Aided by the glow of their portable lanterns, they had tried to repair a Bond in order to signal for help.

"We shorted out four Bonds," Teno said quietly. "It's not that easy to repair them after fooling with them. By then a few lanterns had given out and we had to conserve the rest. I was making some progress with my Bond when Gurit came."

It was impossible for her to tell if they had been frightened at all. She gazed at them, trying to discern some difference, then saw one; neither child would look at her directly. "We made a mistake, rigging the Bonds," Ramli said.

"Why did you do it then?"

"We were sure you wouldn't worry about us, and we didn't want others to find us. You know some don't wish us well."

"You could have died." Instantly Josepha wished that she had not spoken so harshly.

"I know. We all thought we might. We didn't want to."

They had said little more on the way home.

"Don't be sad," Josepha said now to Chane. He tried to smile, but his dark eyes remained morose. "They're safe, and maybe they've learned something from all of this, something we couldn't have taught. I'll admit, it's learning things the hard way, but—"

"They've learned they can die," he responded. "And before that, when Nenum was killed, they learned they might have to hide. Do you think those are useful lessons, Josepha?" She did not reply. "They have learned fear."

"I don't know if they have or not, I couldn't tell."

"And they may react the way many of us have, by retreating."

"Is something else bothering you, Chane?"

He put out his cigarette and lit another, passing the box to her. "I will tell you something you won't find in any public record of my life," he said suddenly. "Do you want to hear it? It's not pleasant."

She lit her cigarette. "If you want to tell it, I'll listen."

"You know that during the Transition I was in hiding. I trusted only two people with information about where I was. I wanted to live until it was over and like many in public life I had enemies. A friend contacted me, one of those I trusted. He pleaded with me to return to the capitol, another government had fallen and he wanted me to help form another, they needed my foreign contacts and experience. As you may know, some countries managed to restore civil order before many African countries could. He thought they might help. As an additional incentive, he told me that my wife and one of my children were imprisoned, prisoners of a tribe sometimes hostile to my own. He was trying to get them and others released but needed my aid."

Josepha waited for him to continue, tapping her ashes into a pewter tray. Chane was hunched over, elbows on knees, staring down at his feet. "I didn't go," he said at last, so softly she could barely hear him. "It was too risky, I thought, telling myself I couldn't have done much anyway. I didn't go. I hid. In fact, I moved so that no one could contact me again."

She had to say something. She reached toward him, then pulled her arm back. "But," she began. She swallowed. "You said," she went on, "that your wife and children were still alive."

"They are. Does that make me any less culpable? Do you want to know what she went through during her imprisonment? Her body was repaired and her mind was wiped of the experience afterward, but I am still a witness to it, I was told everything. I will never have it wiped from my memory. That is part of my punishment."

She stubbed out her cigarette. He moved away from her and slouched at the other end of the sofa. "I have wanted to redeem myself since then if I could. That's why I came here and it is also why I left after Nenum's death. At least that's what I thought at the time—I wanted to stay here, but I thought speaking to others was more important. Maybe it was just an excuse to retreat from you."

"Why didn't you tell me this before?"

"Don't you see? At first I didn't think I knew you well enough, and later . . . I couldn't tell how you felt toward me. You never even argued with me very much."

She sat up. "Why should I have argued with you?"

"It would have shown you cared."

"I thought trying to be rational and pleasant was a better way of showing care. There isn't very much worth arguing about when you know sooner or later it'll be forgotten."

He sighed. "That sounds like selfishness, not concern."

"Why?"

He rose and paced to the window, then turned to face her. "It keeps you from getting involved, from committing yourself. I know, I'm guilty of the same thing. Why didn't you get angry over Warner?"

Josepha opened her mouth to speak, but Chane continued. "Because you would have had to admit your pain and maybe that it was partly your fault as well. Why did I do it? Maybe in some way I was testing you, Josepha. Why didn't you do the same thing? Because you could make me feel guilty by not retaliating, yet avoid any real confrontation where we might have had to make a decision one way or another."

"But I love you," she said, feeling the words were almost useless. "I have for a while. What you did long ago doesn't matter to me now. All of us did things like that or we wouldn't be alive today." She paused, then forced herself to continue. "I worked for a shady cryonic service, even though I suspected many of their clients would never be revived. I bought longevity shots illegally. I didn't do much to make anyone's life better. And before that, out of fear, I ran away from the only man I ever really loved, and when I was an adolescent, I tried to run away through suicide."

"I guess," Chane replied, "that we have at last laid our cards on the table. We humans are peculiar, aren't we? I can see why Merripen wanted a change."

She stood up. "What do we do now, Chane?"

He crossed the room and put an arm around her. "We settle things with Teno and Ramli, between ourselves, and then . . ." He paused. "Right now, I think we need rest."

The children, Josepha noticed, looked almost guilty. They poked at their bananas and milk, gazing obliquely at her and Chane across the table.

"You caused us a lot of pain and worry," Chane began. "I want to know the reasons."

"Chane," Josepha said hesitantly, "can't we wait until we've finished breakfast first?"

"No."

"We made a mistake," Teno said softly. "We needed to be alone for a while, we had some things to work out and decisions to make."

"Couldn't you have made your decisions here?" Chane asked.

"We had to be by ourselves. We didn't think you would worry and we wanted to make sure no one hostile to us knew where we were."

"But you could have gone to the lodges," Josepha said. "You could have had robots protect you there."

Teno stared directly at her. "That didn't help Nenum."

"We're sorry," Ramli said. "Maybe we should have told you. We thought you'd have more trust in us. We forgot that you don't see things quite the way we do. And we didn't count on an accident, though we should have. We were too busy protecting ourselves from other people."

They were trying to twist it around, Josepha thought, trying to make it their fault. It should not have surprised her; quite naturally the young people thought themselves more rational than their parents. "Have you decided anything?" she asked.

"We had to decide," Teno said calmly, "whether to stay here, voluntarily exile ourselves, or pursue a third course."

"Wait a minute," Chane interrupted. "Don't you think your parents have anything to say about what you're going to do?"

"Please let me finish," Teno replied tonelessly. "You were right when you decided to speak to people outside the village and to have more visitors here. The problem is that you didn't go far enough. We need to live with other people now. Maybe we should have been brought up with other children from the beginning. We want to move away from here. It will be hard—I don't know how well we'll get along, but we have to start."

"You want us to build another village somewhere else?" Chane said.

"No," Teno responded. "That would be the same thing we have now. We want to live with others. Some of us may live off-planet, the others in different societies here. It won't be easy, having to leave each other, but it's the only way. People won't see us as a group then, but as individuals. And we'll be forced to learn, to get along, to find out what to do, each of us, because we won't have the others to lean on. Instead of isolating ourselves, we'll learn how we can help."

"But you're so young," Josepha said, looking to Chane for support. "You're children, you don't know what you're doing. You can't decide something like that yet."

"We're not like you, Josepha," her child said. "We don't have much experience, but that doesn't make us children. Physically, we're grown. We don't have the hormonal changes and emotional problems others do at our age."

"It's time for us to lead our own lives," Ramli added.

"And what are we to do?" Chane said, sounding weary. "Go with you? Stay here? Do what we want? Did you think of us at all?"

"Do what you think is best," Ramli said. It sounded cold to Josepha; the child seemed to realize that. "We're not abandoning you," Ramli went on. "You'll see us often, you can advise us. You'll have to tell us if we're doing something wrong."

Josepha, looking at the two serious young faces, knew that they and the others would have their way, whatever the parents or Merripen or anyone else thought. The children would take their leave; she and Chane would have their own decisions to make. They would leave the village; there would be no point in remaining. It all reminded her of death, the end of one thing, the beginning of another.

V

The autumn leaves, bright spots of orange, red, and yellow, covered the ground near the creek. They rustled under the feet of Josepha and Teno, muffling the cracks of dead twigs. Overhead, sunlight shrouded by gray clouds penetrated the webbing of bare tree limbs.

Teno, clothed in sweat pants and a heavy red jacket, walked with hands shoved into pockets. The child's gray eyes matched the cloudy sky and seemed to hide as much. "I'll call you from Asgard," Teno was saying. "I may go to the Moon afterward."

"I've never been off Earth," Josepha murmured. "It seems silly now, sort of unenterprising."

"Maybe you'll visit me," her child said. "Isn't it about time you went?"

"Probably. I hope I can bring myself to set foot in a shuttle."

"The future may be there. We talked about it, all of us. We want to find out more. We're curious, I think we'll go on a long journey someday, or our descendents will. They probably won't be anything like you or ourselves."

"Probably not."

"Even we might not be the same. We've talked about somatic changes, readjustments in our bodies, but I think we'll need more experience before deciding what to do."

They turned from the creek and walked back toward the house. The old maple tree still remained; the apple tree Josepha had planted still lived, although its fruit was small and bitter. The house itself looked the same but felt old, unused, musty. She had left the village hoping to gain some strength from her old home and had felt only displaced. She could no longer live here.

"Will you go live with Chane, Josepha?"

"Yes, at least for a while. He wants me to travel with him, meet some of his friends. He feels he has to continue speaking for you. He's probably right."

"He is right. Our plans may not work out. Some call us infiltrators—as if we're subversive." Teno sniffed loudly. "It's good that you'll be with Chane. Without Ramli and me to worry about all the time, you'll be able to work things out between you."

Josepha stopped and turned to her child, gazing into Nicholas Krol's gray eyes. "Teno," she said hesitantly, "there's one thing I have to ask, it may seem strange or silly to you, but humor me for a bit." She paused. "I don't know how to put it exactly. Do you have any feelings for me at all, as a parent? Do you really, deep down, feel any sort of an attachment, any concern? I just want to know."

The gray, quiet eyes watched her calmly. "It would be strange," the child answered, "if we could have lived among you without coming to some understanding of your feelings. Of course I'm concerned. I care about you and I'd feel a loss if I no longer saw you or couldn't speak to you. If one loses a friend or companion, one loses another perspective, another viewpoint, a different set of ideas and the personality that has formed them."

"That isn't quite what I meant." Josepha struggled with the words. "Do you feel any love?" She waited, wondering what Teno thought.

Teno was silent for a few moments. Josepha thought: I shouldn't have asked. A person could profess love, but actions were what counted. Teno and the others had tried to show all the love they were capable of feeling if they could feel it at all. One could not ask, should not ask.

"Do you believe," Teno said softly, "that only your physiology, your glands, your hormones can produce love? It isn't true. Love is part of a relationship, it can't be reduced to physical characteristics or body chemistry. I love you, Josepha. I'll care about you as long as I know you or remember you."

She should not have asked. The words could tell her nothing. She could still doubt, still wonder if the child was telling her what would be most comforting.

But Teno's face was changing. As she watched, she saw the child's lips form a crescent, and realized with a shock that Teno was smiling. It was a slow smile, a gentle smile, compassionate but impenetrable. A softness seemed to flicker behind the gray eyes. It was Teno's parting gift.

The smile too might be a comforting mask. But as she entered the house with her child, Josepha decided she would accept it.

Transfigured Night

GEORGE ZEBROWSKI

" . . . pass beyond the service economy, beyond the imagination of today's economists; we shall become the first culture in history to employ high technology to manufacture that most transient yet lasting of products: the human experience.

" . . . blurring of the line between the real and the unreal will confront the society with serious problems, but it will not prevent or even slow the emergence of the psyche-service industries and psych-corps.

" . . . sequences of experience so organized that their very juxtaposition with one another will contribute color, harmony or contrast to lives that lack these qualities . . . frameworks for those whose lives are otherwise too chaotic and unstructured."

—ALVIN TOFFLER,
Future Shock

"I begin with two possibilities which are quite probably realized, though not by normal men; namely, that Smith remembers that twenty years ago he was Jones and also Robinson, while Macgregor and Stuart each remember that twenty years ago they were Johnston. . . .

"If we divide a flatworm in two, both halves may live happily ever after. If each gets a fair share of the nervous system, presumably they get a certain amount of memory from their common parent. And the converse holds when two protozoa fuse. The case of disassociated personality in men is hardly apposite, as two different personalities rarely if ever seem to be fully conscious at the same time. Human consciousnesses do not usually split or unite in this way because human bodies do not. If, on the other hand, as is widely supposed, consciousness may continue without a body, I see no reason why such restrictions should hold. But I leave it as a problem for a person sincerely desirous of immortality whether he would prefer that 100 years hence fifteen distinct spirits each remembered having been he, or that one spirit remembered being he and also fourteen other people. For clearly if 100 years hence someone remembers having been I, I have not died, even though he is less like me than I am now like myself at four years old."

—J. B. S. HALDANE,
Possible Worlds

"The chief implications [of indefinitely extended life] concern the sanity and outlook of the individual . . ."

—R. C. W. ETTINGER,
Man into Superman

1 / Quantum Mutata

Eternals! I hear your call gladly.
Dictate swift winged words & fear not
To unfold your dark visions of torment.

—WILLIAM BLAKE

Thrushcross watched the birth of his father.

As the unclad body was borne upward out of the long-term nutrient bath, Thrushcross selected fitting responses from his repertoire of sensitivities. His face softened into attentive radiance; feelings of joyous love blossomed within him, moistening his eyes, settling him into a blissful acceptance of the event.

The moments of caring passed slowly. His thoughts followed a prayer of understanding. It entered his mind as he watched the crystalline liquid fall from the suspended body. *Death once gave renewal. We die by degrees, discarding memories, keeping what we please of ourselves. We renew our bodies without the sacrifice of death. We shape ourselves. We go on despite forgetfulness . . .*

The frame was never to be forgotten. To receive its meanings was the only prayer permitted by the circling illuminati, who maintained the frame of earth.

Thrushcross's feelings developed. He knelt down trembling before the raised form (to meditate further would result in the recording of special graces); pride, triumph, and delight filled his being.

These sensations had persisted in unconscious forms through the ages before the beginning of the game periods more than five thousand years ago. All life moments within the frame's container were the work of planners and their descendants, the illuminati; their choices were his own.

The pulse of his life was his own creation from one moment to the next, unlike the crude, unchosen flow of experience known by the unchanged. The unchanged men, he thought, are such frail creatures—clinging to every powerless instant before melting back into nature, where death is the only way of summoning up new individuals.

Emerging from renewal, his father would live his next sequence as desperately as the unchanged still lived their struggle for mere survival.

The last words of the prayer entered him. *Free actions and formless things shaping themselves into intense contrasts and varieties: a goal worthier than all others . . .*

All this the planners had taught.

Droplets of remaining liquid glistened on his father's body. The skin was smooth and hairless. The flesh was new; the brain and nervous system were new, yet retaining the vital past.

Thrushcross stood up behind the clear partition, anxious now to rejoin his own life. In the flow of time he would often impinge upon the sequence of a relative or known person. At times he would be older than his parents; at other times he would not know them. To intersect with recognition was rare. Thrushcross stood motionless as his father's eyes opened to look at him across the centuries . . .

It was only half a recognition; the youthful green eyes did not know him. Thrushcross wondered suddenly why he had come to his father's reanimation.

✳

In the private time of his own sequence, Thrushcross sought colors in the void. His will reached into the cube's black field and folded out a visible pattern from the spatial infrastructure.

A triangle of light.

The points glowed into stars.

Yellow. Orange. Red.

He relaxed his concentration and the field went blank. Why was it taking so long for the sequence to quicken? A pale shimmer of light marked his unease. His sudden lack of interest turned the cube's inside a hopeless black, a space larger than everything outside it.

He looked around at the bare studio, got up, and went up the flight of stairs leading out into the alcove in the north corner of his living room.

Beams of light, focused by the giant lens of the picture window, crossed the green carpet. It was spring outside. Thrushcross stepped out of the alcove and walked through the streaming light into the center of the room. A soft wind fluttered the short grass in front of the house. The black road was a chasm running through the tall oaks, a section of night where no one traveled.

Thrushcross thought of the estates beyond the roadway, dwellings for two million persons around the world; behind each person lay the memories of countless lifetimes. How often had he lived through the stored sequences of others? Somewhere someone was now living one of his own forgotten lifetimes. Among the unchanged someone had died; another would certainly die tomorrow; and one would be born, to grow into self-awareness for the first time, with no promise of a past. He thought of Evelyn in her house down the road. She was waiting for him.

Thrushcross stood perfectly still, waiting for the sequence to quicken.

✳

Slowly, the substance of darkness spilled out of the roadway and ate the spring day. Stars pierced the night.

He went up close to the picture window and peered outside. A wind rustled the tree near the house. By the light streaming out from the living room, he saw the leaves change color as the night wind turned them over; they relaxed, turned, fluttering like fingers plucking invisible harpstrings . . .

He turned back to the brightness of the living room. A vague fear constricted his chest, and he took a deep breath.

The lights went out. He looked around at the dark shapes of motionless furniture transformed suddenly into crouching beasts. The picture window was a cave mouth with a howling wind outside. The dull gong of the doorbell seemed to float up from his bowels.

He walked to the front entrance, turned the brass knob, and opened the door. No one.

But as he looked up, he thought he saw a black, shoulder-like silhouette obscuring the stars. The ground trembled slightly and he gripped the door frame with both hands. The warm wind quickened its soughing through the oaks. A great figure of some kind had bent down to the house to ring the doorbell.

Thrushcross closed the door and went back into the living room. The lights slowly dimmed and flickered.

He looked around the living room, noticing how dusty it seemed to have become, as if years had passed in the few moments he had taken to check the front door.

He went to the picture window and saw that the eastern sky was filling with orange light and great low-lying cumulus clouds. Beams of light stabbed down onto the roadway.

He stepped back and sat down in the high-backed chair that faced the window. Feelings of concern for Evelyn stormed into him as he summoned the sight of his father's eyes. Inertia imprisoned him in the chair as a desire to visit Evelyn seized him.

The orange light grew brighter, passing through the window like a threatening tide. He got up and forced himself to walk to the door. Opening the door seemed a slow process. He stepped outside.

The clouds drove quickly from the lighted east, staining the night sky. He turned around and saw the house lights blinking through the open doorway, as if a fire were raging inside.

Memories flickered just beyond recognition.

Urgently he turned from the house and ran down to the road. From there he looked back at the assembly of interconnected domes, in reality, globes set in the earth; the windows flickered with white light, and the picture window suggested the eye of a giant. At any moment Central would activate the buried colossus and he would tear his way out of the ground, scattering dirt and rock around himself.

Thrushcross felt his body readying itself, preparing him for the dangers of the sequence. He walked into the center of the road and started to run toward Evelyn's house. He slowed suddenly and continued in a fast walk, puzzled by the involuntary reversal.

He felt apprehensive as he walked. The road curved right and he saw the house, three interconnected pyramids with flattened apexes and triangular windows. The lights were blinking inside.

The wind was growing stronger; the clouds were darkening, creating enclaves in the orange expanse. There was a smell of flowers on the wind. Despite the rush of air in his ears, Thrushcross felt the stillness inside the house as he came up to the open front door.

He went inside, turned right, and entered the oval living room. Looking up through the skylight, he saw the ghastly heavens pressing down on the house. The orange light fell into the room like a fog, discoloring the red rug.

Her body lay in the center of the room, headless.

Thrushcross slowly became aware of a man standing in the far right corner of the room. He held Evelyn's head by the hair. In the flickering light, Thrushcross saw that the intruder wore long black hair to the waist; his features were coarse, thick lips open in a sneer.

Catlike, the figure rushed him, knocking him down as it went past into the hall and out the front door. Fixed in Thrushcross's mind was Evelyn's face, eyes shut in sorrow, long red hair drawn tightly by the weight of the head. As he got up, Thrushcross could not decide which to do first—go after the head or attend to the body.

He ran outside, down to the road, and continued into the lighted east. The wind pressed him back, thickening the air into a barrier which struck him in the chest and face. Ahead of him, his mother's head was a black ball swinging back and forth in the running shadow's hand.

2 / Line of Darkness

"I believe the moment is near
when by a procedure of active
paranoiac thought, it will be
possible to systemize confusion
and contribute to the total
discrediting of the world of reality."

—SALVADOR DALI

The orange brilliance of the east was becoming a bright yellow. Thrushcross could no longer see the fleeing marauder. He slowed to a walk. His heart beat steadily, an acoustical sun at the center of his universe, sounding loudly over the rush of air in his ears.

The yellow glare swept toward him, dissolving all sight of road and horizon. Thrushcross stopped, turned around once, and lost all sense of direction. Dust rose from the ground around him.

He felt frustration and anger. Images of mutilation played in his brain. He pulled the arms and legs from the intruder's body; he dug the eyes out of the head; ripped the tongue from its mouth; shattered the teeth with a stone. The mouth filled with blood, becoming a deep pool of thickening liquid.

He ran, legs working furiously, but they did not carry him out from the realm of yellow light. He tried another direction, and another, with no result.

He stopped and was still. He breathed, he saw, he heard the sound of his heart; but who was he? There was something he had to do—

—the moment of discontinuity passed. The light cleared and he saw a red plain ahead, dunes to his left and right. Overhead the sun was too bright to look at, a smear of white heat in a deep blue sky. A warm, dry blast of sand hit him; as he turned away he glanced back in the direction from which he had come—

—blackness where the cadmium sands ended, a wall of darkness at the edge of the world, as tall as the sky, right and left into the vanishing point. Its blackness seemed to be absorbing daylight, as if reality had been cut open here to reveal the night beyond.

He ran up a high dune to his left and looked away from the barrier. Heat waves rippled the image of a plateau. The view jiggled into clarity and he saw white cliffs.

Squinting, he noticed that something spiderlike was climbing up a portion of cliff face. The heat magnified and distorted the limbs, making them even more insectlike.

The fleeing figure reached the top and disappeared over the edge of the tableland. As he watched, Thrushcross noticed the faint images of two cloud-wrapped peaks standing far back on the plateau.

He turned again to the black wall. Its surface changed into a front of billowing storm clouds filled with silent lightning. He thought he

heard an ocean, the crying of sea birds, beached fish flapping on the packed wet sand until the waves rushed in again to pull them out—
—and the clouds pulled themselves over the desert like a blanket of steel wool unrolling to the sound of grinding gears. Rain fell slowly, sorrowfully, with the rhythm of a rhyming verse.

The desert melted into brown mud. The sky was an inverted black floor pierced with small holes; right side up it would have been a fountain instead of a drain.

A yellow glow was trying to break out from behind the peaks on the plateau. The rain ran down the cliffs, staining them dark gray.

Thrushcross looked up into the raindrops, expecting that at any moment he would fall into the sky, to the surface below; but the setting remained the same, refusing to flip over according to his anticipation. *Good, Good,* he thought as the water washed his face. He waited.

The rain stopped, leaving small rivulets running away into the sand. A great creature had been slaughtered beyond the sky, and the desert was soaking up the fallen blood, reddening itself further. Heat mists rose from the sands, vapors swirling around Thrushcross, closing up space until he could not see five feet in any direction. He sat down on the wet sand and waited for the universe to open up again.

A crablike creature crawled out of the mists, a moving death's head leading with a single claw. Thrushcross looked at it carefully as it jerked slowly forward on the loose sand, past him and back into the fog.

He stood up and saw that the mists now extended only as high as his waist. A giant, he had poked his head through the clouds and wondered why he could see only snow fields. The shallow mists floated gently over the sands, secure and lazy, as if waiting for the world to change beneath their cover.

Far away the cliffs floated on the whiteness. Beneath a bleached sky the twin peaks imprisoned an orange fire in their valley. Thrushcross thought of Evelyn's head, consciousness scattered from behind its eyes, sparks wandering now in a starless waste of the unclaimed.

I remember, I remember, he thought as he began to run slowly toward the plateau. Halfway there he quickened his pace; his eyes searched for a way up as he came close.

He saw a series of handholds cut into the white chalk wall. Inhaling white dust, he climbed, feeling the softness in his palms and fingers.

As he reached the edge and looked over across the tableland, a strange quiet drifted into him. Tall grass moved in a slow breeze. The two peaks dominated, casting sharply cut shadows across the grainlike plain of grass.

Thrushcross stepped over the edge with one knee, then the other. He stood up slowly, at peace. A permanence hung over the land, as if thoughts were draining out of the world, to come back, in time, as new physical objects for his appreciation.

As he began his walk to the mountains, he pictured a vast hollow area inside the plateau, a region of resonances, where thoughts and wishes aspired to musical utterance, where the dreams of all who lived within the frame of earth were channeled into a mighty river running out of chaos into the reality of, for him, a green plain, unbroken blue sky, mountains, and the lure of what lay beyond. *I remember, I remember,* he thought again as he hurried.

Beyond the jungle of the valley ahead of him, the horizon was a blinding wall of light, its upward glow suffusing the blue sky. The rocky barrens of the mountain pass were behind him. Ahead, the earth sloped downward into the tangled greenery.

The smell of corruption reached him on a sudden gust of wind, the whisper of a desperate messenger. The way became steeper, and he saw the swamp.

Here the forest's knotty roots were met in vast networks of crotches, elbows, and open-fingered hands. Mist rose into the mass of leaf and vine overhead, but some of the glow from outside still filtered through, bathing the swamp in a bleak yellow. The vegetation seemed to breathe with an endless sadness, concealing a pathos which mocked profundity. The thought surprised and puzzled Thrushcross.

He came to the water's edge, stopped for a moment, and tried to remember, then continued to his right along the sandy shore. A hundred feet ahead stood a tree, its drooping branches dipping into the stagnant water, weary limbs straining to lie down upon their own reflection.

Thrushcross walked closer and saw Evelyn's head hanging on a branch like a rotting fruit. Her mouth was an open *o*, eyes closed to shut out the stroke of her attacker's blade.

Thrushcross summoned a shudder; his body shook and he tasted sweat on his upper lip. *Good*, he thought. He searched for the intensity of fear, and found it coiled snakelike in his stomach.

Suddenly a spear of light left his mother's mouth and lanced out across the green water, a hundred yards across the oily stillness, to a small encrusted island, to touch a shining slender metal shaft standing there on spidery undergear, pointing like a cathedral spire to the sickly yellow sky.

Thrushcross saw a dark figure step out from behind the tree. Evelyn's murderer raised a spear and hurled it—

—directly into Thrushcross's solar plexus. The jolt of penetration threw him back; his arms flew out as the message of pain traced out the complex circuit of his nervous system. His hands closed around the lance and pulled it out. The attacker drew a machete and reached Thrushcross in two leaps, swinging the blade in a whistling arc that caught him in the neck, throwing his head upward—

—he saw his trunk fall with hands still clutching the spear, felt the blood rush up after his head, pulse out from his heart. It took forever for the head to fall; he was suspended within an instant of time, buoyed up by the force of his denial. He tried to shout, but his sound shot out as a cord of light touched the spire point on the islet, and faded.

Below him, the blood from his body soaked into the sand.

He lay in a dream-filled night. The pain in his open neck vessels reached out after his severed head to lure it back. He felt no pain in his head. Liberated, it floated in the starry darkness, jealous of its freedom, wondering how it could ever have been part of the broken thing lying on the pallid sands below. *An accident in the game sequence, was it possible?*

The past came into his brain, comforting him with its age—

—his body agonized, welling blood—

—memories fell like stones into the mirror surface of an azure pool, creating circles of wave fronts drifting into the past—

—he was looking down into a valley of dying stars, glowing coals left over from the fire of a devouring creation. Time reversed itself and the stars flared up as if a sudden wind had breathed upon them—

—he stood in a hot wind under a desert sun. The speed at which life passes slowed, and he was speaking to his warriors in the dusty square of the village. " . . . we must hew our days," he was saying, "as if from stone. We are better for this than those who have changed their bodies and spirits, who leave the earth for an outer darkness, which is also within them . . ."—

—*what a savage I was in those endless days of my first century, living among the unchanged. I was one of them—Herdal, who lived long enough to fall in love with an outsider—*

—"I've been awake all the nights of this year," Rydpat said to the cocked ear of his diary, "hoping for peace, for some kind of contentment, no matter how small, before dawn comes. Day is turmoil, unfocused, uncontemplative, a scattered light. Night is space to think in . . ." He stopped and listened as his mind-linked harpsichord dusted the space of his house with tinkling notes. Each series was the direct analogue of preceding thoughts, which had to be clearly stated and elegant. "Only my most painful memories create the best sounds . . ."—

—*To what purpose are these selves retrieved? Who is forcing me to see them again?* The unchanged Herdal, Rydpat the composer, and others had long ago passed from his self during renewals. It was not part of sequences to look back so overtly.

—*Who are you?* he thought, wondering why the illuminati were failing to protect him. Was the intruder more powerful?

There were no answers to his questions. Alone he was powerless to bear himself out of the transfixed state. Plucked one by one, he knew, from the stores of the illuminati, memories began to exist once more, living things, invasions sharper than any spear point, fears of origin, kindly murdered long ago . . . crying to be restated, examined, redeemed, understood, accepted . . .

2-1 / *The Unchanged*

" . . . any sweeping change in man is
likely to become worldwide; there
will be no reservoir of unchanged
men to follow alternate possibilities,
unless we consciously choose
to maintain such a reservoir."

—GERALD FEINBERG,
*The Prometheus Project: Mankind's
Search for Long-Range Goals*

Herdal lay under the desert stars, shivering in his blanket. A fire
would only reveal him to whoever had been tracking him for the last
two days.

At his right towered The Eye's Bright Treasure, snowy peaks with
rock like blue metal, lower reaches draped in shadows. In those
shadows lay the cave of those who had gone before, all now lost
forever. To reach the cave was a difficult journey across swamp,
desert, stone-sharp foothills, glacier—a test of his right to lead. One
day in years ahead he would fail to come back, and the one who
came after him would arrange the bones on his first visit, mingling
them with all the others in the great pit at the back of the cave deep
within the mountain.

Did they think him so weak that they would send the next one so
soon? He had led his people for only six years. It had to be a
stranger, maybe from outside, from the dreamlife that had taken his
mother long ago . . .

Herdal turned away from the mountains, pressed his cheek to the
cooling sand flat, and watched the dark line of horizon. The sky was
deep blue in the bright starlight; it would be easy to see the
silhouette of anything moving toward him. .

A bump appeared at the edge of the world, the black center of an
unseen spider, growing larger as it crept toward him; it stopped.

He watched for a long time, as he had for the last two nights; the
pursuer was motionless, asleep. Slowly Herdal closed his eyes and
rolled on his back—

Eyes followed him as he left the village. Toothless women sat in front of their adobe houses. Children stopped to watch him as he walked through their playing. The men were in the swamp forest, hunting small game, snakes and fishes. The younger women were planting grain in the field. The oldest men were asleep.

He saw his father's eyes inside himself. All his life Rastaban had gone to the invisible wall, to gather the food which appeared daily. Those who followed the way of honor hated him and those like him. Herdal hated him also, but gave his protection. The old man ate the leavings of the powerful ones who had taken his wife; he had traded his young son's mother for a lifetime of eating without effort. Herdal walked the way of honor for himself and for his father; and the village knew that for this reason Herdal would always come back from the cave, even when he became old. For his father's faults Herdal would not die in the cave; his bones would belong to the desert. There would be no one to take them to the cave, even if they were found.

—bright lights blinded him, brighter than the sun, yet it was too early for sunrise. He threw off his blanket, jumped up and shouted at his pursuer, "Come and face me, coward! What trick is this!"

Something fell over him and he began to claw his way through it, straining to break the strands. He struggled, but the net was pulled tighter and he fell. The lights went off and he lay still in the dawnlight.

A figure came and knelt down over him, touching his thighs, tearing open a few of the leather stitches that held the pieces of his pants together. Hands reached in to check his genitals, then pulled at the hair on his chest. He heard a laugh, like a boy's giggle.

A sliver of sun pushed up over the horizon, spilling light across the barren flat. Herdal looked up and saw a tall woman standing over him, her face pale under a dark, wide-rimmed hat. The rest of her was covered in unbroken silver. She was thin and bony, her hips protruding grotesquely. An outsider for sure, he thought. Behind her stood a three-wheeled vehicle, its twin lamps still bright in the daylight.

"You smell horribly," she said in his own words, "but we'll clean you up and you'll do fine." She knelt down to him again. "Were you going to that awful cave with all the bones?"

He nodded, and poked his right hand through the net to grab her face. She fell back on her heels and kicked him. "You'll like it better after some changes." Her nostrils flared and he wondered if she really had two hearts and had lived more than one lifetime.

She looked at him intently, then reached forward and seized his left wrist with a grasp of iron. "I'll let you out if you behave."

He nodded again. She took out a pair of metal jaws and began cutting the net. "You're really magnificent, you know."

When he was free and standing, he saw that she was a head taller than he, and larger in chest and shoulders despite her bony frame. He watched her as she went back to her three-wheeler. She turned off the lights, took out a small package from behind the seat, came back, and dropped it at his feet. "Take off those rotting things and put these on."

"No," he said.

"Why not?"

"My parents and friends made what I have to last a long time—"

"That won't be long from the way it looks."

"—and it would show I have little respect for the labor of my people."

"I can't wait that long," she shouted. "Put these on!" She came up close, grabbed his shirt, and ripped it off with one motion, burning him with the leather; then she grasped the waist of his pants and pulled, tearing the seam as he was thrown to the ground.

He lay on his back, humiliated. She was strong, and unafraid to use her strength. It would be best to do as she wanted, until a better moment; he would use her garments until he could repair his own. He sat up, pulled the bundle to himself, and began unfolding it. Standing up, he looked away from her as he put on the thin one-piece garb; he knew that she was watching him, enjoying his shame. The white suit felt comfortable.

Forcing himself to turn around and look at her, he asked, "Why do you follow me?"

She looked out from under the rim of the hat, tilted her head back, and he noticed that the hat hid all her hair, if she had any; her eyes were very large. "From time to time," she said, "we're interested in seeing what you unchanged beasts have come to. Some others will look you over, then you'll stay with me." She smiled. "You can change too, if you want; of course you don't know what that means now, but you won't want to come back after you've seen the outside."

"What do you mean?" He was beginning to feel a vague fear.

She came up to him and closed the lock seam on the open chest of his new clothes. "You'll be like us," she said. He looked down at the smoothness of the fabric and wondered about the lack of buttons.

"Why should I want to be like an outsider?" he asked, looking up at her.

"Don't look so frightened—we were all here once, a long time ago. The whole world lived as you do, died as you do—"

"Outsiders took my mother."

"She's alive, somewhere. You won't have to die," she added.

He had heard that they would open his head, spill his blood, take away his pride, giving him pain and forgetfulness in return. He struggled with his fear, as it stole into his arms and legs, urging them to move: *hit her in the face and run.*

"If you run, I can catch you easily with my wheels. Old-fashioned, but fast."

He looked at his feet, and the fear he had never known made him tremble inside. "Please let me go on to the cave," he said without looking up. "If I am to die, let me die there, so that the one who comes after me may lead without fear . . ."

She touched his arm. He looked up and saw the hairless skull of death smiling at him. She had taken off her hat, revealing her emaciation.

He tried to jump back, but she reached out and held him in place. He made a fist with his free right hand and swung at her face, but she pushed him away and he hit the sandy flat with his back. She fell on him before he could get up, spread-eagling him on the ground. Her eyes were soft and brown, examining him intently as she pressed herself down to hold him still. She blinked and smiled, eyes without eyebrows, skull bones set in pale flesh.

He shouted and tried to push up, but she hit him in the chest. Stunned, he lay still as she touched him through the seam of the suit. "Quiet now," she said stroking him, "quiet." After a few moments she again closed the seam. "You're a wonderful beast. I'll want you for a long time."

He was gasping for air when she stood up and went back to her vehicle. She came back with a device of some kind strapped to her waist. She held another exactly like it in her right hand. Kneeling down, she lifted him into a sitting position and attached the small metal box to his waist, pulling at the device once to make certain it was joined to the suit. "We're going to fly," she said. She touched both boxes once and took his right hand in her left. Herdal felt himself lifted into the sky and hurled toward the high mountains. She turned her head to smile at him, and let go his hand. He cried out but did not fall. She drifted close to him and said, "You'll feel no cold or wind—we can go as high as we want."

The peaks were below them. His fear was gone as he stared down at the impossible ridges of rock and snow and valleys like plowed furrows. He tried to glimpse the trail that led to the cave of his ancestors, but it was too small and probably behind them.

There would be no bones for the one who came after him to arrange.

Sleep was a ship drifting on waves of darkness. Orbion could not open his eyes. A giant blue sun blazed in his dream-space, illuminating his insides with a cold, electric glare. The star burned upward into his brain, showing him the moisture-filled universe inside his body. The star pulsed with his heartbeat. Its life was his life. Slowly the personal sun brightened, turning yellower, whiter and hotter, permeating his body. The light coursed through his circulatory system, correcting time's deposit of random incoherence in cell structures. *I want to die, but only for a short while.* Light flowed through his nervous system, cleansing his brain—

He saw gangs of unchanged men breaking into the sleep centers to destroy the flasks. He saw himself waking at the end of time, crawling out of a damaged flask to silence and a blood red sun, knowing that they had forgotten to reanimate him. All of life was past now; he had missed it. A day in the springtime of creation was now worth more than a million years in a dying universe—

—and the sun was bloating into a giant red blot upon the sky; slowly the redness evaporated as seconds turned into ages, leaving only a small bright star which sent a chill through the cooling liquids of his body. Soon the star would give in to the closing hand of gravity, collapsing into a black cyst in space, locking up in a fist the energy it had once so freely given, until the moment when all space-time became one point readying to reveal a new unwinding of possibilities . . .

"*Do you wish to remember all your previous lives?*" a voice asked.

"*They hurt,*" he said.

"*They can all be retrieved.*"

"*It's enough that they are safely stored.*"

He trembled at the edge of an abyss, then fell and could not close his eyes.

Herdal became Rydpat, and lived three centuries. Rydpat became Kolem, who edited all his memories, forgetting Herdal. Kolem became Solion, who lived a thousand years without changing—his pride stopped him from admitting that he was bored with himself. Tooz, Esteb, and Versh lived a thousand years of borrowed lifetimes, inventing nothing, finally disappearing into the first Thrushcross. Anfisa, who had brought Herdal out of the wilderness, returned to the second Thrushcross as Evelyn, revealing that she was his mother from the time of Herdal, greeting him now through twenty lifetimes. Thrushcross revised himself for the third time after Evelyn told him that as Anfisa she had brought out his father, Rastaban . . .

Stop, Thrushcross thought. *The past runs away like water.* A cool stream of water washed through his brain cells, removing small grains of unimportant memory, bits that would in time fill him to capacity with useless information. "*I don't want these memories,*" he said to the intruder. Life without end made one a sieve through which eternity flowed, each deposit of personal identity to be washed away by the next. The unchanged solved the problem through birth and death, through the peace of dissolution which followed too soon the pain of beginning. The unchanged accepted death as he welcomed passage in the sleep ship; the unchanged dead would never return again, but he craved the life to come, the returns to come.

He saw his body wrapped in yellow incandescence, the fine tracery of brain and nervous system visible as a whiter design. As the intensity of light increased, he felt himself dissolving into consciousness. His eyes ached to open. His ears strained to hear. His skin tingled warmly. Desire focused itself in his groin. His arms and legs sought to stretch . . .

"*Not yet, not yet,*" the intruder whispered in a hiss. "*Your life is not your own. The imagination of others, long gone, preys upon your life. You exploit urgently, ruthlessly, and are yourself exploited within a web of needs and contrasts, spun from the irrational past still present in the lower structures of your brain—a brain still awash in an ocean of blood.*" Thrushcross saw a massive artery snaking down from a red sky into his chest. The voice was encamped in his center, as close as the protective illuminati. "*I will not be dislodged easily. That you will have to do for yourself, because I have bypassed your protectors.*"

Silence. A memory quivered . . .

. . . *and the third Thrushcross became Tross* . . .

2-2 / *Eyes of Satin, Rimmed with Gold*

" . . . this very abdication of human
control over the direction of events
might be regarded as a positive step
by some, especially those who feel
that the proper concern of mankind
is the complex psychic world within
each person. The desire to be
master of one's fate is not universal . . .
even in the West, where a few
centuries ago this would have been
regarded as dangerous heresy."

—GERALD FEINBERG
The Prometheus Project

All over the green countryside the stables were quiet, waiting for the dawn that would release their charges. Tross stood on the hillside watching the houses where the masters slept behind stone walls. He trembled slightly, startled by his own existence, his presence in the world at this very moment out of all possible moments, as if there had never been other moments, other places, other awarenesses turning inward in recognition; everything had just been created, including himself; the sense of the arbitrary, of the newness of things named only as he looked at them, was compelling. He was alive in a puzzle, trapped in a tide of things readying to follow this moment; he would act, and he felt the pleasure of anticipation, but he did not know what he was going to do next. The grass glowed in the morning night, drops of moisture still trembling with the light of steel-cold stars.

He lay down among the dew-laden blades and took a deep breath. Creepers groped toward his body, slowly attaching themselves to the fleshy valves on his arms and chest, filling his bloodstream with the liquid that held all knowledge of rooted, growing things. He felt his senses sharpen; he breathed in the fragrant festival of warming air wafting in ahead of the sun.

The grassy vines covered his body now, and he felt the movement of living things in the soil around him.

The sun pushed up slowly over the edge of the world, throwing a carpet of orange across the green land. The grassy vines withdrew as Tross breathed in the air of morning day. The dew dried from his body, leaving him washed and satisfied.

He stood up and went down to the villa below, through the open gate, across the court now flooding with light like a pool, through the open double doors into a room, surprising the waking lady as she lay naked in her bed. The master would by now be at the stable, preparing to release the beasts for the morning hunt of the unchanged, those who still lived in a chaotic freedom, resisting direction.

He fell on her just as she opened her three eyes, pushing up into her natural place. Her four arms beat on his back as he moved. She tried to squeeze his waist with her legs, stopping when she saw that it caused him no pain.

She was limp, resisting him with her contempt, glaring at him, trying to turn him to stone with her disdain.

He reached to her side and slipped his fingers into one of her orifices. It was moist and yielding between the ribs. With his left hand he found another on her left. Her face was without expression, but she almost cried out when yellow sunbeams cleared the court wall and shot into the room through the open double doors. He stopped and held her, as if she were wounded and her life was slipping away.

Her eyes were satin, rimmed with gold; the pupils were black. Her white hair flowed out of her head and fell back in a solid waterfall over the edge of the bed to the charge area terminal on the floor. His body tingled from the low level energy flowing through her body.

He thrust harder, using her side opening as handholds. She grew dewy in her sides; her face reddened and her lips parted to release a gentle puff of warm air. She closed her third eye, but left the two open, staring up at him. He heard a rush as she released a strongly scented musk. The fragrance quickened the flow of his blood to his muscles. He took deeper breaths as her arms began to stroke him lightly on his back and buttocks.

Suddenly her legs again encircled his waist. He felt the suction of openings near her navel, as they sought his valves. The short hairs of her soft white skin began to vibrate as she drew more power into her body, a million needles trying to pierce his skin.

Her breasts hardened. "Drink quickly," she said, "before I burst."

The sweet liquid pumped down his throat, sending fire into his limbs. As the flow stopped, his lips seized the other breast. In a few moments he felt swollen.

She grasped his head with two hands and guided his mouth to the openings under her breasts, forcing him to kiss the lips, first one and then the other. He drank the heat coming out of her, then tumbled into a cold abyss.

He shivered, grasping her back, grinding his palms into the bony hardness of her shoulder blades. She called to him in an endless procession of sounds, no two alike, leading him down a long corridor of musical notes.

A flood rose within him and filled her; but before he died he renewed his longing, suspending him again between desire and fulfillment. Eyes closed, he drifted in a blue space.

"He's back," she whispered, "but don't go!"

Tross opened his eyes, turned his head, and saw the figure standing in the doorway, just at the edge of vision. Pulling away from her, Tross turned on his back in time to see the tall leathery master rushing toward him, red lizard eyes open wide, blade raised to kill, as the lady began to laugh . . .

3 / Flame of Life, Memory of Death

"Father, O father! what do we here
In this land of unbelief and fear?
The Land of Dreams is better far,
Above the light of the morning star."

—WILLIAM BLAKE

Thrushcross waded into the muddy water and pushed his way toward the island. He fell down once and his palms pressed down on the yielding bottom. He stood up and staggered forward, finally reaching dry ground.

He walked up toward the cylinder, through the open portal, and up a short ramp into a room lit in electric blue. Black cubes sat in a circle on the floor.

Thrushcross sat down on one of the shapes and the floor dissolved. He saw himself from above, standing near the tree, looking up at Evelyn's head. The interruption was over and the sequence was running forward again; the intruder had been eliminated.

Thrushcross felt himself flow into the nervous system of his simulacrum, while still watching the scene from above.

—the spear entered his chest, his attacker came at him with the machete, and his head flew upward—

Thrushcross withdrew as the simulacrum tumbled to the sand. He watched it bleed at the edge of the swamp.

He had looked through death more than once, tasting its supper of ashes, knowing that without it and its cousins, sleep and danger, there would be no quickening of sequences, no sharp edges, no welcoming of safety, no release of pleasure. The sight of his simulacrum faded from beneath his feet, ending the poem of death.

"Besides sensation there would be knowing," the intruder said, *"regions of music and reguli, without illusion."* Perhaps, after all, the intruder was part of the sequence?

"No. The sequence is not going forward. I have stopped it."

"You—who are you? Why do you intrude again? Where are

you?" Thrushcross stood up from the cube and waited for an answer.

"Intrude? I have spoken and you have forgotten countless times, as you have forgotten identical lives, identical sleeps, endlessly alike returns."

"Where are you?"

"Right here." One of the cubes lit up inside, revealing a small frog-like body with four eye-stalks. The eyes were large globes filled with snow, regarding Thrushcross questioningly.

"Who are you?"

The light in the room brightened into warm crimson. "Later," the stranger said, "I'll tell you who I am." The voice was soft, louder than the previous thought-whispers. "Let me tell you a story. There will be a choice for you to make at the end, a choice you have never made before. After you have made it, I will tell you who I am. The choice will be one you will either forget or one which will make forgetfulness forever impossible, because you will leave the game cycles. I know this seems unclear to you, but it will be clear when I am finished." The four eye-stalks came together graciously.

Thrushcross sat down on the cube again and waited for the alien to speak. The forward eye-stalks floated slowly apart, one to each corner of the cube face, as if signaling some division of the subject at hand.

"When humankind reached a high level of control over biological materials five thousand years ago, intelligent life on earth split into various branches . . ."

Suddenly Thrushcross thought that the transparent face of the cube was a prison wall, and the alien was speaking to him in desperation, each eye a human fist pounding from within.

" . . . the relatively unmodified humanity left the earth in mobile, self-reproducing worlds, societies which sought through new forms of social organization the attainment of individual happiness. The remaining unchanged clung to ancient ways, fearing any changes in the original organism; some of these still remain. Others accepted creative modifications, developing the gaming civilization. These are yours, seeking complex pleasures, successive lives, dramatic forms, the manipulation of the senses; all drawn from stored memory. You see, the position of individuals in ancient times was defined through a varying control of abundance and scarcity; after the great changes, when scarcity ceased to be a problem, the abundant life still reflected the natural life, vastly stylized, of course. Sequences varied in quality, from banal, anarchic creations given up to simple vitality, to fluid movements mirroring the will that moves all things. Yet even in the best could be seen the gesture of the beast, the pain of the fish swimming upstream to its spawning ground, the cruelty that does not know its own face . . ."

Thrushcross felt uncomfortable, nervous.

"You don't like standing aside from your game?"

"Why should I have to do it?" Thrushcross asked. "There's nothing of interest."

"Don't you feel curious? There are those who seek knowledge as the only way of life . . ."

"To examine like this," Thrushcross said, "to seek knowledge is for unchanged fools—the ancients showed us that it breeds a painful and unproductive self-consciousness, leading only to discontent. There is nothing beyond what I see and feel, and I will never know more."

"All you have is repetition, endless drifting . . ."

"I have not known it to be that."

"I will make you see it."

Thrushcross stood up, enjoying the anger which stiffened his body, curling his hands into fists. "I don't want you tampering with my sequence anymore. Who are you?"

"I study the forms intelligence has taken in the galaxy. The humankind left here on earth, for example, is a strange mix of unconscious evolutionary residues and rational awareness; an exceptionally curious adaptation. Most races, when they reach the time of biological fluidity, choose a more cooperative, rational set of physical and social characteristics; these intelligences often leave the cradle of the home world to live in worlds of their own design, leaving the surfaces of natural planets to the unchanged, the inevitable portion of the naturally adapted for whom further change is a terrifying extravagance." The alien seemed to sigh for a moment; the eye-stalks quivered. "The debate follows a predictable form on countless worlds: in the name of humanism, or whatever name it goes by on a particular world, technical progress is denied;

humanity saw basic flaws in itself once, faults which could not be remedied through technical progress or social reform. But if psychological forms become fluid, so do social and physical forms; there is no immutable nature and all the old objections are seen as brakes born of fear . . ."

"We please ourselves," Thrushcross said as he sat down again. "Now what is this choice of yours?"

"Look."

The floor dissolved again, revealing an endless deep of stars. Thrushcross leaned forward and fell on all fours, trying to press himself away from the openness of lanterned darkness. "That pale red star just below you," the alien said. "My world encloses that sun. I am a hybrid of intelligences from earth and one other world. I offer you the choice of turning away from your life of endless returns and forgetfulness. I can give you clear, unbroken memory, with no accumulation of noise and useless impressions . . ."

Thrushcross managed to stand up and stagger back to the cube. "But why should I want to?" he asked as he sat down.

"If I were to open the gates of your suppressed memory, which still exists at basic levels in your brain despite removal techniques, you would see the endless sameness of your life, its poverty. Your society is trivial and changeless. Its existence is a problem to my understanding . . ."

"Why?"

"You do not direct your own lives."

"I don't care. Why should I listen to you?"

The eye-stalks seemed to look down, as if looking for the answer among the multitude of stars shining in space below the floor. "I cannot convince you by discussion alone," the alien said, "but I can affect you in ways that will help you understand . . ."

"I don't want to be affected," Thrushcross said.

" . . . that you have no understanding of your past, hence no identity. Try to understand what I am saying . . ."

Thrushcross considered for a moment. He saw a male face, a woman's face, children's faces, forest land, a small village.

"You were once an unchanged man," the alien said.

Thrushcross felt a silence inside him. In the stillness something entered his mind and began to direct his thoughts. He felt a new sense of power; a feeling of relief took hold of him. His protectors had come at last to help him. He began to answer the intruder.

"We have been freed from the chaos of reproduction, the pains of scarcity and competition, the limits of reality; we have created endless delight through simple physical health, friendships, and curiosity. Life for us is intentionally varied in ways we cannot predict; and we have destroyed death . . ."

"You must know that these are not your words," the alien said, "and that I am now speaking to the illuminati, not you."

"The illuminati lead, plan, and protect," Thrushcross said, "leaving us to our lives. All that was of the planning, shaping impulse in us lives in them. They are our other half. They are the living, incorruptible reguli of our lives, but they are part of us."

"But how do you know if what they do is right?"

"Their origins warrant our trust."

"You speak with more awareness, for the moment. But you will forget all this—"

"—as soon as I no longer need it."

"For you to see what I mean, Thrushcross, you would have to divest yourself of the very controls and inputs that cannot be removed, since you have given up that choice. The illuminati feed you thought-toys, billowing dreams—"

"Do you have a name?" Thrushcross asked.

"Issli."

"You're very foolish, Issli, if you don't see that in your *mind* anything can happen; there can be no final difficulty, no restriction when all of material reality is made of thoughts."

"But in reality no species is omnipotent . . ."

"We don't have to be—except in ourselves. That is our great perfection. Your drab reality, with all its spaces and terrors, does not impinge—"

"—except through me, or through the natural catastrophes that one day will consume the earth and sun."

"Why should I choose your life? What would I gain except restrictions?"

"You would gain a sense of reality and identity—the satisfactions of truth."

"Would there be happiness?"

"Only moments, but satisfaction and knowledge are more substantial."

"Your reality would not be very satisfying in its limitations, which is why the illuminati were created, and they built the frame of earth for us to live in. Go away."

Issli was silent for a few moments. Thrushcross watched the eye-stalks come together over the body, as if trying to become one eye. "You assume," Issli said suddenly, "that your sequenced illusions are as real as the reality outside them—that you would perceive both in the same way, as well. Do you want to be wakened, to make the comparison, to see which world is the facade?"

"No. If you are right, it makes no difference. I don't want to make the comparison. If I don't know, I won't know the difference. I now think my world vivid and interesting. Why should I spoil its intensity? We reject what you call reality, whatever it is. Whether you are telling the truth or a lie makes no difference."

"But the real world is profound, mysterious, inexhaustible."

Thrushcross felt nothing at the thought. "I want you to disappear," he said. "Even if you are right, we will in time reproduce all that your world contains. Now go away."

"But your powers do not reach that far . . ." The alien's body seemed to swell in a visible sigh. "It's always the same . . . the growing power over the physical environment leads to dimorphism . . . a species splits into those who leave the natural world, thereby extending knowledge, and those who stay to develop the unbounded energy of evolutionary flesh . . . the ones who leave choose the future of fate, of real limits painfully pushed back . . . the ones who remain choose the future of desire, which always finds a way of making failure feel like success. Desire is all will and inwardness, all that was cruel in screaming, competitive evolution, the central devil of all intelligent life in the universe. Those who leave natural planets, those seething caldrons of will boiling itself into first consciousness, first intelligence, meet other intelligences, thereby gaining an external viewpoint on their science and social organization; they gain a comparison of cosmologies, thereby satisfying in part their hunger for uncovering the nature of the universe. Their fate is the search for the given reality, which is multifarious. All these things you will never know."

"We create universes," Thrushcross said, "knowing that imagination is superior to all things outside it."

"Not true, not true," Issli said. "Fate will overtake your world when the sun dies; or, if you should escape through the intervention of some kindly passerby, you will die when the cosmos dies."

"By then we will have placed all things inside ourselves." As he said the words, Thrushcross saw the stars and galaxies glowing inside his body; he would open his mouth and draw in all the suns shining at his feet, all the flowing darkness, all the worlds still awake . . .

"For you," Issli said, "there is nothing external; only the eye which sees a sight, a hand which feels. Your kind is quite insane. I am glad that you are not mobile."

Thrushcross felt distrust and fear. Words formed in his mouth: "There is no choice for me to make."

"Very well," the intruder said.

In a moment the cube was empty. The chamber darkened, leaving only the open doorway at the bottom of the ramp as a source of light.

3-1 / *Resonance*

> "And what is good, Phaedrus,
> And what is not good—
> Need we ask anyone to tell us these things?"
>
> —PLATO,
> *Phaedrus*

Outward, away from Earth's rivers and mountans, oceans and deserts, valleys and plains, across the moon's orbital distance, the planet shrinking first into an oasis, then into a small green stone, finally becoming nothing, its locale marked by a fading star; across fleeing light-years to a world not grown in time's natural soil, a world which has captured its own sun within a shell: here Issli, ninth son of Earth says, "I have returned." Even though he is used to space travel of one kind or another, he is not untouched by the vastness he has traversed.

Esteb, his co-researcher asks, "What do you think?"

Issli's cube drifts out of the enclosure and settles to the floor. "They are a disappointing lot," he says.

Esteb brings his eye-stalks together and is quiet. Finally he asks, "Will we leave them to live as they do?"

Issli considers for a moment. "I think we'll have to . . . I don't know, maybe they know something we do not, though I was not able to find out what that might be. In any case, it will be wise to leave a reservoir of such worlds, to let them develop in their own way, just in case."

"But they do not develop—we've seen that again and again."

"I will consider them again one day."

"You seem affected."

"As one is affected by a story, a certain planned experience produced in the art forms of natural worlds. In these dramatic forms, experience was judged to be meaningful when it referred to some aspect of the real world, relating it to inner experience; but when reference was made only to the form, and imaginative fabrication—by which known sights and sounds of the culture were rearranged in some bizarre fashion—then the form became trivial and meaningless, a clever entertainment, lacking in all conviction. For us, the creation of beautiful things and the search for knowledge are the only things worth doing in the prison of the universe. Those of our brethren who still walk the earth have chosen a terrible form of beauty—beauty without knowledge. They have no clear view of their condition in the cosmos. Are we who know better off? What shall become of us as we huddle around one star, then another? I don't know, but I am grateful for the openness of the question . . . "

And to convince himself he thinks: *in seeking happiness they forgot the virtues of satisfaction. Happiness is a bottomless pit, requiring infinite power with which to conjure. Thoughts become things, dreams reality—the cruelest wishes have no consequence, a river of stored information becomes flesh, solid material is projected to any part of the planet, data fed by the libido of endless power; and forgetfulness wipes away identity and all sense of good or evil. When the sun bloats into a red giant, this vast journeying of souls will scarcely notice the end of their billion-year playground. They will never have known the pursuit of knowledge, the satisfaction of curiosity, which requires great racial projects, the limiting of*

bodily energy through reason. They will never have known cumula-
tive expansion, historically meaningful as a binding up of time, so
that the latest may say, I am loyal to the first, and the last may feel
kinship with all those who have gone forever into the dark. . . . O
Earth, I suffer with you in your blindness . . .

"Let me tell you about our time-travel project," his companion
starts to say and stops.

"There is no one to oversee," Issli says. "They have no one person
or group which sees what they have come to. The interior life is all-
pervasive and nothing else is known."

"Maybe we should wake them up," Esteb says.

"If we disturbed them, only the illuminati would speak to us, the
ghosts they have set to rule. The humanity of earth would be happy
to dispense with physical objects completely; then they would not
need the earth. They would dream until all nature decayed. My
friend, what prevents me from ignoring this form of life is the fact
that too many intelligences in the galaxy engage in it for me to think
it insignificant. Perhaps solipsism is a form of transcendent reference, like the ancient mathematics which relates the forms of all
possible universes?"

"I think the dismissive posture is truest in this case," Esteb says.

"Theirs is a charming madness. Sampling it saddened me. Hoping
to find something of myself in those who contributed to our form, I
found only a crossroads . . . "

"There is not that much of their genetic input in our hybrid
forms, Issli."

"If knowledge comes first, then perhaps I should have given
myself up completely to their life before I could understand it."

"Not if it would mean a loss of consciousness. I would have to
come and waken you—but you say that might not be possible."

"I would like to explore the memory of their artificial intelligences which circle the planet. Perhaps there is a record of some
accident that brought a halt to all development, placing the entire
society of immortals into a process of self-reference, a Moebius strip
of self-awareness, producing the illusion of a high consciousness and
new knowledge as the culture spiraled back into rearranged memories, internalizing all reality . . . "

"How could you even consider studying a circular system? There are enough other backward types which don't refute themselves so obviously."

"I thought there might be something I've overlooked," Issli says.

"Let me tell you about the new cosmology coming out of the equatorials ... "

Issli floats out of his cube, and together with his companion drifts to the open view of their star, which is enclosed by millions of worlds, making up a porous shell several astronomical units in radius. The worlds drink the yellow sun's energy and will continue to do so for as long as the sun's mass permits an outflow ...

And Issli thinks: *Ultimately there is a universe out there which is not what we are; we may be made of the same stuff, but it is not what we are at our level of organization, the level of complexity that makes possible the qualities of intelligence and self-awareness. We fail to grasp this universe at its most basic levels of organization; when we try, we alter, splintering reality. Yet we know something of it, even if we cannot be its complete masters. This surely must be better than denying the difference between a self-reference inwardness and the vast sea around us which crystallized our forms ...*

"There is something of Earth in you," Esteb says, "in the way it draws you, in the way you are troubled."

As he looks across the sun's intimate space, at the many-shaped worlds set in a globular mesh around it, Issli worries about the resonances created in his mind by the visit to Earth. *A zoo of strange lives, Many a culture leaves such living relics behind it in the climb away from the mad vitality of origins. Earth is a place of rituals, illusory knowledge and false wisdom ...*

And something in me loves its desperate beauty.

4 / Memory Is No More

"If a man could be sure
  That his life would endure
  For the space of a thousand long years—"

—Song

"Add and alter many times,
Till all be ripe and rotten;"

—ANONYMOUS

"But even at 'death's end' men will remain finite beings in their accomplishments if not their expectations. I do not know whether the opportunity to exercise our abilities over an indefinite time period will itself be an answer to the unhappiness over our finitude. . . . If this should not prove the case, then some other kind of reconstruction of man appears called for to deal with finitude."

—GERALD FEINBERG,
The Prometheus Project

Shapes stood in the sky, morning clouds outlining a pair of vast, contemptuous intelligences scrutinizing the landscape. Thrushcross sat on the terrace looking out over the plateau, waiting for the end, for the sleep that would renew him. Sometimes he sat here at night, when the world was lit by lightning, each flash a spider of electricity as it moved away from him over the Earth. Mornings he would lean over the small table, setting down marks on the rolls of white parchment, noticing the leatheriness of his hands and the white hairs from his head touching the table. His eyes hurt at the end of each day, and he wondered why renewal was taking so long. When he slept, his dreams were filled with sharp stones, and he felt that he had failed to complete some task. Daily he set down the red marks, imagining that they represented a vast cycle of musical sounds, and he would hear them played during his next return to life.

The red notes flowed endlessly from his hand, more varied and complex as he cut the roll into sheets. The protectors had failed to take him into the sleep ship. The illuminati had forgotten that he had lived past his measured sequence. Throughout the world, he knew, others were passing into new lives, leaving him to die like one of the unchanged.

He looked out over the grassy plateau below his earthen terrace set in the mountainside, and beyond to the lowlands. Suddenly his eyes filled with tears, and he longed to enter the landscape, transfigure every particle of it with his own consciousness; every tree, stone, blade of grass and grain of sand would become an aspect of himself.

Gone would be the terrible isolation of waiting, of looking down at the red marks whose meaning lay just beyond his grasp . . .

Moments passed. A cool breeze touched his face, drying his tears. A sudden realization of his own existence surprised him. He looked down again at the characters on the parchment. They seemed to writhe as he tried to read their meaning, transparent snakes filled with blood, an endless, animated frieze of memory, each echo unrecognizable, empty, except for the pain he felt.

Clouds passed, uncovering the sun's warmth. His sense of self was slipping away. He closed his eyes and watched shapes glide across a bloody background. When he opened them, he did not know what he was seeing. Light flooded his field of vision. He looked at his hand and found it strange, as if he had picked up an oddly shaped piece of wood at the shore. He had no name, no shape, only a waking awareness. He was concealed in time, in a grain of sand in a river bed, as the water rolled on. He looked out through eyes as hard as glass, feeling an empty attentiveness that craved to be filled.

I want to be a child again, naked, without knowledge or memory. He remembered a choice, a chance at renaming the universe, and he had chosen memory, endless desire, possible only in the world at the center of his will. The illuminati knew his will. They would provide and protect. *I want to die, but only for a short time.* A bell knelled somewhere like a broken wail.

He leaned forward and saw his father coming up the path to the house. Evelyn walked with him, brushing away the foliage that threatened to cover the clay path. At last they were coming to take him to the sleep ship; at last Thrushcross began to feel again the tug of time, drawing him forward into a new private place, among endless places to come. Rastaban and Evelyn were youthful and smiling as they walked in the lush greenery.

Thrushcross closed his eyes. A prayer of understanding entered his mind. *Death once gave renewal. We die by degrees, discarding memories, keeping what we please of ourselves. We renew our bodies without the sacrifice of death. We shape ourselves. We go on despite forgetfulness.* The pen dropped from his hand and he leaned back in his chair. His will expanded to fill the world, until such time when it would again fall back into the limits of individual awareness. Memory rushed away from him, emptying into an infinite sea, where all things were possible, where all distinctions were obliterated, all pain dissolved . . .

Emtio awoke. He turned his head and saw two faces watching him from behind the clear partition, a man and a woman. *I remember, I remember*, he thought as the faces turned away and disappeared from sight.

Further Reading

Nonfiction

Ettinger, R. C. W. *The Prospect of Immortality*. Doubleday, 1964.
    Man into Superman. St. Martin's Press, 1972
    "People Freezing: The Establishment Thaws," 1971. Reprinted in
    Ahead of Time, ed. by Harry Harrison and Theodore J. Gordon.
    Doubleday, 1972.
Feinberg, Gerald. *The Prometheus Project*. Doubleday/Anchor Books, 1969.
Harrington, Alan. *The Immortalist*. Avon, 1970.
Kavaler, Lucy. *Freezing Point*. John Day, 1970.
Prehoda, R. W. "The Conquest of Senescence." Reprinted in *Ahead of Time*.
Rosenfeld, Albert. *Prolongevity*. Knopf, 1976.
Segerberg, Osborn, Jr. *The Immortality Factor*. Dutton, 1974.
Thomas, Lewis. *The Lives of a Cell*. Viking, 1974.
Tuccille, Jerome. *Here Comes Immortality*. Stein & Day, 1973.

Fiction: Novels

Abe, Kobo. *Inter Ice Age 4*. Knopf, 1970.
Amosov, Nikolai Mikhailovich (as N. Amosoff). *Notes from the Future*. Simon & Schuster, 1970.
Anderson, Olof W. *The Treasure Vault of Atlantis*. Midland, 1925.
Barjavel, René. *The Ice People*. Morrow, 1970.
Berger, Thomas. *Vital Parts*. Barron, 1970.
Bester, Alfred. *The Computer Connection*. Putnam, 1974, 1975.
Blish, James, and Robert Lowndes. *The Duplicated Man*. Avalon, 1959.
Bodelsen, Anders. *Freezing Down*. Harper & Row, 1971.

Boussenard, Louis. *10,000 Years in a Block of Ice.* Tr. by John Paret. F. Tennyson Neely, 1898.

Bunch, David R. *Moderan.* Avon, 1971.

Clarke, Arthur C. *The City and the Stars.* Harcourt, 1956.

Dick, Philip K. *Ubik.* Doubleday, 1969.

Gray, Curme. *Murder in Millennium VI.* Shasta, 1951.

Gunn, James. *The Immortals.* Bantam, 1962.

Hamilton, Edmond. *The Star of Life.* Dodd, 1959.

Heinlein, Robert A. *Methuselah's Children.* Reprinted in *The Past Through Tomorrow* by Robert A. Heinlein. Putnam, 1967.
Time Enough for Love. Putnam, 1973.

Herbert, Frank. *The Eyes of Heisenberg.* Berkley, 1966.

Hilton, James. *Lost Horizon.* Morrow, 1933.

Hjortsberg, William. *Gray Matters.* Simon & Schuster, 1971.

Pohl, Frederik. *Drunkard's Walk.* Ballantine, 1960.
The Age of the Pussyfoot. Trident, 1969.

Randall, Marta. *Islands.* Pyramid, 1976.

Shaw, George Bernard. *Back to Methuselah: A Metabiological Pentateuch.* Constable, 1921.

Sheckley, Robert. *Immortality, Inc.* Bantam, 1959.

Silverberg, Robert. *The Book of Skulls.* Scribner, 1972.

Stapledon, Olaf. *Last and First Men: A Story of the Near and Far Future.* Methuen, 1930.

Smith, Cordwainer. *Norstrilia.* Ballantine, 1975.

Swayne, Martin. *The Blue Germ.* Doran, 1918.

Vance, Jack. *To Live Forever.* Ballantine, 1956.

Van Vogt, A. E. *The Weapon Shops of Isher.* Greenberg, 1951.
The Weapons Makers. Hadley, 1947.

Weinbaum, Stanley. *The Black Flame.* Fantasy Press, 1948.

Wolfe, Gene. *The Fifth Head of Cerberus.* Scribner, 1972.

Wyndham, John. *Trouble with Lichen.* Ballantine, 1960.

Zelazny, Roger. *This Immortal.* Ace, 1966.
Lord of Light. Doubleday, 1967.
Isle of the Dead. Ace, 1969.

Short Fiction

Benford, Gregory. "Knowing Her." Appeared in *New Dimensions 7,* ed. by Robert Silverberg. Harper & Row, 1977.

Disch, Thomas M. "Things Lost." Appeared in *Again Dangerous Visions,* ed. by Harlan Ellison. Doubleday, 1972.
"The Pressure of Time." Appeared in *Orbit 7,* ed. by Damon Knight. Putnam, 1970.

Gunn, James. "The Immortals," 1958. Reprinted in *Bio-Futures,* ed. by Pamela Sargent. Vintage, 1976.

Knight, Damon. "Dio," 1957. Reprinted in *Alpha Four,* ed. by Robert Silverberg. Ballantine, 1974.

MacLean, Katherine. "And Be Merry," 1950. Reprinted in *Omnibus of Science Fiction,* ed. by Groff Conklin. Crown, 1952.

Plauger, P. J. "Child of All Ages," 1975. Reprinted in *The 1976 Annual World's Best SF,* ed. by Donald A. Wollheim. DAW Books, 1976.

Scortia, Thomas. "The Weariest River," 1976. Reprinted in *Bio-Futures.*

Silverberg, Robert. "Born with the Dead," 1974. Reprinted in *Born with the Dead* by Robert Silverberg. Vintage, 1975.

Simak, Clifford. "Eternity Lost," 1949. Reprinted in *The Best Science Fiction Stories: 1950,* ed. by Everett F. Bleiler and T. E. Dikty. Frederick Fell, 1950.

Smith, Cordwainer. "A Planet Named Shayol," 1961. Reprinted in Seventh Annual of *The Year's Best SF,* ed. by Judith Merril. Simon & Schuster, 1962.

Tiptree, James, Jr. "She Waits for All Men Born." Appeared in *Future Power,* ed. by Jack Dann and Gardner R. Dozois. Random House, 1976.

Tushnet, Leonard. "In Re Glover," 1972. Reprinted in *Bio-Futures.*

Vonnegut, Kurt, Jr. "The Big Trip Up Yonder," 1953. Reprinted in *Assignment in Tomorrow,* ed. by Frederik Pohl. Doubleday, 1954.

Wilhelm, Kate. "April Fool's Day Forever," 1970. Appeared in *Orbit 7,* ed. by Damon Knight. Putnam, 1970.

About the Authors

Thomas M. Disch grew up in Minnesota and attended New York University. His novels include *The Genocides, 334, Echo Round His Bones,* and *Mankind Under the Leash.* His story for *Immortal* is excerpted from his forthcoming novel, *The Pressure of Time.* He is the author of two short-story collections, *Getting into Death* and *Fun with Your New Head.* He has edited four anthologies, *New Constellations* (with Charles Naylor), *The Ruins of Earth, Bad Moon Rising,* and *The New Improved Sun.* He is the author of a volume of poetry, *The Right Way to Figure Plumbing,* and his short stories have appeared in *Playboy, Mademoiselle, Paris Review, New Worlds,* and many other magazines and anthologies.

R. C. W. Ettinger is a physicist, lecturer, and a leading figure in the cryonics movement. He wrote science fiction in the forties and is the author of two nonfiction works, *The Prospect of Immortality* and *Man into Superman.* Mr. Ettinger lives in Oak Park, Michigan.

Pamela Sargent is also the author of three novels, *Cloned Lives, The Sudden Star,* and *Watchstar.* She is the author of a short-story collection, *Starshadows.* She has edited four anthologies: *Bio-Futures, Women of Wonder, More Women of Wonder,* and *The New Women of Wonder.* She lives in upstate New York.

Gene Wolfe was born in Brooklyn and lives in Illinois, where he edits the trade publication *Plant Engineering.* He is the author of *The Fifth Head of Cerberus, The Devil in a Forest,* and *Peace.* His stories have appeared in *Analog, Orbit, Universe, Future Power, Again Dangerous Visions, The New Atlantis, The Ruins of Earth, Bad Moon Rising,* and many other anthologies and magazines. He received a Nebula Award for his novella "The Death of Doctor Island."

George Zebrowski is the author of more than thirty stories, articles, and essays appearing in various magazines and anthologies. He is the author of many novels, among them *Macrolife* and *Free Space,* as well as editor of *Faster Than Light* (with Jack Dann) and *Human-Machines* (with Thomas N. Scortia). His work has been translated into foreign languages, and he has lectured and taught widely on science fiction, the future, and writing. He lives and writes in New York State.

About the Editor

Jack Dann was born and raised in upstate New York. He has been a Nebula Award finalist twice, taught science fiction at Cornell University, and has edited several anthologies. He is the author of two novels, *Starhiker* and *Junction*. Mr. Dann lives in Johnson City, New York.